Praise for these bestselling authors

Julie Kenner

"Julie Kenner is one of my favorite writers.
Funny and sassy, her books are a cherished delight."
—*New York Times* bestselling author Sherrilyn Kenyon

"Kenner's star is definitely on the ascent."
—*Publishers Weekly*

Nancy Warren

"Nancy Warren's wonderfully realistic characters, positively
charged, compelling romance, and too-hot-to-handle loving,
dished up with spicy humor, will leave readers breathless."
—*Romantic Times BOOKclub*

"Sexy and wonderfully witty."
—*USA TODAY* bestselling author Lori Foster

Jo Leigh

"Jo Leigh knows how to blend heartwarming romance
and witty dialogue into sheer joy."
—*Romantic Times BOOKclub*

"Jo Leigh delivers lots of laughs."
—*Romantic Times BOOKclub*

Dear Reader,

Spring is on the way, and the Signature Select program offers lots of variety in the reading treats you've come to expect from some of your favorite Harlequin and Silhouette authors.

The second quarter of the year continues the excitement we began in January with a can't-miss drama from Vicki Hinze: *Her Perfect Life*. In it, a female military prisoner regains her freedom only to find that the life she left behind no longer exists. Myrna Mackenzie's *Angel Eyes* gives us the tale of a woman with an unnatural ability to find lost objects and people, and *Confessions of a Party Crasher*, by Holly Jacobs, is a humorous novel about finding happiness—even as an uninvited guest!

Our collections for April, May and June are themed around Mother's Day, matchmaking and time travel. Mothers and daughters are a focus in *From Here to Maternity*, by Tara Taylor Quinn, Karen Rose Smith and Inglath Cooper. You're in for a trio of imaginative time-travel stories by Julie Kenner, Nancy Warren and Jo Leigh in *Perfect Timing*. And a matchmaking New York cabbie is a delightful catalyst to romance in the three stories in *A Fare To Remember*, by Vicki Lewis Thompson, Julie Elizabeth Leto and Kate Hoffmann.

Spring also brings three more original sagas to the Signature Select program. *Hot Chocolate on a Cold Day* tells the story of a Coast Guard worker in Michigan who finds herself intrigued by her new downstairs neighbor. Jenna Mills's *Killing Me Softly* features a heroine who returns to the scene of her own death, and *You Made Me Love You*, by C.J. Carmichael, explores the shattering effects of the death of a charismatic woman on the friends who adored her.

And don't forget, there is original bonus material in every single Signature Select book to give you the inside scoop on the creative process of your favorite authors! Happy reading!

Marsha Zinberg

Marsha Zinberg
Executive Editor
The Signature Select Program

COLLECTION

Perfect Timing

Julie KENNER

Nancy WARREN

AND

Jo LEIGH

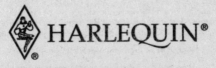

HARLEQUIN®

TORONTO • NEW YORK • LONDON
AMSTERDAM • PARIS • SYDNEY • HAMBURG
STOCKHOLM • ATHENS • TOKYO • MILAN • MADRID
PRAGUE • WARSAW • BUDAPEST • AUCKLAND

ISBN 0-373-83703-8

PERFECT TIMING

Copyright © 2006 by Harlequin Books S.A.

The publisher acknowledges the copyright holders of the individual works as follows:

THOSE WERE THE DAYS
Copyright © 2006 by Julie Kenner

PISTOLS AT DAWN
Copyright © 2006 by Nancy Warren

TIME AFTER TIME
Copyright © 2006 by Jolie Kramer

CONTENTS

THOSE WERE THE DAYS

Julie Kenner

CHAPTER ONE

"I THOUGHT WE WERE going to an exhibit on butterflies," Sylvia Preston said, staring into the glass case at the formidable ivory object that was—quite clearly—*not* a butterfly.

Beside her, Tina shrugged. "You don't need butterflies, Syl." She made a sweeping gesture, her arm encompassing the ornate room and the exhibit cases that filled it. "*This* is good for you."

Ever since the first day they'd met as freshman roommates at UCLA, Tina had presumed to know what was best for Sylvia. A trait that Sylvia had—and still did—found both endearing and annoying.

"*This* is a sex exhibit," Sylvia said, her feelings for Tina today leaning toward the annoying side of the equation. "And *this*," she added, pointing to the ivory object in front of her, is a *dildo*." She said the last in a hushed voice, her cheeks burning.

"It certainly is," Tina said, her tone almost reverential.

"Are you insane? It's the size of a...of a...of an I don't know what!"

"They say Catherine the Great did it with a horse," Tina said.

Sylvia put her hands over her ears. "I don't even want to hear about it." She walked away, Tina following.

"See, that's your problem," Tina said, as they moved into the next room, this one apparently devoted to electronic enhancement of the sexual experience. The Sex Through The Ages exhibit was touring the country, and this week it was in Los Angeles, on display at the Greene Mansion in Beverly Hills.

By happy coincidence, Tina and Sylvia were both in town and could visit the exhibit and the house. They'd lived in Southern California during their undergrad years, but for graduate school, they'd left the sunny beaches for the lure of a Stanford law degree. Sylvia had graduated in the top one percent of her class, with Tina not far behind in the twenty-fifth percentile. The nature of their friendship had shifted when Tina had moved to Las Vegas to take a job with the district attorney's office. Sylvia had stayed in San Francisco, snagging a very coveted position with one of the major law firms in the country.

Now that Sylvia was making the move to a Los Angeles firm, Tina had taken some vacation time, flown up to San Francisco and had driven down the coast with Syl. The trip had been a blast, with Syl and Tina playing tourist at every little town they came across. They were even doing the tourist thing in Los Angeles, even though they'd both called the city home during college. They'd gone drinking and dancing, and Sylvia had flirted and chatted, making a concerted effort to get more into the social thing.

The rest had been even more fun. They'd done shopping, the beach, the Pier, Hollywood Boulevard and the Universal Studios tour, including the totally fun tram ride through the back lot, an experience that had been Syl's favorite so far. Corny, but she was a movie buff, and seeing the *Psycho* house and all the other bits of movie history had been a huge thrill.

They'd also been hitting a few museums and exhibits, including the Getty and this exhibit at the Greene Mansion, which clearly was *not* dedicated to butterflies. But despite Tina's deviousness, Syl was glad they'd come. She'd always loved the Greene Mansion. It had been the home of Tucker Greene, one of her favorite film directors from the 1930s, but she'd never been inside before. And, honestly, she had to admit that while the chance to visit the mansion was what made the excursion palatable, the sex exhibit was interesting, too.

Despite her friend's devious behavior, Syl was sad that their trip was coming to an end. Tomorrow she started her new job. And later this evening, Tina was off to the airport. It might be months before they saw each other again, what with the pressure of their jobs. Bittersweet, but time changed everything. She knew that. And she also knew that she and Tina would always be best friends, even if her friend did sometimes drive her insane. Like, for instance, now.

At the moment, Tina was gesturing to a glass case filled with vibrators. "So tell me the truth," she was saying. "Have you ever even used a vibrator?"

Around them, other patrons glanced in their direction, and Sylvia felt her cheeks flame. "Tina," she whispered, grabbing her so-called friend's arm and tugging her toward a secluded corner. As she did, she noticed that one of the security guards was watching her, and she caught a twinkle in his blue eyes before he looked away. She resisted the urge to melt with embarrassment, and instead focused on Tina. "Of course I've used a vibrator," she said, turning her back to the guard.

With any other friend, Sylvia would have put a quick end to the conversation. But the truth was that Syl had no other close friends. She wasn't a loner by any means, but her whole life she'd been selective about who she let in close to her heart. Tina had barreled her way in that first day in their dorm, when she'd thrown her arms around Sylvia and said—absolutely earnestly— "Thank God you're rooming with me. I don't think I could make it through freshman year without a best friend." And even though Syl had never seen the girl before in her life, it was as if Tina's mandate had magic. Tina, quite simply, became her best friend. And that was that.

Some things, however, a girl didn't have to put up with even from her best friend. And discussion of the use of vibrators was tops on that list, Sylvia thought as she scowled daggers at Tina.

Her friend, as usual, was unconvinced. "You?" Tina said, her voice dubious. "You've used a vibrator?"

"Yes. And I've watched dirty movies and I've made out in the back seat of a car."

"Oh." She frowned. "But I thought your whole problem with Dwight was, you know, *sexual*."

"That doesn't mean I'm clueless about vibrators," Sylvia said. "God, Tina." She stifled a sigh, telling herself she was grateful to have a friend like Tina with whom she could talk about things like sex, even while kicking herself for ever hinting to her friend about her hideous childhood, her asshole stepfather, Martin, or the problems in bed that had plagued her ever since.

"Sylvia? You wanna clue me in here? What exactly am I missing?"

Sylvia sighed, then cocked her head toward the side of the room, urging Tina toward the relative privacy of the far wall. "Sex with Dwight was fine," she said. "Except, it's not fine. I mean, I'm not, you know, comfortable with him. With telling him what I want. Does that make sense?"

"You're the quiet type in bed," Tina said with a shrug. "A lot of girls have trouble telling a guy what they want. Not me, of course. But a lot of girls."

"Sure," Sylvia said. "You're probably right." Not that she believed that, but this was hardly the time to talk about it.

"I mean, it even makes some sense," Tina said. "Your early experiences with men weren't exactly warm and fuzzy. Martin totally dominated you. It wasn't like you could ask him to stop doing something, right? So now you don't feel you can ask, either. For what you want or for what you don't want."

"Absolutely," Sylvia said, wishing Tina would just drop it. She didn't want to talk about this. Not when she was still dripping with guilt from having left San Francisco for Los Angeles. Everyone—her mom, Tina, Dwight—thought she'd left because she'd had an amazing job offer from the largest law firm in California. But what none of them knew was the reason she'd applied for the job in the first place—to escape.

Dwight was on the verge of popping the question. He'd been hinting around for weeks. But Sylvia didn't want to marry him. Hell, she was only so-so on the subject of dating him. He was nice enough, and she did love him. But she wasn't *in love* with him.

But she couldn't tell him that any more than she

could tell him what she wanted in bed. Instead of dealing with Dwight as a normal, rational, reasonable adult, she'd called a Los Angeles headhunter and been snatched up so fast that Sylvia had called it fate in an attempt to alleviate some of her guilt.

Of course, she'd known the job offers would flood in. That was a given considering her résumé. In a perverse way, she supposed she even had Martin to thank for her success. She'd delved in to enough pop psychology to realize that her overachiever personality was her way of fighting back. Of proving to him—and to herself—that she was worthy.

She'd aced school and landed an amazing job in San Francisco. Now she was moving to Los Angeles for an even better job with an even better salary. Would she have accomplished all that if it hadn't been for Martin's vile whispers every night after her mom had gone to bed? The kisses he'd planted on her mouth and between her legs, making her feel ashamed and dirty? His hushed tones telling her she was worthless, and her screaming inside her head that she wasn't?

Martin might be the root cause of her desperation to succeed, but he was also the reason she so often escaped into fantasy. If she wasn't buried in her work, chances were she was lost in a book or curled up in the dark with a classic movie playing on her television.

Martin was also the reason all her relationships failed. Why she couldn't communicate sexually with a man. And why she was running now from a decent man who loved her. She couldn't simply escape into a book or movie where Dwight was concerned. So instead of dealing with the question he was about to pop, she'd escaped real life by taking a job hundreds of miles away.

When she'd accepted the job offer in Los Angeles, she'd told Dwight that this was simply too good an opportunity to pass up, somehow neglecting to mention the part about how she went looking for that opportunity. Their relationship was strong enough to handle this, she'd said. And all the while, she'd had her fingers crossed, hoping, that in their case, distance didn't make the heart grow fonder.

"I think you just need to go balls to the wall and shift into dominatrix mode. *That*," Tina said, "will work wonders for your self-esteem."

"Excuse me?" Sylvia asked, her voice climbing higher.

"When Dwight comes down to visit, you jump his bones. Tell him exactly what you want. If he can't handle it, well, then you're in a new town with new men. Send him back up San Francisco way."

"I…but…" Sylvia blinked, feeling more than a little befuddled. "It's not that easy."

Tina deflated a bit at that. "Maybe not. I mean, you've got a history with the guy. That would make it harder. I know," she squealed, her features flushing bright. "Just find someone you like and pick him up. No strings, right? Surely you can tell some stranger exactly what you want in bed. I mean, why wouldn't you? No expectations. Just wham, bam, and tell the boy thank you very much."

Sylvia just shook her head. "This conversation is *so* over."

"I'm serious, Syl," Tina said. "You spend your life watching movies. Just pretend you're some uber-hot starlet. Like Uma in *Kill Bill*. Or Kathleen Turner in *Body Heat*. Find a man you want and take charge. No strings, no expectations. Just make it all about Sylvia. Get exactly what you want from the guy. And once you do that, you'll be free of Martin. I promise."

"I mean it, Tina," Sylvia said. "We're not talking about this anymore."

Her friend pouted but didn't say anything else. Instead, she just raised one hand, then took a step back. "I guess I'll go check out a few more of the exhibits."

"Right," Sylvia said. "You do that."

As Sylvia watched, Tina went off to look at a display of vibrators shaped like various animals. Beavers, bunnies, even a bright yellow ducky with an, um, *useful* beak and tail. Sylvia didn't follow. Instead she moved out of the room and into another, finally settling on a plush bench. Antique, obviously, but Sylvia knew about as much about history as she did about dildos, so she couldn't guess the period. Whenever it was from, it was comfortable, and she sagged a little, suddenly exhausted but still interested in the room.

The inside of the Greene Mansion was just as fabulous as she'd imagined it would be. Built in the 1800s by industrialist Carson Greene, the house overflowed with graciousness, the carved wood ornate and warm, the furniture inviting, and the many windows giving the interior a cheery, light-filled quality. Of course, there were dozens more rooms that were off-limits to patrons of the exhibit, and Sylvia was disappointed about that. For one, she'd hoped to see some Hollywood memorabilia. So far, though, she'd seen nothing.

She'd also simply wanted to explore the house. Her

whole life, Sylvia had been fascinated by old houses. Or, rather, not her whole life, but at least from age six. That's when Martin Straithorn had married her mother. They'd moved into his ramshackle farmhouse. Old, but hardly stately or elegant.

Even so, Sylvia had soon learned that the house was the best thing about her mother's marriage. Maybe even the only good thing. Because the farmhouse had lots of nooks and crannies. And that meant lots of places for Sylvia to hide. Lots of places where she could hole up with her books and sit quietly after school, wishing the sun would never go down and she'd never have to go to her bedroom.

Because she couldn't sleep in her hiding places. At night, she had to come out. Had to go into her bed. Had to pull the covers up to her chin and hope—no, *pray*— that for that one night, she'd be allowed to sleep, blissfully and peacefully. And, most importantly, alone.

Books had been her daily companions, the characters her best friends. How many times had she wished that she, too, could find a secret doorway so she could escape to another world? Sleep in another land instead of in her own bed, watched over by Aslan's gentle eyes instead of Martin Straithorn's deviant leer.

She shivered, hugging herself, the memories closer now than she liked them to get. She forced her mind away from the past, deliberately focusing on the room she'd stepped into. The drawing room, perhaps. Or a morning room. As much as she loved old houses, she'd never bothered to learn the names for all their various parts. It was the whole she cared about. The elegance and warmth. The detail in the woodwork. Not the strip-mall type homes that seemed to be taking over America.

She stood and wandered through the room, wondering if she was supposed to be in here. It wasn't cordoned off, and yet none of the exhibits from the Sex Through The Ages tour were set up in here. Honestly, Sylvia had to admit she felt a bit of relief at that. She probably wouldn't have come with Tina had she known the subject matter of the exhibit. She knew she had issues with sex, thank you very much. And she didn't much appreciate Tina blatantly *lying* and telling her the exhibit was about some damn butterflies.

She saw a brochure for the exhibit sitting on one of the tables, and she picked it up, almost snorting as she skimmed through it. *Some butterflies.* Instead the brochure showed pictures of key elements from the exhibits, and even had an inset photograph of the guard who was traveling with the exhibit as it toured around the country. An older man, with a friendly face and unkempt gray hair escaping from under his cap. The same guard, Sylvia realized, that she'd seen in the other room. Not a bad job, she supposed. Hang around sex toys all day and watch women come and go in various stages of embarrassment or delight.

Mostly, though, the brochure described the various exhibits that now filled the rooms of the stately house. Sex as shown in the paintings of Picasso and others. Sex and technology. Plus exhibits on fertility goddesses and fetishes and the Kama Sutra. Basically, anything remotely relating to sex was there.

Definitely *not* butterflies. Although Sylvia wouldn't have been surprised to find a butterfly-shaped vibrator.

The exhibit covered the range of sex and sexuality, and she knew in her heart that Tina had tricked her into coming because her best friend loved her. Tina was the only person in the world that Sylvia had ever confided in about Martin. And even then, the truths had been minimal. Mostly, Sylvia had only hinted about the past. But Tina was bright, and Sylvia knew that her friend had figured out the truth.

But while she knew that Tina only wanted to help, that didn't change the fact that it felt like interference. Not that Sylvia didn't find the traveling exhibit fascinating—she did. But she would have liked full disclosure before coming down here. After all, her sexual issues were hers and hers alone, and she was aware of them and dealing with them. She knew the cause—he'd married her mother, after all, so how could she *not* know—but wandering through rooms filled with dildos and vibrators was hardly going to make her more comfortable with her sexuality, or help her learn to communicate with men so that they knew what she wanted.

Enough.

She wanted to kick herself. She'd escaped the stupid exhibit and yet here she was, thinking about sex all over again. *Think about something else*, she ordered. This room. The ornately carved mantel over the fireplace. The portraits.

She got up from the bench, then walked the perimeter of the room, examining everything critically and with such an eye for detail that she had no room in her head to think about anything else. Which probably explained why she jumped a foot when the hand settled on her shoulder.

"Oh! Goodness! I'm so sorry I startled you!"

Sylvia turned, and found herself looking into bright green eyes, sparkling from a well-aged face. The woman looked to be close to seventy, with regal posture and an air of confidence. "I'm Louisa Greene," she said with a smile. "I live here."

"Oh. *Oh.* I'm so sorry." Sylvia took a step toward the door. "I just wandered in from one of the exhibit halls. I didn't mean—"

"Nonsense!" Louisa placed a hand on her arm. "Please, don't run away. I saw you admiring the portraits. I thought I'd found a kindred spirit." She lowered her voice to a stage whisper. "I agreed to host the traveling exhibit here because I find the subject matter so very fascinating. But one does have to step away every once in a while, don't you think?"

Sylvia blushed, and wasn't quite able to meet the woman's eyes. She was twenty-six—right at the age where sex and work were supposed to be the two things at the forefront of her mind—and yet here she was desperately avoiding the subject while this grandmotherly woman blatantly admitted to being fascinated by it. Whatever happened to decorum?

"Darling!" Louisa said, her voice lilting. "I've made you uncomfortable. I'm so sorry. Here, please sit and let me make it up to you."

Louisa gestured toward a divan and though Sylvia's instinct was to run—to *race*—from the room, she couldn't quite convince her feet to go along with that plan. And so she found herself sitting.

Louisa signaled to one of the docents, who came over, looked at the two women, then nodded. Then, as Sylvia watched, wide-eyed, he left the room, shutting the double doors behind him.

"Where's he going?"

"He'll ring Thomas for tea and will ensure we're not interrupted. You looked like you could use a bit of a break, and I feel I must apologize for embarrassing you."

"It's really not—"

"Nonsense. Besides, you were enjoying the room and I interrupted. It's the least I can do."

Despite herself, Sylvia relaxed. There was something about Louisa she found comforting, even familiar.

"I think it's the way I was raised," Louisa said, making Sylvia blink with the change of subject.

"Excuse me?"

"Sex, I mean," the older women said casually. Then, "Oh, thank you, Thomas. You can just set the tray right here."

A butler in full livery had appeared in the doorway carrying a tea tray with a pot, two cups and an assortment of tiny desserts. Sylvia thought she ought to be impressed by the speed at which he'd prepared the tray—it was almost as if Louisa had been expecting company—but she couldn't quite work up the energy. The whole day was turning out a bit baffling and surprising.

As soon as Thomas left, Louisa turned back to Sylvia. "It was my grandparents, you see. They were so incredibly in love, they couldn't keep their hands off each other. Considering the era, it was probably quite scandalous, but I learned early on that sex is an expression of love, no matter how many electronic devices might be involved," she added with a wink.

"I…um…oh."

Louisa sighed. "I've gone and done it again. I was trying to make you feel more comfortable and I've just embarrassed you more."

"Not at all," Sylvia said. Which, of course, was a lie. "But I do think you're naive."

The second she spoke, she was afraid she'd insulted the older woman. To her surprise, though, Louisa just laughed. "Naive? My dear, I'm getting close to seventy. I'm a lot of things, but I'm no longer naive."

"It's just…well, your attitude about sex. It's not always love, you know. Sometimes it's about control. Power. Sometimes," she whispered, mortified to realize her eyes were filling with tears, "it's not a good thing at all."

"Oh, sweetie," Louisa said, taking her hand. "I certainly didn't mean to belittle anything you've gone through. But it's all a question of semantics, really. Don't you think?"

Part of Sylvia wanted to race from the room. Another part wanted to protest. To clear up the perception— accurate though it might be—that Sylvia had been talking about herself. She *never* spoke about Martin. About what he did. Even to Tina she'd talked around the subject. Bits and pieces that let her friend draw her own conclusions. And Syl had only managed to reveal that much after ten years of friendship.

But to this woman, Sylvia had opened her heart in no time and with no warning. It terrified her, but for some inexplicable reason it also calmed her. And so instead of running, she stayed on the divan, leaned over for her tea, and asked simply, "What do you mean by semantics?"

"What you describe isn't sex. It's assault and battery. Using a sexual organ as a weapon, sure. But it's not sex. It's not a union."

"I…" Sylvia trailed off, not entirely sure what to say

to that. She wanted to believe it, actually. But wanting was a lot easier than doing.

"Don't worry about answering me," Louisa said. "Just smile and nod and indulge me my idiosyncrasies. It's a wonder I haven't gone completely batty what with strangers wandering through my home four days a week."

"So you meant it," Sylvia said. "When you said you lived here." She sighed. "It's a grand house. I've just moved into an apartment in the mid-Wilshire area. But someday, I want a house like this."

"Do you?" Louisa cocked her head, looking at Sylvia in a way that made her squirm. "One day, I think you'll get one."

"Why do you open it up to the public like this?" Sylvia asked, realizing as she spoke that it was an incredibly nosy question. "I'm sorry," she said, backpedaling. "That's really none of my business."

"No, no. Not at all. I can understand your interest. So many of these stately mansions have been turned over to charitable foundations. The upkeep on a house like this is…well, I have to have a very strong glass of sherry every time I go over the numbers with my accountant. But we're actually one of the few that is self-sufficient." She patted Sylvia's hand. "Not that I'm bragging. It's simply a fact of life."

"A nice fact," Sylvia said.

Louisa's smile was soft and genuine. "Indeed."

"So, if you have the money to keep the place operational, why all this?"

Louisa stood, gesturing for Sylvia to follow, then moved across the room to stand in front of the wall of portraits. She pointed to the one in the center. "Because of her," Louisa said.

"I'm sorry?"

"That's my grandmother," Louisa explained. "She was a bit of an oddity in my family, but we always took everything she said very seriously."

Sylvia studied the portrait, noticing with interest that it seemed somehow familiar. The woman there looked calm and self-assured, with light brown hair and green eyes highlighted by a slightly large mouth and high cheekbones. Not to mention ears that stuck out just a little too much.

With a start, Sylvia realized that the woman resembled *her*. How strange. But perhaps it explained why Louisa was so open. Maybe Sylvia's resemblance to her grandmother made her feel more comfortable.

Louisa apparently hadn't realized that Sylvia's attention had wandered. She was still talking about the woman, and when Sylvia tuned back in, her interest was piqued. "She's one of the reasons the family is so well-off," Louisa was saying. "Had a head for speculative finance. Made a fortune in the stock market and real estate."

"Nice," Sylvia said. "But what does that have to do with opening the house?"

"Grandma insisted. For as long as I can remember, she would tell me that when I was older, I had to make sure the house was opened to the public. That we must allow traveling exhibits to tour. She made me swear." A soft shrug. "And I agreed."

"And you don't know why?"

Louisa's smile was almost shy. "I have my theories. At any rate," she said, changing her tone and moving away from the portrait, "she was right. There's a lot of history in this house."

"Well, sure," Sylvia said. "I mean Tucker Greene. He was a force in Hollywood. An amazing filmmaker. Who hasn't heard of him?"

"And the Ragtime Strangler," Louisa added.

Sylvia cocked her head, trying to remember. "That's right," she said. "I read something about that. A serial killer, but back in the twenties. Went after young, pretty flappers." She frowned, her memory fuzzy. "I'm not an expert on Hollywood or anything, but I like Greene's movies, so I've read a few articles and watched the extras on DVD remasters and stuff. If I remember right, the Strangler was stalking Beverly Hills before Greene got into film, right? He was doing something else. Radio, wasn't it? One of my DVDs even included a new performance of one of his radio plays. It was pretty cool."

Sylvia shut up then, realizing she probably sounded like an obsessed fan. Louisa, however, only smiled and looked delighted with Sylvia's recollection. "You're exactly right."

"But what does this house have to do with the Strangler?"

"My grandparents caught him," Louisa said. "Right in the next room."

"Wow," Sylvia said, truly surprised. "Thank you for telling me all this. It's a beautiful house. It's nice to know some of the history that goes along with it."

The door opened, and Tina poked her head in. "*There* you are. I've been looking everywhere for you!"

"I'd better let you two finish touring the exhibit,"

Louisa said. "It's been wonderful talking with you, Sylvia. You take care."

And with a quick smile, she glided out the doors with a regal nod to Tina.

"Who was that?"

"The lady of the house," Sylvia said. "But—" She frowned.

"What?"

"I never told her my name."

Tina looked at her dubiously. "Well, obviously you did."

The hair on Sylvia's arms seemed to tingle, as if she'd walked too close to a high-voltage fence. "Of course. I must have." She nodded toward the door, but took one last look back at the portrait, struck by the feeling that she'd seen it once before. "Let's go."

"You haven't said anything for ten minutes," Tina said. They'd moved into the Roaring Twenties room, filled with flapper gowns and silk stockings and the first bit of Hollywood memorabilia that Sylvia had seen—a large poster advertising the 1922 version of *Robin Hood* starring Douglas Fairbanks. The poster had been framed and propped on an easel. Sylvia squinted at it, noting that Fairbanks had signed it to "My good friend Tucker Greene." Apparently Greene had had Hollywood connections even before he tried his hand at directing.

Sylvia smiled, feeling she'd learned a secret fact. Because certainly the poster had nothing to do with the exhibit. It was original to the room, unlike the rest. The flapper gowns and jewelry, along with the sheet music and photographs, had come with the exhibit. At first,

Sylvia had thought this section of the exhibit seemed su-
perfluous, but then she started reading the information
printed on cards next to the various displays. The
Twenties, it said, had been a coming-of-age period for
young women. Affluence and postwar giddiness had
combined to create a new sensuality and freedom, particularly felt by females. Exploration and sensual
delights were at a high point.

"Sylvia!" Tina said. "Are you listening to me? Why
are you so quiet?"

"Sorry! Just thinking."

"About that woman? Or about flapper gowns. You'd
look great in that, you know." She pointed to a beaded
gold gown with spaghetti straps and a fringed hem. The
gown had no waist, just a thick band that seemed to
settle around the mannequin's hips. The outfit was
topped off with a beaded headband highlighted by a
dyed feather.

"You think?"

"Oh, sure. That's the perfect style for girls without
boobs."

Sylvia shot a look to her friend. "Thanks. Thanks a lot."

Tina shrugged. "It's true. So, are you gonna tell me
what's on your mind or not?"

Sylvia wandered away from the gown. "I was just
thinking about Louisa. The way the past is so alive for
her." She shuddered slightly. "Me, I'd just as soon
forget my past."

Tina snorted. "Who could blame you? And maybe
then we could have a normal conversation about
boyfriends and vibrators without you going all defensive on me."

"I'm not defensive," Sylvia said, even though she probably was. "And what's so normal about discussing vibrators anyway?"

Tina just rolled her eyes. "I'm going down to the food cart. Coming?"

Sylvia started to say yes, but then she noticed the guard in the corner. And even though there was something oddly creepy about the way he watched her, there was something compelling, too. "I'm going to stay a bit," she said, turning back to Tina. "I'm not hungry."

"Suit yourself," Tina said casually. "But let me have the backpack." They'd both shoved their wallets, makeup and other tourist-girl essentials into a nylon Venice Beach daypack that Syl had picked up from a street vendor. Now, they were taking turns shouldering the thing.

Sylvia handed it over. "Spend *your* money," she admonished with mock severity. "And stay out of my makeup."

"Oh, sure," Tina retorted. "Just spoil all my fun." She aimed a grin at Syl, then headed out the door. "Catch you in a bit."

Sylvia watched her go, shaking her head in amusement.

"Letting go of the past," a voice said. "Now that's something I bet a lot of people would like to do."

Sylvia spun around, surprised to see that the guard had moved silently to stand beside her. "Pardon me?"

"I overheard you and your friend," he explained, his smile friendly. "Sometimes it's not about escaping your past, you know. Sometimes, it's about confronting it."

Sylvia squinted at him. "Aren't you…" She trailed off, lifting the exhibit brochure and glancing at it. Sure enough, the guard she was talking to was pictured right there. How odd.

"I travel with the show," he said. "Keep an eye on things. Make any adjustments that might be needed. That kind of thing."

"Oh. Right." She frowned, not really in the mood to talk to strangers, no matter how kindly. "I'll just go catch up with my friend."

"Of course, miss." He stuck his hand in his pocket, pulled out a quarter, and started twirling it between his fingers. She watched, fascinated by the agility with which the coin danced over his hand, weaving in and out, over and under and then—*snap!*—falling to the ground and rolling under the easel with the Fairbanks movie poster.

"Oh! And you were doing so well, too."

He nodded toward the easel. "I don't suppose you could snatch that thing back for me? These old knees don't get down on the ground like they used to."

She hesitated, not entirely sure why, then realized she was being ridiculous. "Sure. No problem." She edged toward the poster, keeping her eye to the ground as she looked for the coin. "There you are," she whispered, bending down. As her fingers closed around it, she felt something shove her from behind. She toppled forward, slamming against the poster and then actually tumbling *through* it.

But that couldn't be right. Just her mind playing tricks as a wave of dizziness crashed over her. Her knees went weak and she sagged to the floor.

And the last thing Sylvia remembered thinking was that if she was going to faint, that guard had damn well better say "thank you" when she gave him back his coin.

CHAPTER TWO

TUCKER LEANED AGAINST the railing and watched the swirling, whirling melee below him. His sister, intent on garnering a reputation for throwing the best parties in Beverly Hills, had gone all out with this one. Everyone who was anyone had been invited, and even more had breached the door without invitations. The masquerade theme was fitting, allowing the guests to quaff the illicit alcohol with less fear of recognition. And, surely, the family's social position assured that they would not be troubled.

Mostly, though, Tucker knew that the guests had come to slide into the oblivion of amusement and temporarily forget the undertone of fear that so recently colored the neighborhood. Fear of a killer who had attacked the community's women. The Ragtime Strangler they were calling the beast, and the very thought made Tucker's blood boil, his hatred of anyone who would so intentionally cause pain to a woman cutting at him like the blade of the knife the killer had wielded.

With effort, he forced himself not to think of that, turning his thoughts back to the party and his sister. He looked down, surveying the scene. Women in white with gossamer wings. Men with harlequin collars, their faces painted with black and white greasepaint. And everyone dancing, flirting, laughing. And, of course, drinking.

Honestly, he should be down there with them, but somehow he couldn't quite work up the energy. He didn't begrudge his sister her need for entertainment, but he didn't feel lighthearted enough to join in the fun. The horrors he had seen during the Great War had robbed him of a certain ability to escape into mindless fun. And the specter of the Strangler made him wary, unlike his peers who danced and drank to forget.

Mostly, though, Tucker was occupied with his own worries. Specifically, his mind was whirring, busy plotting ways to kill off Detective Spencer Goodnight, Los Angeles Police Department.

He needed something spectacular, of course. Something that did justice to Spencer's illustrative career. Something that pitted Spencer against a formidable enemy, like Holmes against Moriarty.

Too bad Tucker had never created a Moriarty-like character within the *Goodnight: Los Angeles* cast. An astonishing lack of foresight on his part, but he'd certainly never planned on ending the show. Why would he? Of all the radio shows broadcasting from Los Angeles, his was one of the most popular. Families tuned in each week for Spencer Goodnight's next adventure. Certainly Tucker would never get another job in radio after pulling the plug on such a popular—and profitable—enterprise.

That sad fact weighed on him, but bearing down equally hard was the fact that he had no choice. His father had spoken. And in the Greene household, the Colonel's word was law.

Some things, it seemed, were simply too good to be true. And some dreams were destined to die.

As, apparently, was Spencer Goodnight.

Perhaps an ocean liner. Something along the lines of *Titanic*. Goodnight could be on a pleasure voyage. A deb murdered in a grisly fashion. Goodnight finds her killer. But the victory is bittersweet when the ship hits an iceberg and—

"Desperately dull, isn't it, love?"

Tucker jumped, yanked from his fantasy by his sister Blythe. She took a long drag on a cigarette, precariously settled at the end of a silver holder. She tapped the holder against the railing, releasing a flurry of ashes to the crowd below as she watched him, her expression filled with ennui.

"My dearest Blythe, if the hostess is bored, whatever does that say about the quality of the entertainment?" He knew, of course, that his sister was far from bored. With their parents in London for the summer, Blythe had made sure that the Greene family's Beverly Hills estate was the after hours destination for anyone who was anyone.

"The entertainment is just fine," she said, with a twinkle in her eye.

Two flappers ran behind them, giggling as two fellas chased them, champagne sloshing from crystal flutes as they ran.

"Must be me then," Tucker said, turning away from his sister to watch the crowd below him.

"Darling, it's always you." She leaned over and pecked him on the cheek. "You're supposed to be mingling, you know. Playing the host."

"And steal your spotlight? I wouldn't dream of it."

She laughed, then snagged the sleeve of a passing woman. "Lizzy, be a love and find me a drink. I'm positively parched."

Blythe's former school chum winked at Tucker, then disappeared into the crowd, returning momentarily with two flutes of champagne. "The best the host has to offer," she said.

"And the host*ess* has very good taste," Blythe said, lifting her flute.

"I have good taste, too," Lizzy said, sliding an arm around Tucker's waist. She batted her lashes, then pressed her hip flirtatiously against his crotch. Lizzie had suffered under an infatuation with him since she'd been in diapers and Tucker in short pants. Never once during those years had he returned her admiration. Even so, since Tucker was neither dead nor a saint, he found himself immediately standing at attention, his body suddenly interested in the young woman who'd never before captured his eye.

Lizzy noticed, of course, and cupped his crotch. Then she giggled, and he had to wonder just how much naughty salt had tickled her nose. Not that the effect would lessen her appeal in bed. Quite the opposite, actually. A happy side effect of the powder was a certain exuberance among the women in his bed.

Blythe took a sip of her champagne, arched an eyebrow and made a graceful exit, leaving Tucker and Lizzy alone.

He pulled her close, then crushed his mouth over hers, the beads of her dress making a satisfying *shooshing* sound as it scraped against his suit. He grabbed her, his hands tight on her soft rear as he pushed her toward him, their bodies grinding together. So easy, he thought. So easy to lose himself in her. A little sex, a little dance, a little drink. And maybe he could forget his problems. At least until the sun came up.

"Why, Tucker," she said, when they came up for air, "I didn't know you cared."

She was teasing, of course, but the words struck him in the gut, knocking him off-kilter. Because he *didn't* care. Not about the business he was being forced to inherit from his father. Not about the parties his sister lived for. Not about this girl.

He cupped her face in his hands, then pressed a kiss to her forehead. "Go find Roger, Liz," he said, referring to the boyfriend she'd tossed aside a mere two days ago. "Tell him you want to dance."

"I—" Her wide eyes, painted with blue and gold, blinked at him, full of hurt.

Tucker couldn't help himself. He smiled. "Darling Liz," he said. "It's not me you want. It's this." He took her hand and pressed it against his crotch. Then he swept his arm to encompass the room. "And there's a lot of that out there."

He held his breath, afraid he'd pushed her too far, expecting the sting of her palm against his cheek. It didn't come. Instead, the corner of her mouth lifted, and then she laughed.

"Tucker, darling, you are a wonder." She pressed a quick kiss to his cheek, then left in a shimmy of beads and feathers, leaving Tucker not sure whether he should be relieved that she left so easily or insulted that she didn't get into a snit.

He decided to go with relief. Much easier, especially since it was true. Honestly, it wasn't Blythe's party that bored him so much as it was the guest list. Particularly the guests of the female persuasion.

Although they put up a good show—as did he, of course—he had yet to find a woman who was truly interested in him. His money, yes. Or the bit of celebrity that came from writing the Spencer Goodnight broadcasts.

Mostly, though, the girls were interested only in getting in his bed. As if he were there to be conquered.

To a certain extent, he supposed that was true. For that matter, he wasn't entirely sure why he minded. The good Lord knows he'd conquered his share of females. Lately, though, he'd found himself restless. And the idea of bedding another flighty female simply held no appeal.

"Tucker, old man. There you are. Why the devil are you hiding out up here?"

Tucker turned to see Jonathan Straithorn coming toward him, his arms out wide. Jonathan's family lived a few doors down, and he tended to appear whenever Blythe threw one of her parties. A nice enough fella, though Tucker couldn't say he knew the man well.

"So many lovely women for the pickings. Or men, if that's your particular poison." Jonathan cocked his head, indicating the far side of the gallery and the two Ethels, heads so close together Tucker could practically see the heat rise between the two men, so obviously infatuated with each other.

"It's not," he said succinctly.

"Nor mine," Jonathan agreed. "If those two aren't careful, they'll end up in the papers. Rumor is that the Tattletale is here. Along with a crasher toting a camera."

"Bloody hell," Tucker said, irritated that the infamous gossip columnist had crashed the party. He leaned over the rail, scouring the crowd for an unfamiliar face or anyone carrying a camera or a flash pad. The exercise was futile, of course. No one looked familiar. And considering the density of the crowd, he probably wouldn't notice a photographer until the flash powder ignited.

"Bloody hell," he repeated. "You would think with the Strangler still roaming the city the news hounds would have better things to do than chase gossip."

"Ah, but the Ragtime Strangler's a mystery," Jonathan said. "Nothing but questions. Who is he? When will he strike next? Who will be his next victim?" He shrugged. "Not much to report there. But the loves and affairs of the social elite? That, my friend, sells newspapers."

Tucker eyed him curiously. "A very passionate speech. I'd almost think that you are the mysterious Tattletale."

Jonathan chuckled. "I assure you, I am not. Though I will admit to having some secrets."

"Do you now?" Tucker asked, smiling at his neighbor. "You pique my curiosity. Be careful, or I'll have to enlist Blythe's aid. She could coerce a secret out of a priest."

"I imagine she could," Jonathan said with a tight smile. "And I could only dream of being so lucky as to be the subject of your sister's coercive tactics."

"Jonathan, I'm sorry," Tucker said earnestly. "I didn't mean—"

"It's all right," Jonathan said, but his face was still tight and he didn't quite look at Tucker.

Tucker wanted to kick himself. How stupid of him to have suggested getting Jonathan and Blythe together, even in jest. The extent of Jonathan's admiration for Blythe was no secret. Nor, unfortunately, was Blythe's stout refusal to be wooed by the man. "He may be a neighbor," she'd told Tucker, "but I don't like him." No explanation, no second chances. And that, quite simply, was that.

Tucker cleared his throat. "Been two weeks since the Strangler last attacked," he said in an effort to change the subject. "I expect there will be another incident soon."

Jonathan eyed him curiously. "Do you?"

"Seems like a reasonable guess to me," Tucker said. "Like you said, the bastard's getting no press. And my guess is he craves attention. From the world, and from the women he attacks."

"Careful there, Greene. You're turning into your Detective Goodnight."

"I think not," Tucker said. "But the conclusions don't seem out of sorts, do you think? All of his victims have been women with a certain breeding. More, they've all been the types of young women you might see described in the Tattletale's column. Not young women studying abroad or living in a convent."

"Flappers," Jonathan said agreeably. "Women who share our gin. And our beds. Loose women," he added. "Or that's what my father would say, anyway."

Tucker looked at him sharply. "And do you agree?"

Jonathan waved the question away as if it were smoke. "That stuffed shirt? The man has ticker tape where his blood should be. But his attitude does suggest a question. What did the victims do to attract the Strangler's attention?"

"Figure that out, and we can bait the bastard," Tucker said.

"Tell me you're not serious."

"I'm not," Tucker said, though in truth he wished he did have the wherewithal to see such a plan through. That a man was so vilely and violently violating and then murdering Beverly Hills women…well, it made his blood burn.

He'd seen horrors during the war, of course, but those horrors spoke to an ideal. Even though he had been conscripted, and would not care to repeat the experience, he understood and agreed with President Wilson's motives for joining the Allies in the conflict. The vindication of human right, the President had said. And Tucker agreed. To now hear tales of women torn about in the manner of the men he'd crouched with in the French trenches—men less fortunate than he, who had not come home—well, the horror made him ill.

"Speaking of loose women," Jonathan said, unaware that Tucker's mind had wandered. "Isn't that Talia Calvert?" He pointed toward an older woman in orange with an overly large ostrich feather protruding from her head scarf.

Talia Calvert—also known in the gossip magazines as the woman who shared home and hearth with motion picture director R. J. Calvert—tossed her head back in response to something her companion was saying and laughed with delight. She opened her eyes, saw Tucker and waved. Then she aimed her cigarette at him and mouthed, *Don't move*.

Ten minutes later she'd worked her way through the room and up the stairs, flirting and laughing and generally beaming at every male within a fifty-foot radius. She pressed a kiss to each of his cheeks. "Tucker, darling, I'm paralyzed with happiness to see you. And who is your absolutely delicious friend?" she asked, turning to Jonathan.

After Tucker made the introductions, Jonathan pressed a kiss to Talia's hand, sparking a delighted tinkle of laughter. She hooked an arm around his waist and scooted close, apparently claiming Jonathan as hers for the evening. "Have you thought any more about R.J.'s offer?" she asked, tossing her husband's name into the mix even while her hand slid down to knead Jonathan's ass.

Tucker tried to keep a straight face, pointedly looking at Talia's eyes and not the direction of travel of her nimble fingers. "R.J. and I have had this conversation, Talia. I'm not leaving radio to move into film. I'm leaving radio to take the helm of my father's empire."

"Empire," she said with a laugh and a wave of her hand. "Darling, the war is over, or hadn't you heard? Leave the munitions as your father's legacy and move on."

"He's diversified," Tucker said, forcing his voice to stay calm and reasonable even though he wanted to scream at her to drop the damn subject. He had no interest in stepping in to fill his father's shoes. But what choice did he have? He'd been born to this life and, as his father had said, it was his obligation to protect it and the family. Just as it had been his obligation to fight for his country in the war. He'd pursued his own dream for the past four years, writing radio plays. Now it was time to look to duty.

"Diversified?" Talia asked.

"Most of my father's days now are spent overseeing his portfolio."

At that, Talia actually snorted her gin, which had the side effect of forcing her to remove her hand from Jonathan's tush so that she could dab at the front of her dress. Jonathan, always a gentleman, pulled out a handkerchief and dabbed it over Talia's breasts.

"You?" Talia said, pressing her hand over Jonathan's to stop his dabbing, and forcing him to cup her left breast. "Darling, I really can't imagine you spending the day in a dreary room reading a ticker tape."

"I hardly expect you to imagine me at all, Talia," Tucker said, pointedly dropping his gaze to her chest. "I should think you'd have many other things to fantasize about."

"Indeed," she said, apparently knowing when to end a conversation. Or, perhaps, simply ready to find a dark corner. "Too bad, though. You have such talent. R.J. will be disappointed."

Tucker looked at Jonathan. "Yes. I imagine he will."

"Tucker!" They all looked up as Blythe rushed toward them, causing curious guests to turn in her direction as she sped past.

"Darling, what is it?" Tucker asked as his sister clutched his arm, her chest heaving.

"There's a woman on the floor in the drawing room," she said. "I think she may be dead!"

CHAPTER THREE

"THE STRANGLER?" Tucker asked as he ran down the stairs, breathless, behind his sister.

"I don't know. She's just…lying there."

"I can't imagine the Strangler would hit now," Jonathan said. "Too many people. He's never been that bold before."

"Just *hurry*," Blythe said.

They rounded the corner, moving farther away from the grand ballroom and the rear veranda and rushing down the hall toward the front door and the thick, carved oak doorway that led into the drawing room.

The doors were closed, and Tucker shot a questioning glance toward his sister. The room was usually kept open, and during their fetes, the room often saw the still-sober crowd, smoking and discussing philosophy or jazz from the comfort of the oiled-and-rubbed leather furniture.

"I didn't want anyone wandering in," Blythe said. "I left Anna in there with the body," she added, referring to their housekeeper.

"Good Lord, woman," Jonathan cried. "Have you gone mad? Anna with a dead body? The story will be all over the gossip rags by tomorrow. I imagine that wretched photographer has beaten us to the room."

"I'll thank you not to question my judgments in my home, Jonathan," Blythe said, looking down her nose at him. "I trust Anna implicitly. She's been with us for years."

"Perhaps you would do well not to—"

"Enough," Tucker said. "There's no point in bickering. Open the door and we'll see the situation for what it is, whatever it is."

As it turned out, Blythe was right. Their motherly housekeeper hadn't moved, and certainly hadn't brought in any other help. Instead, she was hunched over the prone form of a young woman. She held one of the girl's hands tight against her breast, and with her free hand, she patted the girl's cheek.

Tucker raised his brow. "I know that the dubious bit of combat medicine I gleaned during my infantry days is no substitution for a formal medical education, Anna darling, but I sincerely doubt that a pat on the cheek will prove restorative."

"She's not dead, sir. Just a mite under the weather."

Tucker took a tentative step forward and found himself looking into a very alive—albeit very unconscious—face. A beautiful face, too, with light brown hair framing angelic features.

She wore no makeup, unlike the current fashion, and Tucker tried to recall the last time he'd seen a young woman without her face painted. He'd gotten so used to seeing his sister and her friends, their eyes outlined in kohl, their lids painted blue, their cheeks and lips flush with rouge.

He'd forgotten how fresh a woman could look. Soft and new, as if she'd just woken in his arms after a night of lovemaking.

Tucker closed his eyes, frowning, and wondered where the devil such absurd thoughts had come from. Yes, the woman was attractive, but she was also quite knocked out. And he was behaving like a foolish schoolboy.

Quickly, before anyone noticed his distraction, he bent beside her, shrugging out of his jacket and laying it over her. "Yours, too, Jonathan," he said. "If she's in shock, we need to keep her warm."

"Do you think that's it?" Talia asked. "Shock? Did she meet the Strangler perhaps?" Her eyes, Tucker noticed, were wide with excitement. "And what a strange costume she's wearing. Dungarees and that odd top. I realize this is a masquerade party, but I don't think I've ever seen a young woman choose such inappropriate attire. It's both provocative and entirely unflattering."

"Out," said Tucker firmly.

"Pardon me?" Talia's eyebrows rose in amazement.

Tucker nodded his head, in deference to the woman's years. "Please. I'd like you to step out." In truth, he agreed with Talia's assessment. It all was very odd. And the way the black material clung to her breasts was, indeed, very alluring. "The girl hardly needs to wake up to five strangers peering at her as if she were a carnival sideshow."

For a moment, he thought Talia would argue. But the older woman surprised him, her eyes losing their scandalous gleam and fading to a warm sympathy. "Quite so," she said. She took Jonathan by the elbow and started to steer them both toward the door. Jonathan, however, held back.

"You, too, old man," Tucker said.

"Very well," Jonathan said. "But first, a word."

Reluctantly, Tucker left the girl's side. "What?"

"The way she's dressed. Dark colors. Pants more suitable for a working man." He exhaled loudly. "The woman has a pretty face, but don't fail to consider the obvious, Tucker. Your home is filled with valuables as well as with your guests. You'd do well to ensure the security of both."

Tucker bit back an instinctive response to slug Jonathan and defend the girl's honor. Instead he nodded stiffly. "Of course," he said, then motioned for the door.

"Give a shout if you need anything," Jonathan said, casting one backward glance at them before the oak doors swung shut, leaving Tucker alone with Anna, Blythe and the unconscious woman.

"Anna, go prepare a room. I expect we'll have an overnight guest."

"Of course, sir. Should I send for Dr. Williams?"

Tucker looked at Blythe, who shrugged. "Yes," he told Anna. "I think that might be a good idea."

As Anna scurried out to take care of the various tasks, Tucker bent over the woman, her hand tight in his. Blythe knelt down beside them, her face furrowed with concern. "Whatever could be wrong with her?"

"I don't know," Tucker said. He couldn't remember ever feeling this helpless in his life. Not even during the nine months he spent fighting in the war, with artillery bursting all around him. At least then he'd had a sidearm, had a fair chance of staying alive. And he'd understood the situation.

"Where do you think she came from? Did she come for the party? Does she know one of the guests? Perhaps she's come to work. We hired dozens and dozens of waiters. Could she be wearing some odd new uniform?"

"Blythe," Tucker said, without looking at his sister, "do be quiet."

Blythe made a hurt little noise, but she complied, and for that, Tucker was grateful. He needed to think, and he couldn't get his head around the situation, not with her blathering on and on. He knew the answer to none of her questions, and that one simple fact preyed on him. This beautiful woman had collapsed in his drawing room, and he had no idea as to her identity or purpose. No idea about anything at all, for that matter.

Except for one thing.

Something about the woman fascinated him. He brushed his fingers across her cheek in a soft caress, wishing he knew what had brought her to him. Although he couldn't explain it, the scent of danger filled the air, and just looking at her made him want to ball his hands into fists, leap to his feet and play the savior.

Only, what, he wondered, would he be saving her from?

He didn't know. All he knew for sure was that a compulsion was growing within him. A deeply felt need to watch over this woman. To protect her.

And right then, with her hand held tight in his own, he silently promised to do just that.

SYLVIA OPENED HER eyes, managed to process the bizarre realization that she was flat on her back with a strange man's eyes peering down at her, and screamed.

She sat bolt upright, still screaming, the sound coming clearer and stronger as she changed position and pulled more air into her lungs. The sound—or possibly the movement—drove the man backward, and she told herself that was a good thing, even as a small part of her mind mourned the fact that he was no longer stroking her hand.

"It's okay, it's okay," a woman's soft voice murmured beside her, and Sylvia turned, her head swimming with the motion, and her stomach threatening to lose its tenuous hold on whatever she'd eaten recently. What *had* she eaten recently? She couldn't remember. She frowned, concentrating as she tried to force her mind to feel like something other than warm Jell-O.

Right. Yes. Of course. Pancakes at DuPars at the Farmers Market. Then she and Tina had tooled down Sunset in Tina's convertible, and stopped at the Greene mansion for the sex exhibit.

The frown deepened, and she turned her head, taking in the familiar—and yet oddly different—room. "Where are the exhibit cases?" she asked. She saw the *Robin Hood* poster, framed and on the wall instead of propped on an easel. But nothing else seemed familiar. "For that matter, where's Tina? Or that guard?"

The woman and man looked at each other, shaking their heads in very obvious confusion.

Sylvia fought off a warm rush of panic and forced herself to speak very slowly. "What happened to me?"

The woman beside her shot a frown toward the man. "We're not sure what happened," she said softly. "We think you fainted."

"Oh." Sylvia considered that. As far as she knew, she'd never fainted in her life. Considering all the box-lugging, furniture-moving and shelf-hanging she'd done over the past few days, perhaps she would have been smart to have worried less about calories and eaten more than half a pancake at breakfast. "Okay then," she said, looking into the woman's eyes. "Then who are you?"

"I'm Blythe," the woman said. "And this is Tucker," she added, pointing toward the man. "Who are you?"

"I'm Sylvia," she said automatically, her eyes never leaving Tucker's face. It was an interesting face, to go with an interesting name. And how curious that Louisa had just mentioned her grandfather, also named Tucker.

This Tucker was darkly handsome, with tiny lines at the corners of his eyes, as if he knew how to laugh and practiced often. And those eyes! They watched her with an intensity that should have made her uncomfortable but instead made her feel inexplicably warm and safe. As if his only purpose in the world was to watch over her.

"When I opened my eyes," she said, "I saw your eyes. I thought you were an angel."

His grin shot down to her toes. "So naturally you screamed your head off."

Her cheeks warmed with the blush. "The angel thing only lasted a second," she said. "Then I realized I was lying on the ground and I'd never seen you before in my life."

"I *was* looking out for you," he said. "We thought you were injured. I was trying to help you."

"I believe you," she said, hoping he understood that she was telling the truth. For some reason, she didn't want this man to think she was afraid of him.

She started to climb to her feet, and Blythe moved in and took her arm for support. Her head started swimming about halfway up, though, and she sank back down to the ground. "Maybe it's a little too soon for that," she said.

"Can you tell us what happened?" Tucker said, settling himself comfortably on the floor beside her.

"I'm not sure I can," she said. "I remember looking at the exhibit, and talking with Louisa about the portraits and the history of the house. Stuff like that. And then I went back into the exhibit to find my friend Tina. She went off to find some food, and I ended up chatting with the guard. And then he dropped a coin, and I volunteered to pick it up for him. But then I felt a shove, and…." She trailed off with a shrug, not willing to confess the very odd sensation of falling through a picture. "I guess I passed out."

Tucker and Blythe were looking at each other more than her, and though she tried, Sylvia couldn't interpret the signals that seemed to be passing between them.

She watched them, then decided she might as well ask what had put that look of concerned confusion in their eyes. But when she opened her mouth to ask, a completely different question came out. "So, um, are you two married?"

She clapped her hand over her mouth, completely mortified. "I'm so sorry," she said. "I must be dizzier than I thought. That is *so* not my business."

She wanted to look at Blythe while she spoke, but her eyes kept drifting to Tucker who, she was relieved to see, looked amused rather than upset.

"She's my sister," he said, with a tender smile that made her heart do little backflips. "Who is Louisa?"

"The lady who lives here," Sylvia said. "At least, she lives in the part of the house without the exhibits." She looked around the room again. "Where on earth did the exhibit cases go?"

"The room's the same as it's always been," Blythe said. "As for Louisa, maybe you ended up at the wrong house? Tucker and I live here. Our parents, too, when they aren't in London."

"Oh." Sylvia reached up to rub her temples, trying to process that information. "Is Tina here, then? Did I have some sort of walking blackout?" Maybe she and Tina had moved on to the next event in Tina's packed schedule for the day? Since Sylvia had never fainted before, she wasn't entirely sure how she would react. Maybe losing hours and hours was perfectly normal.

Automatically, she stretched out her arm, pulling her sleeve back to reveal her pink Swatch. The damn thing was stopped, the second hand stuck firmly on the twelve, and the time at eleven forty-five, just about the time Tina had headed off for a snack.

So much for the lost-time theory. That was okay, she supposed. Because as disconcerting as the odd memory lapses were, they weren't nearly as frustrating as this damn headache. She could barely even focus, the pain was so intense.

Experimentally, she concentrated on the wall, squinting until one of the portraits came into focus. A man, in a dinner jacket, a monocle in one eye. She'd seen it before. Near the portrait of Louisa's grandmother.

"This is the house," Sylvia said. "I remember that portrait." She frowned. "But the one of Louisa's grandmother isn't here."

She frowned, wondering what was going on, when she once again saw Blythe and Tucker exchange looks filled with confusion and concern.

"Okay," Sylvia said. "Enough. Why do you keep

looking at each other like that? Am I talking crazy? You're acting like I should be in the nuthouse or something."

"This Louisa," Tucker said. "What was her last name? Do you know?"

"Of course," Sylvia said. "Louisa Greene. I told you. She owns the house."

"She doesn't," Tucker said, looking at Blythe rather than at her. "There is no Louisa Greene. This house is owned by Irene and Carson Greene. Our parents."

She blinked at that, trying hard to get a grip on reality. "Greene," she repeated. "Your last name is Greene?"

"Yes." He frowned at her, his brow creased with worry. "Miss, are you okay?"

She realized she'd put a hand to her head, and she could tell without a mirror that she was pale. "I...I guess I must just be a bit confused." *That* was certainly an understatement.

"I imagine so," he said. "As you can see, there aren't any exhibit cases here," he said. "They're as mysterious as Louisa."

"Right." She licked her lips.

"I think you need a doctor," he said. He looked up at his sister. "Can you go see if Anna's managed to locate Dr. Williams?"

"Of course." She bent down and gave Sylvia's hand a squeeze. "Everything's going to be fine, darling." And then she floated out of the room, her short, beaded gown shimmering in the soft lighting.

"Flapper," she whispered, her mind registering the clothes even before she'd realized. "Like in the exhibit room."

"Pardon?"

"Oh, my God," she whispered, as her heart started to pound in her chest. Her skin went cold, and she felt her insides start to tremble with a sensation that felt remarkably like an anxiety attack. Hell, maybe it *was* an anxiety attack. If the ridiculous theory trying to squeeze into her mind was correct, she had every reason to be anxious. "Oh, my God," she whispered again.

"Are you all right?" His eyes were filled with so much concern that her heart nearly melted, and she was overcome with the urge to touch him. No, not just touch, but to kiss him. The urge was overwhelming for that matter, as if she might be sucked out of this world and into oblivion if she couldn't find her footing in this man's arms.

Prodded by some force she couldn't control, she leaned forward, pressed her palms against his cheeks, and pressed her lips against his. Soft yet firm, his mouth moved beneath hers, first in surprise, and then in response. They kissed deeply, their tongues meeting and mating. Liquid lust pooled in her belly and between her thighs, her breasts tingling with desire, and her body weak with longing.

"Not that I'm complaining," he said when they pulled apart, all too soon from Sylvia's point of view. "But what was that for?"

"I needed to feel alive," she said, only realizing as she spoke the words that they were exactly true. And that it had worked. The kiss had worked a magic on her, sending electric currents through every part of her body. Making her feel safe and alive and grounded.

She drew in a breath, still unsteady from the rush of desire. "Tucker, what day is it?"

"September tenth," he said. "What day is the last you recall?"

"What year?" she asked, ignoring the second part of his question and tightening her hands into fists as she steeled herself for his answer.

"Nineteen twenty-three," he said. "Why do you ask?"

But once again, she didn't answer. Because even though she'd told herself that had to be the explanation—even though she'd expected to hear from his lips that she'd somehow traveled back in time—now that he'd said the date aloud she knew that she couldn't open her mouth. Not right then. Not yet.

Because if she did, she'd surely scream again.

CHAPTER FOUR

DR. WILLIAMS bent over the girl, his hand clutching her wrist, his focus directed solely at his pocketwatch. The woman, Tucker noticed, also had a watch. Hers was strapped to a pink strip and wrapped around her wrist. An usual piece of adornment, to be sure. Like nothing he'd seen before, either among the women of Beverly Hills or during his European travels.

He'd almost pointed it out to Talia and Blythe, but something had caused him to hold his tongue, and by the time Blythe had looked at him, her eyes questioning and concerned, the timepiece had disappeared under the sleeve of the girl's strange garment.

"Doctor?" the girl said. "Am I okay?"

Dr. Williams stood up, stroking his chin. "Your pulse is a bit fast, but not of a level to raise concern. Your pupils are responding properly to light and your reflexes are perfectly normal. Except for your dizzy spells and your inability to remember how you got here, I'd have to say you seem like a perfectly healthy young woman."

"Thank you," she said, with obvious relief.

"I do need to ask you some questions now, though. I conducted the physical examination, first, to rule out any injuries or illnesses. But now—"

"You want to check my head. I get it."

Williams's smile was gentle, and Tucker found himself grateful he was treating the woman with such care. Intellectually, he knew that was a ridiculous reaction. The woman had appeared mysteriously in his drawing room, dressed in dark clothes and unknown to any of his friends or guests. A logical guess was that she intended to steal from them, just as Jonathan had suggested. Their kiss, however, had told him otherwise. The press of her lips against his had been a reaction filled with need and desire, but also with honesty. And the longing that had fired his blood had been like nothing he'd experienced before.

Logic, therefore, had very little hold on Tucker at the moment. He was, quite simply, infatuated. More, he knew—from her face and from her touch—that she did not intend any harm for him or his family. She was in trouble. She needed him.

And, in truth, he needed her, too. He didn't understand the depth of feeling that coursed through him, but he knew that it was real.

"Ask me anything," the girl was saying to Dr. Williams.

"Do you know what your name is?"

"Sylvia," she said, and Tucker couldn't help but notice that she didn't volunteer her last name.

"A pleasure to meet you, Sylvia," Dr. Williams said. "Do you know our president?"

The girl laughed, a little nervously. "Do I look like a girl who moves in those social circles?"

Tucker laughed, and the doctor joined in.

"I don't mean to be flip," Sylvia said. "But I'm fine. Truly. Just a little dizzy. I was disoriented, but I'm better now."

"But you came for Louisa," Blythe said. "And we don't know a Louisa."

"I met her at a party," Sylvia said. "Perhaps I misunderstood her last name. Or perhaps she was playing a trick on me."

"Why would she do that?" Tucker asked.

"I don't know."

"Can you stand?" That from the doctor.

She drew in a breath. "I think so." She started to climb to her feet, taking Tucker's outstretched arm when he offered it to her. "Yes," she said. "See, I'm much better." She kept clinging to his arm, though, a fact that didn't trouble Tucker at all.

"And do you know where you live, my dear?" the doctor asked.

"Doctor, of course. You're acting as if no one has ever fainted before," she said with a charming smile. To Tucker's eyes, though, the smile didn't seem to reach her core. She was, he realized, lying. Or at least not telling them the full truth.

"How's your head?" he asked. "Anna will have made a place for you by now in one of the guest rooms. We should let you get some sleep."

"Oh," she said. "I couldn't. I mean, I should…" She trailed off with a frown.

"You should?"

"I was just going to say that I should go home. But—"

"Later," he said, determined to keep her there. "It's late, and I wouldn't feel right letting you travel in your condition. She should stay for the night, shouldn't she, Blythe?"

Blythe's eyes shifted with remarkable speed from

surprise to delight. "Absolutely," Blythe said. "You can stay as long as you need until you're feeling better." She took Sylvia's other arm and shot a triumphant smile toward Tucker.

He wanted to tell her not to be melodramatic. He was simply concerned for the girl. He was acting out of chivalry, not romance.

But even had they been alone, he couldn't have said any of that. Because the truth was that from the first moment he'd seen her on his floor, Sylvia had fascinated him more than any of the women giggling and dancing in his ballroom or on his veranda. Until he knew why— until he'd explored the possibilities with this woman— Tucker didn't intend to let her get away.

TIME TRAVEL.

Sylvia sat at the foot of the bed, her silk-clad knees hugged to her chest, as she let the words flit through her head one more time.

Time travel.

Could it really be possible?

Considering she was sitting here in a bedroom of the Greene mansion—which was clearly *not* doubling as a museum—wearing silk pajamas and listening to the dying strains of "Has Anybody Seen My Girl" played on a scratchy phonograph somewhere in the house... well, she had to admit that the idea of time travel was feeling pretty damn plausible.

She got up and paced, loving the feel of the soft pajamas against her skin. Blythe had told her to help herself to anything in the room, and she'd taken the girl at her word, pulling on the decadently soft outfit, like something she'd find in a vintage-clothing store, and certainly not like the ratty T-shirt and panties she wore to bed in her own time.

No, these pajamas made her feel feminine. Sexy even, and she felt her cheeks heat at the thought—and at the image of the man that flashed into her head. *Tucker Greene*. And not the vague concept of him, either, as some force in Hollywood. No, this Tucker Greene was flesh and blood and devilishly sexy. Their kiss had fired her blood, heated her soul. And although she'd not been thinking clearly when she'd put her mouth to his, now her thoughts were focused and clean. She wanted him. She wanted him with a fury like nothing she'd ever felt before.

She'd been attracted to many men in her life, but none so strongly—or so instantaneously—as Tucker. Under the circumstances, the attraction seemed bizarre. After all, she was time-traveling here. Sex should be the last thing on her mind. And, honestly, it was. But even through the haze of confusion, her body had tingled with his proximity, and she'd mourned a little when Blythe and Anna had escorted her to this room.

"God, you're as bad as Tina," she whispered to herself, getting up to pace the room and force the prurient thoughts from her head. She was in another decade. Another millennium, for that matter. Best she focus on that, and forget about the supersexy man of the house. At least for the moment.

Resolved, she made a quick pass of the room, confirming what she already knew: no television, no digital alarm clock, not even a radio even though she was certain radios existed in the twenties. But back then the family had gathered around it, right? And they all sat together like a family listening to *The Shadow* or Jack Benny or whoever it was that was around during that time. Honestly, if she'd known she was going to be time-traveling, she would have paid more attention in history class. Or at least watched The History Channel more often.

Time travel. Now that was something for the Discovery Channel, and unfortunately she hadn't watched much of that, either. She still couldn't quite grasp it, despite all the evidence. Her hesitation probably made sense. After all, the whole concept wasn't exactly within the realm of normal.

She should be in shock. Freaking out. Borderline hysterical. That was the proper way to act when the unimaginable happened to you, right? Except she wasn't any of those things, because to Sylvia, the situation wasn't unimaginable at all. Instead, it was the culmination of all her dreams.

That was the real reason she couldn't quite wrap her head around the concept. Because if it were true—if she had really traveled through time—then all of her hopes and fantasies really had come true. And that seemed like too much to wish for.

With a sigh, she sat back on the bed, the intricately embroidered pillows propped behind her back. *It was true.* Being here meant that all those afternoons of wishing she could be swept away to a different land—of wishing she could find the magic wardrobe and Aslan the King—had paid off.

Dear God. She'd finally gotten her childhood wish, but it had come too damn late. Martin had been dead for years now. If Fate was going to toss her backward by almost a century, then why in hell couldn't it have happened when she truly needed the escape?

She got off the bed and started pacing again. She had to get back, of course. She had a fabulous job she was supposed to start in the morning. Not that she had a clue *how* to get back.

Still, she had to figure out a way. She had obligations and a life that she'd fought for tooth and nail despite the specter of Martin always hanging over her shoulder. He may have tried to screw up her life—both literally and figuratively—but in the end she'd come out on top. She'd aced every school she'd attended, and the bidding war when she'd graduated law school had been a beauty to behold. She was a success now—one hundred percent—and that was all in spite of Martin Straithorn.

Of course, just thinking his name made her shiver, and she rubbed her hands over her arms, trying to make the goose bumps disappear. "So much for coming out on top," she whispered, the sound of her voice making her feel a little crazy because, honestly, who talked to themselves?

All of a sudden, she wished Tina were there. That wish, however, wasn't going to come true. Sylvia was all alone, just as she had been so much of her life. Alone, and always running away.

She paused for a moment, her mind in a whirl as she thought about how she'd run toward academia and work, even while she was running away from Martin and the memories. She'd used her work to substitute for a relationship because she couldn't handle the intimacy. She couldn't handle the give and take that came with an honest relationship with a man, because all Martin ever did was take. She *knew* that. Her motivations were so clear any Psych 101 student could see them.

But knowing and changing were two different things. Blame the man, sure. But she still had to wriggle out from under his thumb.

She just wasn't sure how to do that.

She'd reached the window and now looked blankly down toward the manicured lawn, watching the men in suits and the women in colorful dresses flit away into the night.

One turned, looking up toward her window. *Tucker*. She gasped, realizing her heart had started pounding double time. She didn't even know the man, and yet his touch had fired her blood.

Pheromones. She'd learned all about them in biology. Their effect on fruit flies, animals and, of course, people.

Sexual attraction, chemistry, lust at first sight. Whatever you called it, it was real. Scientifically established. Her body chemistry reacted to his. That was all. That was what had compelled her to kiss him.

But she couldn't help wondering if his body reacted the same way to hers, although she was pretty sure it had. There'd been real passion in his kiss, after all.

She smiled a little at the possibility, at the same time thinking that she must be an idiot. Because how many girls who found themselves thrust into the 1920s spent their time lusting after a man instead of trying to figure out how to get back home?

She didn't know the answer. But even with the question hanging out there, she knew one thing—she wanted Tucker Greene.

The thought took her a little aback. Sure, she'd been attracted to guys on and off all her life. After all, Martin may have screwed up her ability to communicate sexually, but he hadn't put a dent in her ability to lust after a man. But she'd never felt for a guy anything like what she now felt for Tucker. A desperate longing. An almost physical need. The sense that if she couldn't touch him again, the world would never shift back and everything would be slightly off-kilter from now until the end of time.

Melodramatic, but that was how she felt. And because of that, she took a deep breath and allowed herself to consider the decadent little thought that had been seeking entrance to her mind: Tina's words, loud and clear in her head. *"Find a man you want and take charge. No strings, no expectations. Just make it all about Sylvia. Get exactly what you want from the guy. And once you do that, you'll be free of Martin. I promise."*

Tina's plan had seemed unlikely and frivolous while standing in the museum, now it seemed not only palatable but promising.

Tucker Greene could be the focus of her Grand Experiment. A chance to follow Tina's advice and to take what she wanted. Not her usual behavior, to be sure, but nothing about this situation was usual. She could be gone in a split second, right? For that matter, she wasn't even really here. After all, she wouldn't even be born for another sixty-some years.

So why not—as Tina said—take what she wanted?

She took a deep breath, steeling her resolve. She was going to seduce Mr. Tucker Greene. And for the first time in her life, she intended to be the one in charge between the sheets.

Scary to be sure. But mostly, Sylvia simply couldn't wait.

SYLVIA COULDN'T SLEEP.

She tried. Everything from counting sheep to singing lullabies to herself.

Nothing worked. She told herself that she simply wasn't tired. For all she knew she'd been blissfully asleep for the equivalent of days as she traveled back through time. It wasn't as if she understood the physics of going back, after all. For all she knew, it had taken a full month of "her" time to get here.

A nice theory, but probably not true. More likely, she couldn't sleep because she couldn't get her mind to calm down. Having come up with a plan, now she wanted to implement it.

Trouble was, she wasn't very good at first steps. At least not where men were concerned.

A soft tap at her door startled her, and she jumped. Probably Blythe, come to check on her. She drew in a breath, slid out of bed and called, "Come in."

A rattle and then the door pushed open. Sylvia's heart did a skittering number as she saw that it wasn't Blythe standing there at all. It was Tucker, and her pulse immediately picked up its tempo. This was her chance, she thought, even as she wondered if she could see it through.

"Ah," he said, looking at her, then immediately at the floor. "I beg your pardon, Sylvia. I thought I heard you say come in."

"I did," she said, wondering what was wrong with him. The thought had barely entered her mind, when she realized the answer. She was in pajamas. True, they covered up more of her body than many of the outfits in her closet at home, but they were pajamas nonetheless. Intimate apparel. And this was, after all, another era.

"I'm so sorry," she said, slipping into a robe she'd found earlier. "I don't know where my head is. Please, I'm decent now."

He looked up then, and the heat she saw in his eyes sent a trill of power through her. Without a doubt, he'd had the same reaction to her that she'd had to him. And if she wanted to take advantage of the situation, now would be a perfect time.

The trouble, of course, was that she had no clue what to do. She took a step toward him, wishing she had Tina's bold confidence. How could she be so confident in the courtroom and so muddled with a man? It really defied explanation.

"Did you—" She broke off, cleared her throat, and tried again. "Did you need something?"

"No, I…" He moved closer, and she matched him step by step until they were separated only by inches, the air between them crackling with need. She wanted to touch him, but although she had the desire, she couldn't quite find the courage.

"I saw your light on," he said. "I just wanted to make sure you had everything you needed."

Not everything. But she couldn't say the words aloud. Instead, she nodded. "I'm fine," she said, watching his chest rise and fall. His eyes stayed on her, dark brown and intense. Filled with concern and something else, too. A familiar heat that she was certain was matched by her own steady gaze.

Do it! Walk one step toward him and kiss him. You've

already kissed him once. Just do it again. Take control, just like Tina said.

Right. She could do that. This was fantasy. She was in a world not her own, and when would she ever have such an opportunity to be bold again?

Before she could stop herself, she shifted her weight, starting to take the last step toward him. She froze, however, when he started to speak.

"I also wanted to make sure you weren't uncomfortable."

She peered at him, confused, and something in his tone making her wary. "Not at all. It's a lovely room. Blythe gave me carte blanche with the closet. And these pajamas are awesome."

"Yes," he said, clearing his throat and not quite looking her in the eyes. "I noticed." He cleared his throat again. "Ah, what I mean to say is that I understand you were a bit dizzy and delirious earlier. I hope you don't think that I would be so bold as to presume any intentions on your part because of our earlier, ah, kiss."

It was Sylvia's turn to blush. "Oh. Right." Damn. So much for her ability to read men. In the moment, she'd thought he'd been enjoying the kiss. Apparently, he'd only been indulging her particular neurosis. "Um, thanks for telling me."

"You're welcome," he said. It was essentially an exit line, and she expected him to turn and leave.

Except he didn't. He stood there, looking at her, his expression soft, his eyes warm and inviting. So inviting, in fact, that she almost took another step toward him.

She tried to channel Tina. Tried to conjure up some

semblance of control. Of a woman who could, in fact, have the upper hand with a man.

But whatever confidence she'd gathered only moments ago had vanished, and she found herself unable to meet his eyes. Even as she cursed her hesitation, she heard herself say, "Thanks for coming to check on me. That was very sweet of you."

"Of course," he said. "You're our guest. We want you to be comfortable. If you need anything during the night—"

Butterflies fluttered in her stomach, riding waves of hope. "Yes?"

"—Blythe's room is the last door on the left. Or you can ring for Anna."

"Oh. Sure. Thanks," she said, the butterflies turning to lead weights.

He turned then and left, his departing gesture nothing more sensual than a smile.

Sylvia stood there, staring at the door and cursing herself for her failed attempt to take control. Even in the twenties, she thought, some things never seemed to change.

TUCKER PACED THE length of his room, not sure if he should be thanking his parents or cursing them. Because it was only their constant drilling of manners into his head that had made him walk away from Sylvia.

Damn.

He'd wanted her—still wanted her. And it had cost him dearly to walk away.

Even now, he could imagine the way the soft silk of those pajamas felt under his hands. The buttons hard against his fingers as he made short work of them. The softness of his skin against his palm and the beat of her heart pounding in time with his own.

He pressed his hands to his head, cursing himself. It was as if the woman had worked a spell on him. She was beautiful, yes, but she was also confused, possibly sick, and most definitely lost. He wasn't a scoundrel. And only a scoundrel would take advantage of a woman in her condition.

He paused in front of his window and looked down at the yard. Only a few stragglers remained. Understandable since it was almost four in the morning. Still, if he went down now, surely he could find someone to share a drink—or five—with. He needed to sleep. And with Sylvia on his mind, sleep wasn't going to come without a bit of gin to help it along.

Armed with a plan to keep his mind off the girl, he crossed to his door and yanked it open, then gasped as he saw her standing there, her hand raised as if she were just about to knock.

"Sylvia!"

"I— Oh, I didn't realize you were stepping out. I'm…I'm sorry."

"No, no. It's—"

"Wait." She closed her eyes, drew in a breath. When she opened her eyes again, she seemed calmer, less confused, and certainly more in control. She squared her shoulders, lifted her chin and pointed at him. "You," she said, her voice trembling just slightly. "Back in the room."

"Pardon?" But she was already stepping toward him, and he had no choice but to move backward. As soon as she cleared the threshold, she kicked back, catching the door and slamming it shut. "Does it lock?"

"Yes," he said, then watched with increasing fascination as she engaged the lock and handed him the key.

She drew in a breath, looking nervous and determined and positively delicious. "I hope I'm not intruding."

"No," he said, feeling himself harden, and hating himself for so desperately hoping that she'd come to him in that way. "Not at all."

"Good." Her features relaxed a bit, and her mouth curved into a smile. "I had second thoughts," she said.

"About what?"

"About letting you leave my room."

Heat coursed through his veins, and he felt a wave of relief. He'd been right. Thank God, he'd been right. "I see," he said, hoping he really did.

"Did I misunderstand?" she asked, her voice losing some of its power and taking on a vulnerable tone. "I thought you had wanted to stay. That you'd only left to be polite. Proper." She licked her lips. "Was I wrong?"

He could practically hear his parents screaming in his head for him to send the girl back to her room. She'd had a difficult evening. She was confused. No gentleman would take advantage of her in that state.

Tucker, however, wasn't concerned with being a gentleman. Not then. Not with her.

Slowly, he shook his head, his eyes never leaving hers. "No," he said. "You didn't misunderstand." And then, when he saw the flare of heat in her eyes, he knew that he'd said exactly the right thing.

SYLVIA COULDN'T believe she'd done it.

After he'd left her room, she'd cursed herself, trying

to talk herself into following him. She'd never expected to convince herself, though. And the fact that she had— that she'd actually ended up outside Tucker's door— both delighted and baffled her.

Fantasy, she reminded herself. She wasn't even born yet. This wasn't real, no matter how much it might feel real. This was just a chance. A chance to be in charge. A chance to work out the demons of her personal past here in the temporal past. Because right now she should have no demons. Martin didn't exist any more than she did. All that mattered in this world was her and Tucker and that zing of desire she'd felt arc between them.

Fulfill the promise embedded in that zing, and she could go back to her own time with a new confidence. The kind of confidence she'd wanted to take with her to Los Angeles, leaving her sexual shyness behind with Dwight in San Francisco.

That had to be why the guard had sent her here, after all. Because she was certain he *had* sent her. All that talk about the past, and then the business with the coin. She didn't know how he did it. But she was absolutely certain that the exhibit guard was responsible.

Only time would tell if she should thank him or curse him. But as she stood there looking at Tucker, her heart was filled only with gratitude. And desire.

"I convinced myself I needed to come after you," she said, distilling the lecture she'd given herself in her room to its most basic components.

"I'm glad you did," he said.

"Are you?" she moved toward him, her voice low, her body humming.

"You may think me very ungentlemanly, but I've craved you from the first moment I saw you." He'd moved even closer to her as he spoke, and now he was mere inches away, so close she could feel the heat of his skin, and the scent of him made her light-headed.

More than his proximity, though, it was his words that thrilled her, firing her confidence. "Kiss me," she said boldly, forcing the demand out before she could stop herself.

He didn't give her any time to change her mind. The request had barely left her lips when his mouth blocked any further words. His lips were soft, yet firm, and captured her fully. One hand snaked around her waist, and the other held the back of her head, holding her captive as his tongue sought entrance and explored the heat of her mouth.

Her body reacted, melting against him even as her head screamed for her not to give in, to take charge. To take *him*.

But the connection between mind and body had been severed. She was losing herself to the sensations. His mouth. His hands. The way his fingers stole down the pajama top, managing to combine skill and fumbling as he unfastened the buttons and freed her breasts.

His hands cupped them, his thumbs rubbing her rock-hard nipples. She tilted her head back and lost herself to the pleasure. And it *was* good. His touch, the heat that coursed through her, the trembling in her belly. Nothing dangerous. Nothing scary.

But also nothing in her control.

It's okay to give up control when you *want to.* The words ricocheted through her head, and she told herself they were true. Martin had *taken* her control away. Here, she was giving it freely to Tucker.

His mouth left hers, and she gasped, sucking in delicious air to cool the heat raging within her. A heat that didn't dissipate when he pressed his mouth to her neck and started kissing his way down, lower and lower, his lips caressing the curve of her breasts even as his fingers kneaded and pulled, igniting a fuse that ran from her nipples all the way down to between her thighs.

She pressed her legs together, not sure if she was trying to quell the need building there or satisfy it. All she knew was that she couldn't keep still, and she writhed against him, desperate for his touch.

His lips didn't disappoint, as he continued his southward journey. His tongue played across her skin, tickling her navel as he teased and promised with his lips and hands.

His fingers tugged at the soft drawstring on the pajama bottoms, and she gasped a little when they came loose, then pooled around her feet. She hadn't worn her panties, instead rinsing them out and hanging them in the bathroom to dry for the morning. Now she heard his gasp as he saw her naked before him.

He eased his thumb between her thighs and found her clit. She tossed her head back, her eyes closed as he stroked her, her entire body shaking from the thrill of it. She wanted to lose herself to him in a way she'd never done before. Certainly not with Dwight. Not, for that matter, with any man before.

But then he did the unthinkable. He bent his head closer, his breath tickling the soft skin of her inner thighs. And with his tongue, he teased and tasted her.

She froze. Fear and revulsion fought to take over, and she fought back. Not with Tucker. She didn't want those feelings with Tucker. The sense of being lost, of losing herself. Of having to take whatever was given even if she didn't want it at all.

But she was. She was standing there taking it even though inside her head she was screaming for him to stop. She felt a tear trickle down her cheek, and she knew that she'd lost the battle. She'd foolishly believed that Tucker was different. That even though she'd come in here with Tina's plan of being in control, that she could surrender to him and still not lose herself.

She'd been wrong, and now everything between them would be tainted.

Tucker. Dear Lord, not this. Not when a fantasy had been laid at her feet. This was *her* fantasy, and she was determined to take it back.

It wasn't real. *It wasn't real.*

And as she repeated that mantra in her head, her heart pounded in her chest, fear fighting courage, until she had to force the word out in a single breath even as her hands cupped the side of his head. *"Stop."*

He looked up, his eyes soft but surprised. The surprise faded quickly to alarm, and he was on his feet, his finger brushing away a tear. "My darling," he said. "Forgive me. I was too bold. I thought—"

She pressed a finger to his lip. "Shut up," she said, then kissed him hard. She fumbled for his belt and loosened his pants. "The bed," she demanded, determined to take control. To take back this moment, and not let anything about Tucker be tainted with the revulsion she felt for her stepfather.

He hesitated, but when he looked into her eyes, something seemed to shift. He pressed a kiss to her lips, then scooped her up, carrying her bridelike to the bed and laying her there.

She refused to stay down, though. She climbed to her knees and then, with a soft hand on his chest, she laid him back, then straddled him. Leaning forward, she captured him with a kiss, her hands stroking his chest as she went to work on the buttons of his shirt.

Her pulse pounded in her ears, a testament to her nerves. But she wanted this. Wanted to take this man on her terms and prove that she could do it. And so she pushed onward, stroking his shoulders as she eased off his shirt, delighting in the way his muscles tightened as she ran a finger down the smattering of hair leading to his navel.

She eased his fly open, then tugged his pants down, noticing with delight how he lifted his hips to help. He was rock hard, and that fact both thrilled her and urged her on.

"Sylvia," he whispered.

"Shh." She pressed a finger to his lips. "No talking," she said, then replaced her finger with her lips.

With one hand, she took his and pressed it between her thighs, easing him back and forth until he took up the motion, his fingers sliding in and out and making her even hotter and wetter than she'd been before.

He drove her to the edge like that, and she moaned against his mouth, her hands tight against his chest until she couldn't stand it any longer. With a sharp sigh, she slid onto him, impaling herself on the length of him. She arched back and moaned. His throaty groan matching hers, and his hands reached for her, cupping and stroking her breasts even as his hips rose and fell in a rhythmic motion that matched hers.

They fell into a pattern full of wild and desperate need, more and more until, at last, the world exploded around her and she sagged against him, totally spent.

He was, she realized, still hard. He started to ease her over, but she shook her head, spooning up tight against him. "Later," she whispered, even as fatigue took over.

She thought he might argue, might fight her for this moment of control. But he didn't. Instead, he pressed tight against her, his hands softly stroking her back. She felt safe in his arms. Safe and right and free of her demons.

And with that thought, she drifted to sleep, secure in Tucker's arms.

CHAPTER FIVE

"MORE TEA, MR. GREENE?" Anna asked, holding the teapot as if she were determined to pour whether Tucker wanted more or not. He didn't, actually, but neither did he want to leave the patio yet. After an incredible evening with Sylvia, then falling asleep in each other's arms, he'd awakened quite alone.

Honestly, he wasn't entirely sure what to think. The woman had taken over their lovemaking, a scenario that had thrilled him more than he'd anticipated. He hadn't quite gotten all that he'd wanted out of the encounter, though, and he'd ended up taking a cold shower after she'd drifted off.

Despite the cold shower, he'd awakened this morning hoping that his own satisfaction was on the agenda, only to be disappointed by the discovery that she'd disappeared during the night.

He'd come down to breakfast, hoping to see her here, and instead found only his sister.

Though once again frustrated, he supposed it was for the best that she'd sneaked back to her room, especially since Blythe had announced to Tucker that she'd popped her head into Sylvia's room and told her where to find them for breakfast. As soon as his sister had told him that, Tucker had slowed down his attack on his poached eggs and toast, hoping she would appear before he finished his breakfast.

So far, he was eating by himself.

He shot a glance at his sister and amended the thought. Not by himself, but also not with the woman with whom he wanted to be.

"If you keep staring at the door, she'll never come," Blythe said, a teasing smile dancing across her expression.

"I've no idea what you're talking about," Tucker said, reaching for the newspaper.

"Certainly not," Blythe said. But the smile widened and she eyed the paper knowingly. Tucker never read the blasted thing. That was his father's domain and until he was forced to sign the papers putting him in charge of Carson Greene's financial empire, Tucker preferred the chatter of the society gossip pages and the entertainment news reporting on film and radio.

Unfortunately, he'd already perused the entertainment rags. Which left him with two choices—leave the table or read the only other printed material available. Since he had no intention of leaving, he'd chosen the newspaper.

Not that he could have concentrated on it even if he wanted to. He was too anxious, waiting for Sylvia to show. He needed to look into her eyes and know that last night wasn't a fluke. That she wasn't simply another loose girl playing games with him.

He hated the fact that he'd already fallen so hard for the girl, but fallen he had. And Tucker knew that he'd be devastated if she was simply an airheaded flapper out to play the tease in his house and in his bed.

Unfortunately, he wouldn't know the truth until he saw the girl. Until then, he was having breakfast with his fears and frustrations.

"Sylvia, darling," Blythe called out, her waving hand appearing above his newspaper. "Come and have some eggs and toast."

Tucker closed his newspaper, trying not to appear too eager as he looked at the woman who'd appeared so mysteriously in his home and had, just as mysteriously, captured his imagination. Not to mention his libido. She wore one of his sister's dresses, black and covered with a red fringe that shimmered when she walked. It had no sleeves, only thin strips of red silk holding it up, and her shoulders looked soft and kissable. Her legs, he noticed, were covered by ivory-colored stockings, and her feet were adorned in a pair of red shoes that he also recognized as belonging to Blythe.

Sylvia tossed each of them a quick smile, then ran her fingers through the fringe of the dress. "I hope you don't mind. I just love this dress. I couldn't pass it up."

"You look wonderful," he said, straightening the place setting next to him in a not-so-subtle attempt to direct where she sat. It worked, too, and she settled in next to him, her thigh brushing his as she leaned sideways for glass of orange juice that Anna had poured in anticipation of her arrival.

"Thank you," she said, smiling at him, her expression a mixture of happiness and modesty. "And Blythe. Thank you for inviting me down to breakfast. And of course, for the outfit."

Blythe looked between the two of them, her expression one of delight. "We can't have you feeling that the household is inhospitable," she said, as Tucker wondered just how much his sister had figured out.

He cleared his throat. "I trust you're feeling better this morning?"

"I feel terrific this morning," she said, her eyes dancing. "Thanks for asking."

"I hope the music didn't keep you awake," Blythe said. "I thought about sending everyone home since you seemed so ill, but trying to get a crowd to leave a party is quite impossible."

"I'm glad you didn't kick everyone out on my account," she said. "I slept just fine," she added, with a quick glance toward Tucker.

He threw caution to the wind and took her hand under the table, twining his fingers through hers, his senses springing to life as she squeezed back, then rubbed the pad of her thumb rhythmically over the back of his hand.

He was just wondering if Blythe would notice if he reached for his coffee cup with his left hand when the clatter of footsteps echoed from the hallway. Soon Jonathan and Talia stepped through the open French doors and onto the marble tile of the patio. "Darling!" Talia enthused, her eyes fixed on Sylvia. "I told Jonathan last night that we had to come by and check on you. You don't remember us, I'm sure. I believe you were quite unconscious when we saw you. But do tell us, how ever are you feeling?"

"Much better, thank you," Sylvia said, aiming a bemused expression toward Tucker as Jonathan took the empty seat next to Blythe.

Tucker cleared his throat. "Sylvia, this is Talia Calvert and our neighbor, Jonathan."

She nodded politely, but her gaze lingered on Jonathan a moment, her brow furrowing.

Tucker almost inquired, but then Blythe stood and put her napkin next to her plate. She nodded briefly at Sylvia and then Talia. "Ladies, I apologize, but I must run. Sylvia, darling, make yourself at home. I hope you're not too bored rattling around in this old house."

"I thought perhaps she could join me today," Tucker said, both because it was the truth, and because he wanted to toss something into the conversational mix before the expression of anger and hurt on Jonathan's face got any more heated.

"Absolutely," Sylvia said, so quickly and with such enthusiasm that Tucker had to assume she'd also noticed Blythe's snub of Jonathan. "Where are you going?"

"Hopefully to see R.J.," Talia said, looking down her nose at them both. She shifted her focus to Sylvia alone. "Perhaps you can talk some sense into the boy. His sense of familial duty is going to ruin his career."

"Oh." Sylvia looked around, baffled. "I, um…"

"Ignore her," Tucker said firmly. "We're not going by the studio, Talia. I have to run a new script over to Charles at the radio station."

"A script?" Sylvia asked.

"A radio play," Tucker said. "My most recent project is *Goodnight: Los Angeles.*"

Her eyes went wide and her grip tightened on his hand. "How fun! I listened to one of those. It was on a DVD!"

"On what, dear?" Talia asked, leaning forward with a hand cupped to her ear.

"Oh, right," Sylvia said with a nervous little laugh.

"My, um, darling velvet divan. I call it a D.V.D." She smiled at Tucker. "Silly, but I like to sit on the divan and listen to the show. It's wonderful."

"*He's* wonderful," Talia said. "Which is why R.J. is desperate to sign him."

"R.J.? Wait. You're Talia *Calvert.* You're married to R. J. Calvert?" Her voice rose with excitement. "Oh, my gosh. I'm flabbergasted. He's a legend. Or, I mean, he will be a legend. Someday. You know. Because he's so talented."

Talia arched her eyebrows. "Some people apparently don't have the faith that you do," she said, without once looking at Tucker.

"Fine," Tucker said. "You win. I'll talk to the man." He turned to Sylvia. "How does spending the day alternating between radio and film sound to you?"

"It sounds perfect," she said.

Talia clapped her hands together, beaming. "Wonderful!" She eyed both of them sharply, though. "You have the girl back in the house before dark, Tucker. And you don't leave her side."

"Of course not," he said, his thoughts turning to the Strangler. "What have you heard?"

She waved a hand. "Nothing definitive. But the police are concerned. The Strangler hasn't struck recently, and they're anticipating an attack soon."

"Perhaps he's moved on," Tucker said. "Or quit."

"I doubt that," Sylvia said under her breath. "Predators like that don't quit."

"Exactly," Talia said.

"Don't worry," Tucker said, his hand closing protectively on Sylvia's arm. "I'll keep her safe."

Talia nodded. "Good." She turned and patted Jonathan's hand. "Dear boy, you've been so quiet."

He jerked and Tucker realized he'd been silent and brooding since Blythe left the table. Now he looked up, the fire in his eyes intense enough to make Tucker wince.

"Steady there, old man," Tucker said. "You okay?"

"Fine," Jonathan said sharply. "Excuse me." He rose quickly, then left the way he'd come.

"Well," said Talia. "I don't think your friend likes rejection of the feminine sort."

"Apparently not," Tucker said. For a moment, Tucker considered going after him, trying to calm him down and encourage the man to play the field. Blythe wasn't the only attractive woman out there, and Jonathan would make a fine catch.

He stayed seated, though. At the moment, his own love life was all that he could focus on, and right then he was flying high. Not only had Sylvia praised his radio work, but she'd agreed to spend the day with him. His fears that she'd today spurn him, choosing to forget last night or, worse, run from it and him, faded into a dim memory.

He glanced toward her, caught her smile and felt his heart do a little flip. The woman had secrets, to be sure. But what woman didn't? And considering that no woman before had made him feel quite so giddy, Tucker thought that wading through secrets was a very, very small price to pay.

After all, every week he turned in a new Spencer Goodnight mystery, each one wrapped up and solved right before the last commercial. If he could manage that feat with such enduring regularity, surely he could learn the secrets of the mysterious Sylvia's heart.

And even if he couldn't, he fully intended to enjoy trying.

"AMAZING, DON'T YOU think?" Tucker asked. "All that sound delivered through these small microphones."

Sylvia looked up, momentarily unsure what he was talking about. Her mind was still at breakfast, thinking about Tucker and radio plays and Hollywood. And, also, thinking about the strange, familiar man who'd joined them. *Jonathan*. She supposed he was okay since he was a friend of Talia and Tucker's, but something about the man gave her the creeps. Considering the way Blythe had departed, she had to assume she wasn't the only one who found the man somewhat disturbing.

She frowned, trying to put her finger on it, and then decided that maybe he was just too eager. He had a crush on Blythe, that much was for sure. And it wasn't reciprocated. So maybe the uncomfortable vibes she'd felt were simply the awkwardness of the two of them in the same room.

"Sylvia?" Tucker prodded. "Did you even hear me?"

"What?" She started, looking at him sheepishly. "I'm sorry. The microphones. Yes, they're, um, awfully small, all right." She hoped her acting skills were adequate, because the mikes weren't small at all. They were the overly large kind that always appeared in movies and television sets during the early age of broadcasting. And compared to the mikes of her time, they were positively gigantic. But remembering the DVD incident, she was smart enough to keep her mouth shut this time. Instead, she just nodded, smiled, and made appropriate oohing and aahing noises.

Not hard, actually, because her enthusiasm was real. She was completely fascinated by what Tucker did. Working even before the Golden Age of Radio, Tucker was one of the pioneers of the serial story. Working so early in the format, in fact, that the story she'd heard on her DVD had been a recreation based on scripts tracked down by collectors. At the time, the broadcasts were live. They went into the air, and were lost.

An amazing concept considering the world she was used to, where anything could be seen over and over again with DVDs and TiVo and the like. And it had made her stupid, *stupid* comment about hearing the show on DVD that much more dangerous. Because she couldn't tell Tucker the truth about where she came from. In her own time people would consider her a loon. In this era, they'd probably have her locked in a sanitarium before she could say "digital broadcast medium."

"So what's the script you're working on now about?" she asked as they left the station.

He held the car door open for her, a beauty of unknown make and model, but just like she used to see at vintage car shows. "That's the question of the hour, actually. How to wrap up the entire *Goodnight: Los Angeles* story. Important work, you know. Can't be rushed."

"Wait. You're ending the show?"

"I'm afraid so," he said. He shut the door, then walked around the front of the car and cranked the engine. Since the model was topless, his activity didn't hamper their conversation. Not that there was much conversation to hamper, she realized. She was gaping at him, her brow furrowed and her mouth hanging open, forming a little O.

"Sylvia?"

"I don't understand. *Why* are you ending it? It's doing well, right? And don't you enjoy doing it?" She couldn't remember the details of his radio career well, but maybe now was when he went into film. That had to be it, of course. Because he *did* end up in the movies. She knew. She'd seen dozens of them.

Tucker looked at her, pausing before answering. With any other woman, he might dance around the issue. With Sylvia, he wanted to be honest.

Before he could answer, though, she grinned at him. "Wait! Don't tell me. You're going into the movies."

The look of delight on her face was so great that he hated to disappoint her, but he couldn't lie, either. "No," he said. "Finance."

She stared for a second, baffled and clearly expecting the punchline. He could hardly blame her. He'd been expecting the punchline for months, ever since his father insisted that he take over the business.

"My father," he said. "Apparently, I'm his legacy."

She nodded slowly, sinking back into her seat. He climbed into the car, released the throttle and started down the road. He wanted to look at her, to read her expression. Inexplicably, he wanted her approval for the decisions he'd made in his own life. An absurd reaction, he knew, considering he'd only met the woman, despite the intimate nature of their first evening of acquaintanceship. Somehow, though, it felt as if he'd known her all his life. That she'd always been beside him.

"I've never had a father," she finally said as they tooled along, her hair wild in the breeze.

"I'm sorry," he said, expecting her to pull out a scarf and tie it down, the way his sister always did. When Sylvia didn't, he wondered if perhaps she didn't have a scarf. He almost offered her one of Blythe's, but he enjoyed too much the image of her looking wild and unkempt beside him.

She turned and caught him looking at her. He smiled sheepishly and focused on the road. But not so focused that he didn't sneak another sideways glance, gratified to see the smile curving her lips.

She was quiet as they maneuvered through the dusty streets toward the Mammoth Studios Lots. Tucker had only been half aware of driving the winding canyon roads. But he wanted to give her a treat, and he could think of nothing more spectacular than walking her through the magic of a motion-picture studio.

"I'd imagine it's very hard to turn away from the expectations of a parent," she finally said as they approached the gated entrance.

"I'm sorry?" He had no idea what she was talking about.

"The finance job."

"Ah, yes." He pulled up next to the gate and gave his name to the guard. "Tell R.J. I'd like to stop in and introduce him to a friend."

The guard disappeared into the shack, and Tucker turned back to Sylvia. "I think that sometimes you get to a point in your life where a certain role is familiar. Comfortable, even though you might know that it doesn't fit at all. And you just go with it." Certainly that's what he'd been doing. Playing the role of the dutiful son, even though he wanted to tell his father to stuff it and follow his own path. He thought of the horrors he'd seen in the war by following duty, and hoped that such horrors wouldn't visit his personal life, as well.

He thought she might tell him to sit his father down.

Have a talk with the old man about wants and desires and a son's right to live his own life.

She didn't. She merely nodded and looked at her hands, folded tightly in her lap. "Yes. I know exactly what you mean."

He wanted to ask what *she* meant, but the guard returned then. "Mr. Calvert said to head on over to Rome. He'll meet you there."

"Rome, huh?" Sylvia asked, as Tucker pulled through the gates, then maneuvered between the studio buildings. "I'm impressed."

Tucker laughed. "Ever been on a studio lot before?"

She hesitated, then shook her head. It was weird, but Tucker had the distinct impression that she'd changed her mind about her answer. "It's pretty impressive, though."

Indeed, it was. All around them people rushed about. Actors and actresses wore ornate costumes—members of a royal court, Robin Hood's merry men, cowboys, Indians. Anything and everything imaginable was represented in the flood of life that parted to let their car pass through.

Sylvia, he could tell, was entranced. Not a difficult deduction on his part, actually. She was half standing, her hands on the windshield except when she lifted one to point and squeal. Her eyes stayed on the crowd except when she would turn and smile. He felt like Santa Claus.

Once they were past the buildings maintained for costume and makeup, the crowd thinned, and she sat down again. Next, they turned and drove past the various hot sets, cameras set up, directors perched at the side of the cameramen, and the action rolling. He slowed in front of one set piece, where the actors were involved in a fight atop a moving stagecoach, the movement provided by several stage hands on each side, pushing a lever to make the coach rise and fall.

In front, the director called directions to the actors, urging them to jump back, scream, laugh maniacally. All in all a melee of activity. And Sylvia was taking in every bit of it.

"It's fascinating," she said. "And so cool the way the director talks to the actors like that. I'd never thought about that before."

Tucker frowned, not sure what she meant. "About what?"

"Oh." Her cheeks flushed again, though he couldn't imagine what she could be embarrassed about. "I was just thinking about how someday movies will have talking, too. And I guess the directors will have to learn to be quiet while the actors do their thing, you know?"

"Talking?" Tucker shook his head, grinning at her imagination. "I think talking is for the radio."

"Right," she said. "I'm sure you're right."

They passed through the active sets, then drove along a deserted stretch of lot until they reached the famous Spanish Steps in Rome. Or, at least, R.J.'s version. "An old set," Tucker explained as he parked the car. He got out, then walked around to open Sylvia's door, only to find that she'd already let herself out.

"Um, I was eager to see the steps," she said, apparently noticing his expression of surprise.

"It's pretty impressive," Tucker agreed. He made a frame with his thumbs and forefingers and looked through it. "From the camera's perspective, you don't notice the raw construction on the sides and top. Just the steps. Seems just like Rome, especially when the set is dressed."

She was watching him, not the steps, her eyes sparkling.

"What?" he asked.

"Just you. You light up here. And at the radio station, actually. A big change from a few minutes ago when you were talking about your dad and finance."

"She has a point, old man." A deep voice boomed toward them, followed soon by the stout form of R. J. Calvert. "A wise woman you've brought with you."

"Thanks for letting me show her around, R.J.," Tucker said. "R. J. Calvert, meet Sylvia."

R.J. kissed Sylvia's hand. "A pleasure, my dear. But I'm afraid I had ulterior motives."

"Oh?" Sylvia asked, not at all insulted.

"I'm hoping to entice this young man to work for me. He has a knack for story and an eye for film. Perhaps you'd be an ally, yes?"

"I don't know how much help I'd be," Sylvia said. "He seems to have his mind made up."

"A pity," R.J. said, then turned back to Tucker. "I was hoping you'd write and direct a film based on the Ragtime Strangler. That's what the public craves, you know. Something new. Something different. Not historical fantasies, but real life. The down-and-dirty details of our modern world."

"Careful, R.J.," Tucker said. "They haven't caught the Strangler. Anyone from the gossip rags overhears you, they'll start the rumor you're the fiend, and that you're killing women just to sell movies."

R.J. laughed. "Let them print it. That kind of publicity would sell movies, too."

"Wish I could help you," Tucker said. "But my father would disown me if I spurned his business." He said the words by rote, without emotion, barely even realizing what he was saying. They'd become familiar, as if he were playing the role of the dutiful son instead of living it. Honestly, he supposed he was. Fulfilling his duty to his family just as he'd done for his country.

"Too bad *you're* not the Strangler," R.J. said. "Your father would probably cut you loose, and you could come work for me."

Sylvia laughed. "Yes, but then you wouldn't want him, either."

R.J. gave her a dark look. "No? My dear, the bottom line is the movie. Everything else is just reality."

He left then, his impeccable sense of drama apparently requiring him to depart on the best exit line he could come up with. Sylvia turned to Tucker. "Wow. No wonder his reputation lasted—" She cut herself off with a little shake of her head. "I mean, no wonder he's made such a name for himself."

"He's intense," Tucker admitted. "And usually he gets what he wants."

"He wants you," she said.

"I realize that," he said. "But I'm afraid he can't have me."

She moved closer, and he felt his pulse step up its tempo. "I want you, too," she whispered, her eyes meeting and holding his.

He swallowed, suddenly as shy as a schoolboy despite their earlier intimate encounter. He wanted to grab her and pull her toward him, but he forced himself to hold off, remembering her need to take control. So instead of pressing himself bodily against her, he settled for running his fingertips down her cheek. *"You,"* he said, "can have me."

She moved closer still, and the scent of her filled him with longing. She traced his lips with the pad of a fingertip and spoke a single word. "Why?"

"Because I want you, too," he said, barely able to squeeze the word out past the desperate force of his desire.

"No," she said, taking a step back and shaking her head. "That's not right."

"Believe me, darling, it is," he said, his voice rising to an almost frantic pitch as he tried to halt her backward progress.

She didn't stop. "It's not," she said. "You do want me. I don't doubt that. But you want to make movies, too."

He closed his eyes and sighed, frustration of all kinds—sexual and otherwise—writhing within him. "Yes," he finally said. "The difference is that I *can* have you. Or am I wrong about that?"

Her mouth quirked into a smile and she reached out, taking his hand as she started to walk up the Spanish Steps. "I like it here," she said. "Thank you for bringing me."

"You're welcome." He eyed her, stifling a wave of disappointment as he wondered if he'd made a wrong assumption.

"I've always loved the movies," she said.

"Always?" It was an odd choice of words, he thought.

"I mean, since the first one I saw, I've been hooked. They're all about fantasy, right? A different world that looks like ours but really isn't. It's a bit like magic, I think. And the actors get to be someone completely different. It's almost like a way to live a life that doesn't really belong to you. To live—even if only for a moment—in a fantasy."

"I suppose it is, at that."

They'd reached the top, and now she held out her arms, turning a bit to encompass the entire studio lot, spread out around them. "I used to wonder what that was like," she said. "Now I know. It's like I've been given an amazing gift." She closed her eyes and breathed in deep. And when she opened them, she smiled at him.

He watched her, curious and intrigued. Because as much as he wanted to believe it, he didn't think that the gift she referred to was this trip to the studio. That was something else, and for the life of him, he couldn't imagine what.

"What would you be?" he finally asked.

"Be?"

"If you could be one of the actresses. A new life on film, I mean. What would you be?"

Her brow furrowed as she pondered the question. "A fairy-tale princess, I think. After all, she always gets the happy ending."

"You deserve a happy ending," he said, taking her hand again.

"How about you?" she asked. "What would you be?"

"Ah, that's easy," he said, without taking his eyes off her. "I'd be the frog."

CHAPTER SIX

SYLVIA'S HEART fluttered in her chest. "The frog, huh? Interesting choice. Green. Kind of slimy. I don't know…"

"Trust me," Tucker said, as they moved back down the steps toward the pavement. "I wasn't interested in the slime. And my choice of role was very methodically selected based on your selection."

"Because you're a hop-to-it kind of guy?" she asked, teasing.

"Because princesses are always kissing frogs."

"*Oh,*" she said, then nodded as if she were considering that point. "And you figured that if I was a princess and you were a frog—"

"Exactly," he said, leading her to a secluded area behind a set piece and away from the people bustling around the lot. "So what do you say, princess?"

"That you're very astute for a frog." She leaned in and kissed him, unable to continue the game because she could no longer think clearly—needing the feel of his lips against hers. They stayed that way for what seemed like hours, his hands exploring her body as his lips explored her mouth. He was taking what he wanted from her, and so help her she wanted him to. She wanted so desperately to be able to give in to him, to let him ravage her, and then, in the afterglow, to feel only as if she'd been loved. Not violated or cheated or somehow made less.

"Sylvia?"

She realized she was trembling a bit, and she cursed herself. No, she cursed Martin. "I'm sorry." She tried a weak smile.

"Can you tell me what's wrong? Do you want me to move slower? Let you tell me exactly what you want?"

She closed her eyes, gathering her courage. "It's crazy, especially since we only just met. But—"

"Yes?"

"—what I want is you."

He kissed her then, even harder, pressing against her until they seemed more like one person than two. His hands roamed her body, skimming over her breasts, dipping between her legs, sending her senses spinning with the promise of new heights and new pleasures.

She reached around him, cupping his rear and drawing closer, losing herself in the moment even as some part of her was amazed by her own actions. But this was what she wanted, and she shifted and moved, making sure he was touching her just so, getting their bodies in exactly the right position, exactly as she wanted.

And then, when she felt ready to explode from need and lust and longing, she broke the kiss, putting her hands on his chest to push him back. "I think this princess kissed the right frog," she said.

His smile was soft, in stark contrast to the hard edge of lust in his eyes. "That she did," he said. Then he held out a hand. "Come on."

She frowned, unable to hide her disappointment. "Where are we going?"

"A proper date," he said. "Princesses shouldn't be trapped in the tower."

"Or behind the Spanish Steps," she said.

"Exactly."

She hesitated, not sure what was holding her back. She couldn't stay in this world, as much as she might want to stay with Tucker. Her life was decades in the future, and somehow she had to get back. But she had no idea how long she'd be here. And while she was here—while she was exploring a newfound sexual freedom with Tucker—did she have to hide behind closed doors or the odd set piece? Why not let him take her on a date? What harm could it do?

But as she let him guide her into the car, she knew the harm. She was already falling in love with this man. And when it was time to leave, she could end up breaking both their hearts.

HE TOOK HER TO A jazz club, and to Sylvia it was like being transported back in time. *Exactly* like being transported back. They drank sparkling water until Tucker got them invited into the back room, and then the gin flowed freely. Blythe's red dress flowed around her, making her feel just like a flapper. The music was loud, the dancing wild, and the conversation eager and conducted at a throat-numbing level simply to be heard over the din. Here and there, she caught worried snippets of conversation, people speculating on the Strangler. But for the most part, the party crowd was the same as in her time—oblivious to the dangers of the outside world, focused only on drink and dance and friends.

Like the others in the joint, she and Tucker danced and drank and mingled, and when it was time to leave, she didn't want the evening to end.

Except that she knew once they arrived home, the party that she was really looking forward to would begin. The princess and her frog prince. She shivered in anticipation.

"Cold?" Tucker asked, removing his top coat and placing it over her shoulders. They were back outside, her ears still ringing from the sound of the music as he opened the car door for her. "I'm fine. Thank you."

"I've got a lap blanket in the back," he said, grabbing it then settling it on her once she was seated. "I don't want you to catch a cold."

"It's summer, Tucker."

"With you, I can't be too careful."

They held hands as he drove home, even when he had to shift gears. She simply moved with him as he grabbed the stick and shoved it smoothly into place. The movement was oddly sensual, and Sylvia realized with a start as they pulled up in front of his well-lit and loud house that her panties were damp and her legs were tingling. Were it not for the crowds attending his sister's latest party, she would have insisted he take her right there. As it was, she wasn't certain she could wait until they made it through the crowd to the upstairs.

"The back entrance," he said, apparently reading her thoughts. "We can get up there without having to stop and be social along the way."

"Yes," she said, her voice breathy with desire. "That sounds like a very good plan."

He put the car into gear, then roared to the rear of the house, gravel from the driveway kicking up behind them.

They got out of the car and raced up the service entrance. Laughing like fiends, every look, every word, every near miss with a party guest sent them into peals of laughter. By the time they finally fell into Tucker's room, Sylvia's sides hurt.

And the most amazing thing? She'd been laughing and having genuine fun even though she knew that once they reached the bedroom, she and Tucker were going to have sex. Sex. In the past, the knowledge of impending sex had always caused her to freeze. With Tucker, she couldn't wait.

And her only regret was that it seemed so unfair that this wonderful sense of anticipation—of belonging— had to exist between her and a man she couldn't stay with. Not forever. Probably not even for long.

"Oh no," he said, shutting the door behind them. "I see a look on your face."

"No look," she said, shaking her head and trying to assume a neutral expression. "I was just thinking." She moved into his arms. "I promise I won't do that anymore."

He chuckled, the sound delighting her. "Always a good plan. I think it's best to avoid thinking as much as possible."

"Exactly."

"So don't think. Just tell me. What do you want, Sylvia?"

"I already told you," she said, hooking her arms around his neck. "I want you."

HER ANSWER THRILLED Tucker more than he'd imagined. Because in the end that was what it all boiled down to— she wanted him and he wanted her. And all the rest was just mist filling the space between them. His father's demands. Her secrets. The Strangler. His desperation to avoid the world of finance and enter the more exciting world of movies.

But none of those things mattered right then. Right then all that existed was him and Sylvia and the world within the bedroom.

He drew her to him, letting his hands roam over her, his fingers with an agenda of their own as they stripped her garments off her. She moaned a little, the sound tremulous and somehow all the more enticing for her hesitancy. He slipped his hands over her shoulders, finding the zipper on the dress that Blythe had lent her. Slowly he eased it down, letting the garment hang loose on her.

In one motion, he slipped his hands over her shoulder, hooking his thumbs under the tiny strap and urging it down. He looked at her, his body tightening with lust as his eyes roamed over her breasts. Her bare tummy, smooth and brown, seemed to beckon for his touch. Her panties were different than the current fashion in women's underthings, and he let his gaze pause there, telling himself he was curious when in fact he was merely entranced.

"Tucker," she began, "I should probably—"

He held up a hand, halting her protests. "You should probably do nothing except let me release these stockings from this garter belt. Was that what you were going to say?"

He looked at her, saw the hesitation and held his breath. When she nodded, he exhaled, feeling as if he'd been given a gift.

He made swift work of her clothes, not resting until she was naked beneath him. He eased her back onto the bed, his hands exploring, worshipping. He ripped at his own clothes, somehow managing to free himself from them, then eased down on top of her. He was stiff and hard, about to explode and unable to wait any longer. "Sylvia, I—"

"Yes," she whispered. "Now. Please."

He said a silent thank-you and accepted the invitation, his fingers checking first to make sure she was ready, and his pulse boiling when he felt her slick wetness on his fingers. With one low groan, he slid inside her, losing himself in her heat.

They rocked together, faster and faster, a glorious pressuring building inside him. It grew and grew until he couldn't stand it anymore and lost himself in the glorious explosion of his own release, all the more powerful because it had been denied him the first time they'd made love.

SYLVIA GROANED beneath him, her hips undulating as she tried to find her own release. He'd relaxed on top of her, and now she wanted…what? To come, that was no mystery. But what she needed…

She needed his hands on her, his fingers inside her, and she needed it right now before she went mad from longing.

He wasn't touching her right, though. He was trying, bless the man. His hand making lazy circles between her thighs. But the motions were slow, lacking the desperate strength she needed. *More*, she yelled, but in her head. *Faster, harder, there. Now.* But none of the words left her mouth. As much as she trusted Tucker, she couldn't bring herself to make the demand. Her head knew it was okay, but her heart couldn't believe that he wouldn't reject her if she made demands in bed.

You made all the demands that first day, she told herself. True enough, but that had been different. Tonight, Tucker had been making love to her. That night, she'd been making love to him.

But shouldn't they be making love together? And wasn't this supposed to be her opportunity? A chance in the past to fight her past?

She tightened her already closed eyes and cried in her head for him to touch her the way she wanted. He didn't hear the cry, of course, and she steeled herself, knowing what she had to do, and yet terrified to do it.

Just do it.

"Tucker," she whispered, her voice weak.

"What?" he asked, his lips suddenly at her ear. "Tell me what you want."

"Harder," she said. "Please. Harder and just up, a bit. Yes. Oh, yes. Right there." His fingers moved with her words, his touch drawing her up and up, taking her to a place where her body seemed to shatter in a million pieces, falling back to earth to reassemble into some version of herself.

She moaned and rolled against him, burying her face in his chest, not quite believing she was able to do that. To tell a man for the first time in her entire life exactly what she wanted during sex.

"Hey, my chest is damp," he said gently, stroking her cheek and then tucking his palm under her chin. "Are you crying?"

She rolled over, realizing for the first time that she was. "Sorry," she said.

"I don't mind." His smile was soft and understanding. "I've just never brought a woman to tears before."

She drew in a breath, felt the tremor in her throat as she tried to steady her nerves. Then she sat up, the sheet pressed against her breasts in an attempt not so much at modesty but to forgo any distractions.

"Tucker," she said, squaring her shoulders for courage, "we need to talk."

She wanted to tell him everything. She started with the way Martin had touched her, his demands. His foul breath on her and his fingers taking liberties. She told him the way the abuse had made her feel, and the way it still made her feel, like she was hiding in a shell during sex. "But with you I broke through," she said. "That's why I was crying. I've never been able to do that before. Tell a man what I want, I mean." She blushed, then, remembering the era. "Not that I've had that much experience with the topic or anything," she said.

If he was shocked, he didn't show it. Instead, he pulled her close and kissed her hair. "Now that you've broken through, perhaps you should practice."

"Yeah?" Just from the tone of his voice, her body sparked with anticipation.

"Tell me what you want. Tell me in every tiny excruciating detail."

Sylvia opened her mouth to protest, to tell him that she had more secrets to reveal. But she couldn't quite force the words out. Time had brought her here, after all. Time could damn well wait for a better opportunity.

And so instead of confessing her second secret, Sylvia closed her eyes and lay back against Tucker's soft pillows, prepared to be the director in a little play of their own making. A play designed exclusively for her own pleasure.

SYLVIA WANTED TO stay in Tucker's room until morning, but there were certain things that decorum demanded, and not waking up in a man's room in the 1920s was one of them.

She woke in his arms just before four in the morning, and she carefully extricated herself from his embrace. He moaned a little and rolled over, but he didn't wake up. Under the circumstances, Sylvia thought that was just as well. They'd made love over and over, and she was sore but sated. Still, if she saw those eyes and that smile again—if he patted the bed and urged her over—she knew she would go to him.

As appealing as that sounded, she needed to get to her own room before the morning. She had no desire to explain to Blythe or the housekeeper or any of the party stragglers what she was doing in Tucker's bed. Not that she had any particular qualms, but she wasn't entirely certain what the standard for women was in this era, and she didn't intend to be a feminist pioneer if she didn't have to be.

All of which explained why she was padding down the hall in her bare feet, moving quietly so as to not wake anyone. But her stealth had an added value—she was able to approach people without them hearing her. And that's how she stumbled upon Blythe and the man.

His back was to Sylvia, but they were obviously arguing, and Blythe was clearly scared.

"Hey!" She picked up her pace, hurrying, then grabbed the man's shoulder and spun him around. Jonathan.

"Sylvia! Dammit, girl, what is it?"

"I should ask the same thing," she said, keeping her chin up and moving toward Blythe. "Are you okay?"

"Yes. Thank you." Blythe's voice quivered slightly, but her words were firm. She turned to face Jonathan. "And you, Jonathan Straithorn, have had too much to drink. Please leave now before I wake Tucker and have you forcibly removed."

Jonathan answered, but Sylvia didn't hear the response. She was too focused on the last name. *Straithorn.* As in Martin Straithorn. As in the man who'd filled her childhood with horror.

As if watching one of R.J.'s movies, Sylvia saw herself take a deep breath. She saw her legs buckle, and she saw the floor rise up to meet her.

Then, as she fell, she heard Blythe screaming for Tucker.

TUCKER HAD BEEN watching as Sylvia padded out of bed. She clearly thought he was asleep, and as much as he wanted to pull her back into his arms, he knew that feigning unconsciousness was for the best. He wanted her in his bed, true, but he didn't want her to be the subject of idle gossip.

And, in truth, a small part of him wanted to be alone. He had a flurry of strange thoughts running through his mind, and soon as the door clicked behind her, he sat up in bed, desperate to sort them out.

His mind whirred with absurd thoughts. Jules Verne kind of thoughts, like the stories he'd read as a young man. The types of stories he'd included in his earlier radio plays, with visitors from space and travelers who crossed the barrier of time.

But surely that was all fantasy? Nothing more than his imagination running away with him?

Except there were so many unexplained things. The odd wristwatch, made of a material he'd never seen utilized for an adornment. Her queer undergarments. The references to taking movies in such a matter-of-fact way. Even the patterns of her speech.

Honestly, he couldn't believe he was even thinking along such lines, but he lived his life in the fantasy of fiction, and he'd seen unbelievable things during the war. Very little surprised him now.

And the truth was, it didn't matter to Tucker where or when Sylvia was from. She was with him now, and he wanted her to stay, though he was terrified that if she really was from a different era, that she would be forced return to her own time. Or, worse, that she'd want to.

He was, he realized, falling in love with her, and the warm, honeylike emotion erased all other concerns. He wanted her, he loved her, and he thanked God for bringing her into his life. From wherever He may have delivered her from.

And that was why, when he heard his sister's shrill scream, terror chilled his bones. He raced to the door, afraid that he'd lost Sylvia after having only just found her.

"FOR THE THOUSANDTH time," Sylvia said to Tucker and Blythe, "except for the fact that I'm about to die of boredom, I'm fine."

They'd kept her stuck in her room all day, company to a minimum, Anna making regular visits with tea and meals. Tucker had stayed with her for an hour at first, relief that she was safe coloring his eyes. After that, he'd come in twice to check on her, but hadn't stayed long, not wanting to "wear her out." Apparently, he thought their sexcapades had caused her to faint.

Blythe had come in, too, but only to bring Sylvia a collection of books. "If it isn't your time of month, then you must be catching something. Two fainting spells so close together. It's not right. So you rest. And you eat what Anna brings you."

At the rate Anna was feeding her, Sylvia was going to have to take some of those flapper gowns back with her to the future, because she'd no longer be able to wear anything with a waistline.

Now the sun was finally setting, and she was desperate to talk to Tucker. If he didn't come see her, she was going to him. She'd been thinking about that look in Jonathan's eyes when he'd spun to face her. She'd seen it before in her stepfather's face. Violence. And hate.

She couldn't prove it, but she knew in her heart that the Ragtime Strangler had been pursuing Blythe. And she'd spurned him. So far, she'd lived, because Jonathan seemed infatuated. But when he realized that she truly didn't want him…

Sylvia shivered, not wanting to think about that.

A soft rap sounded at the door, and then Tucker's head appeared in response to her invitation. "How are you feeling?"

"I'm good," she said. "But Tucker, dear God, I know who the Ragtime Strangler is."

His look of disbelief changed to one of guarded concern by the time she finished her story. Anna even came in at one point to bring her soup and, overhearing just the tiniest bit of the conversation, nodded sagely. "That man," she said. "I never did trust him."

"It's not much to go on," Tucker said, after escorting Anna from the room. "That you recognize the look in his eyes from your stepfather."

"You would believe me if you'd seen the way he was looking at her."

Tucker nodded. "I do believe you. But we don't have proof."

She sighed. "I know. But maybe now you can get proof." She licked her lips, realizing she had to tell him the full story. She couldn't keep it from him. And when she left, he deserved to know where she'd gone. "The thing is, it's more than just a familiar look in their eyes," she began. "It's the *same* look. They're related, you see. My stepfather and Jonathan."

"They are? Why didn't you mention it before?"

She shrugged. "I don't know. I'm not even entirely sure how to explain it now."

"Then don't," he said. "It's enough that the connection is there."

"No, you see, there's something I need to tell you." She licked her lips. "A secret I've been keeping."

He nodded. "I see. If you've kept it this long, perhaps

you could keep it just a little longer? I've been working on something all day, and I want to share it with you."

She wanted to protest, but curiosity gripped her. "Working on what?"

"A story idea. For a movie."

She sat forward, surprised. "Really? Oh, Tucker, I'm so glad. Yes, of course my secret can wait." If Tucker was actually thinking about the movies, then that was something she wanted—no, needed—to encourage. After all, history proved that he did end up making films. Surely she didn't want to be the cause of slowing down historical events. "Tell me," she said.

"It's about people who travel from the future," he said, his eyes on her face as he spoke. Her stomach did a little flip-flop, and she worked to keep her expression bland. "They come to visit. Perhaps to study history, I don't know. They have strange ways and odd clothes. And a unique way of speaking."

"I…oh," she said, when he paused. A wave of panic rose in her. What was she supposed to say?

"That's just the background. The main character is a woman. She falls in love with a man from the past. It's a love story, you see. But in a way, the lovers are star-crossed."

"Are they?" she asked, blinking back tears as the real truth of his story—and the extent of his understanding—hit home. "How?"

"That's the part you have to help me with. So far, I don't see anything that can have come between them.

But I have a feeling that I'm wrong. That something's there. Any ideas what that could be?"

"I'm not very good at making up stories," she said, her voice little more than a whisper.

"Then don't make it up," he said. "Just tell me the truth, Sylvia. Tell me, and I promise I'll believe."

CHAPTER SEVEN

"How did you figure it out?" she asked.

Tucker shook his head. "Little things. Your clothes. Your words. Talking about things as if they've already happened." He frowned. "Will movies really start talking?"

She shrugged. "And singing and dancing. It gets pretty amazing, actually."

"Interesting." He supposed he should say more, but he wasn't sure of the appropriate sentiment. "So why did you come here?"

"I didn't mean to. I was touring an exhibit at the house. I talked with the security guard, bent down to pick up a coin, felt a shove on my back, passed out and woke up here."

"What was the exhibit on?"

She rolled her eyes a bit and her cheeks turned a delightful shade of pink. "Um, the history of sex, actually."

"Oh, really?" He couldn't help but grin. Not only at the idea of a sex exhibit, but also because of the absurdity of it all. Time travel of all things.

But he believed her. He really and truly believed her.

"My friend Tina thought the exhibit would do me good."

"Because of your hesitancy during sex," he said. "Do women in the future have—"

He cut himself off. The extent of a woman's sexual experience in the future might be something he really didn't need to know.

"I haven't been with that many men," she said with a knowing smile. "But I will say that you're the only man with whom I've ever felt right." She took his hand and he held tight, almost as if he was afraid she'd get sucked back through time if he loosened his grip.

"It feels right because it *is* right."

Her smile wavered, and she turned away.

"Sylvia?"

"I have to return." Her voice was soft, hesitant and filled with sadness.

"No, you don't," he said, denying the words he'd been afraid to hear.

She turned back to him, holding on tight with both hands now. "But I do. I told you about Martin, right?"

"The one who's related to Jonathan. About what he did to you." He kept his voice tight, his grip on control tenuous.

"But I fought that," she said, tears streaming down her face. "I fought and I built a life and I proved to myself I could do it."

"But do you want it?"

She smiled, then shrugged. "I think so."

He traced a finger down her cheek. "You said that with me you were finally able to ask for what you want. Intimately, I mean."

She nodded, tears spilling out onto her cheeks. "Yes, and for that, I'll always be grateful."

"I don't want you to be grateful," he said. "I want you to do it in your life. Not just in your bed."

She shook her head, clearly not understanding.

"Ask for what you want," he explained. "But not just from me. From life. If you really want to go back, then although I'll hate it, you should. But if you want to stay here, then take what you want. Don't just do what's expected."

She licked her lips, nodding slowly as Tucker hoped he'd gotten through to her. He wanted her to stay with a desperation so fierce he thought it would burn a hole in his gut. Even more, though, he wanted her to make her own choices.

When she finally spoke, her words were nothing like what he'd expected. She looked him in the eye and asked the one question he'd wanted to avoid: "Is that what you're doing? What you want, rather than what's expected?"

He turned away from her, fighting back the urge to tell her this was about her, not him. But the truth was, it was about both of them. And he could hardly expect her to accept his advice if he wasn't willing to listen to it himself.

"Yes," he finally said, realizing as he spoke that he was making the right decision. The *only* decision. "That is what I'm doing."

She blinked at him. "Excuse me?"

"I'm going to wire Father right now. He'll probably cut his trip short and come home to berate and prod me and try to convince me to change my mind, but it won't work. I'm going to keep Spencer Goodnight alive. And I'm going to go work for R.J."

She stared at him, her mouth hanging open for one second. Then she squealed and launched herself at him, practically knocking him over. He spun her around, then held her close, wanting never to lose the feel of her against him. "I'm proud of you," she whispered. "You won't regret your decision."

"What's *your* decision?" he asked, his voice low and his lips barely brushing her ear. "Sylvia, I love you. Tell me that you'll stay with me."

LOVE.

The word flowed over her, making her weak in the knees even when she felt like dancing on rooftops.

He loved her. *Loved her.*

And the truth was that she loved him, too.

The question was, what did she intend to do about it.

She knew what she should do. She should go back. Her life, her mother, her work. All those things were in the future.

But here, in the past, was where she wanted to be. And Tucker was right. She needed to learn to ask for—no, to *take*—what she wanted.

She drew a breath for courage, then looked him in the eye. "I love you, too," she said.

"And…?" He moved closer, his fingers stroking her hair.

"And I'm going to try to stay with you."

His forehead creased. "Try?"

She fought back a wave of exhaustion and frustration. "I don't know how I got here. I didn't do it. It just happened. Who knows if it will happen again?"

"But you want to stay?" he asked. "With me?"

"Oh, yes," she said, and hooked her arms around his waist. She brushed her lips over his, feeling a surge of feminine power like none before. "And I know what else I want," she said, casting a quick glance toward the bed. "I even know how to ask for it."

"You?" he asked. "I don't believe it. You'd better prove it."

"If you insist," she said, then she rose up on her tiptoes, pressed her mouth against his ear, and told him exactly what she wanted.

SYLVIA STRETCHED in bed, naked under the sheet, and watched Tucker get dressed. "You could wait until morning, you know," she said, even though she knew he wouldn't.

"I could, but I don't want to. Besides, if I don't go right now, R.J. might decide to hire someone instead of me."

"Fat chance," she said, sitting up and starting to pull on her own clothes.

"Coming with me?"

She shook her head. As much as she'd like to witness that bit of history, the moment belonged to Tucker. "Nope. You wore me out. I'm going to get a midnight snack." She cocked an ear, making a pretense of listening to the quiet house. "And since Blythe went out for the evening, the house is actually empty. So I can go down to the kitchen in my robe and not worry about causing a scandal."

"Enjoy your snack," he said, then kissed the tip of her nose. "And I'll see you soon."

He slipped out the door, and Sylvia soon followed. She eased down the hall toward the stairs, then let her fingers run along the intricately carved banister. How odd to think that just a few days ago she'd been coveting this house. Now she'd be the mistress of it. Honestly, it was almost too much to comprehend.

She decided not to focus on the vagaries of time, and to instead decide what sort of snack she wanted. Opening a bag of chips wasn't an option, but she was pretty sure that Anna had baked bread that day. Surely she could find some left over. And maybe some cheese and fruit.

As she prepared her snack, footsteps sounded behind her, and she turned, expecting to see Blythe back early from her party.

Instead, she saw Jonathan.

Instinctively, her hand flew to her throat, but she managed a smile. "Jonathan. How nice to see you. Have you and Blythe made up? That, um, looked like quite the fight you were having the other night."

He didn't say anything, just took another step into the kitchen. She picked up the knife she'd set by the bread and started to cut off a slice. "Care for a snack? I'm having bread and cheese." She held the knife tightly, her eyes trained on him.

Terror filled her, but she told herself to be calm. He couldn't know she suspected him. And she had the knife, after all.

Besides, she might be wrong.

Slowly, she tightened her grip as he came toward her, taking the piece of cheese to which she'd gestured. She smiled, trying to maintain a level of confidence. She even thought she was succeeding. Certainly Jonathan seemed to be acting normally, nibbling on the cheese and leaning casually against the table.

She didn't expect the backhanded blow that cut her

across the face, sending her reeling backward. He moved with uncanny speed and trapped her, pressing the small of her back against the hard tabletop. He leaned in, his face mere inches from hers. She still held the knife, but it was useless in light of the way he held her wrist.

"How did you know?" he asked.

She opened her mouth, trying to find words, but it was impossible. This was Martin all over again. No back talk. No nothing. Just shut up and take it.

"*Answer me!* How did you know?"

"I…know what?"

"Housekeepers gossip, little girl. If you're going to speculate on the identity of the Strangler, I'd suggest you do it in private."

She heard a little mewling sound and knew it came from her.

"I'd rather deal with you in my usual way," he said. "But this will have to do." His hand slid down over her wrist, and she realized he was about to take the knife from her.

Inside her head, she screamed, begging herself to find the courage she'd never had in her childhood. Martin had already taken one life from her. She wasn't going to let his ancestor take this new life—take Tucker—away from her.

Fear and rage boiled in her, and as he held her hands tight, she reared back, then lurched forward, smacking him in the face with the flat part of her forehead. Pain shot through her and dots of lights danced in front of her eyes.

But it worked. He backed away in surprise, loosening his grip enough for her to jerk free. She stumbled forward, willing herself not to pass out. She reached the door and felt a tug on her bathrobe. She screamed, looking back just long enough to see Jonathan grabbing the material.

She ripped it away and raced forward, down the hall and screaming for help. But help didn't come. Tucker was with R.J. Blythe was at a party. And the servants had been given the night off.

She was alone with a killer, and all she could do was run.

Although she'd hit him hard, he was still fast, and he was gaining on her. She veered around a corner, turning into the first room she found, the drawing room where Blythe had originally discovered her. Quickly, she slammed the double doors shut, then fumbled with the lock. Once it was secure, she piled furniture in front of the door, then sat on the divan, her chest heaving, as she wished for a cell phone and settled on praying that Tucker would come home soon.

The next thing she heard was her own scream as glass shattered and Jonathan flew through the broken window. He knocked her against the wall, causing the *Robin Hood* poster to fall to the ground. He lunged, and the two of them crashed down, Sylvia on top of the poster as Jonathan whipped a sash around her neck. She struggled, but the room seemed to be turning inside out. She lashed out, grasping, trying to find something—anything—she could use as a weapon.

There was nothing, though. And as consciousness faded, the only thought in her head seemed to come from a voice other than her own: *home.*

THE FIRST THING she saw when she awakened was a pair of clear blue eyes. She blinked, and the entire face came into focus. She squinted, trying to remember. The kindly, older face. The tufts of gray-white hair.

"I know you," she said, struggling to sit up. "You're the security guard."

"And you shouldn't be here after hours," he said with a grin. "And dressed like that. What will people think?"

She looked down and saw that she was still in the bathrobe. "I…I think I must have been sleepwalking."

"Mmm-hmm." He stood up and offered her a hand. "It's okay. I doubt you're as dizzy this time."

She froze midway to giving him her hand. "I was right. You did send me back."

"Indeed I did," he said. "Didn't much expect you to return, either."

She grimaced. "I wasn't planning on it." She drew in a breath, looked around the exhibit room. "It's dark. What time is it?"

"Midnight," he said. "The witching hour."

"Appropriate." She turned to him, not sure if there were rules for dealing with him, but figuring it didn't much matter if there were. "I was trying to get away from the Strangler," she said. "Do you know…I mean, does history tell if—"

"He was caught. Tucker Greene caught the son of a bitch."

She sighed, satisfied. That was as it had been before. At least she hadn't changed history by identifying the man.

"Can you send me back now, please?"

She steeled herself, ready for the thrust back in time. But it didn't come. Instead the old man was staring at her, shaking his head, his eyes full of sadness, "I'm afraid that's not possible my dear. I do one trip, and one trip only. You decide to come back...and you're back."

"No!" Cold panic filled her. "No, I *have* to go back. My life is there. The man I love...he's there."

But the guard just shook his head. "I'm sorry. Truly sorry. But that is the way of it."

Desolation filled her. And fear. She'd made a choice, and it had been ripped away from her. Once again, she'd lost the control that she'd always craved. "This isn't happening," she whispered. "Please, please, help me."

"My dear, I have no help to give you."

"Then let me see Louisa. Please. Wake her up. I know she won't mind. I just...I just want to talk to her." She had no idea how the woman might help, but right then, she felt she had to see her.

The guard, however, didn't move. Instead, he stared at her, his eyes narrowed and his brow furrowed. "Louisa?"

"Yes, Louisa. Louisa Greene. She lives in this house."

"No one lives in this house. It was converted to a museum in nineteen seventy-five."

Slowly, she shook her head. "No, that's not possible. Louisa lives here. The Greene Mansion is one of the few that's still self-sufficient." She knew she was blathering, but he had to be wrong. The house—*her* house—open to the public since seventy-five? It didn't make sense.

He was looking at her, an odd tilt to his head.

"I'm not crazy. I talked to her. Sat right in the next room and talked about the house and her family. She showed me portraits and told me about her grandfather and grandmother. Tucker Greene was her grandfather. You know. The Hollywood guy. Famous director. Loads of Academy Awards."

"You discussed these things with Louisa? With Louisa Greene."

"Yes. That's what I've been telling you. And then I came back in here and—*poof*—you sent me away."

"Come with me," he said, hurrying out of the room and into the next. The one where she'd sat with Louisa. The one with the portraits. Only this one had no portraits. Just a single framed picture of Blythe and Tucker, arm in arm.

"Something's not right," she said, looking around in confusion. "Louisa was very specific. Tucker Greene was her grandfather." Just saying his name caused a knot of longing to rise in her throat. She swallowed, forcing herself to go on. "Her grandmother was brilliant at investing. Their pictures hung right here. This was their house."

"And he worked in Hollywood, you said."

"Right."

"Tucker Greene was a financier. He worked on Wall Street. Lost everything in the crash. He deeded the house to his sister, who had married well. They kept the place in the family until the seventies, when their children decided to donate it to the county."

Sylvia shook her head, not quite able to speak as the real truth settled around her. *She* was the grandmother in the portrait. Why hadn't she seen it before? And she's the one who'd told Louisa to meet her—the young Sylvia—in the exhibit. So she could go back and marry Tucker and history could turn out the way it was supposed to.

"I shouldn't have come back," she whispered. "I wasn't supposed to come back." She turned to him, sure she looked like a crazy person, but who else in the whole world could possibly understand. "My portrait's not here anymore. I think I screwed up history by coming back. I was supposed to have stayed. I would have survived the attack. Louisa said her grandparents caught the Strangler. Not just Tucker. Oh, dear God, I just should have stayed."

"You were meant to stay in the twenties," he said slowly, as if weighing his words.

"Um, yeah. Isn't that what I just told you?" Despite the tears that streaked her face, she couldn't keep the sarcasm from her voice.

He stroked his chin as he looked around the room. "Do you know what this means?"

"That I ruined the lives of people I love?"

"It means that you would have gone back without me. Somehow, time would have taken you back to where you truly belong."

"And this is important because why?"

"Because if you truly belong there—and if returning you will fix the rip in the future that you've caused— then I *can* send you back."

She stopped short, staring at him, certain she'd misheard. "You can send me back?"

"Not at the exact point you left, I'm afraid. Time doesn't run as parallel as we'd hoped."

"But you'd said you *couldn't* send me back."

"There are rules that must be adhered to. But now that I understand the full ramifications…" He nodded. "Yes, yes, I think it must be done." He fixed his blue eyes on her. "Are you ready?"

She took a deep breath, unable to stand another

moment away from Tucker, and fearing if she didn't take this opportunity now, she'd lose it.

"Yes," she said. "I'm ready."

TUCKER STOOD IN the driveway, his bags packed. Everything had been taken care of, all of his California obligations handled.

Even R.J. had taken the news gracefully when Tucker had explained about Sylvia's disappearance. Her whereabouts were still a mystery, with the police assuming that Jonathan had killed and hidden her somewhere. A sordid story that only fueled Tucker's desire to leave this place.

The one small bit of comfort he took was that he knew she was alive. He could feel it in his heart. Jonathan had practically told him as much, blabbering on about how she'd disappeared, sucked down into the floor through a movie poster, of all things.

The incident had driven him over the edge, and he'd confessed his crimes. So the Strangler was caught, but Sylvia was gone.

And now Tucker was leaving, too. He didn't want to stay here without her. And the force of his desire to leave was even greater than his dislike of his father's work.

So he'd be a businessman instead of a filmmaker. Other men before him had done the same, and prospered, so he supposed he shouldn't complain.

"Are you all packed?" Blythe asked, coming up and giving him a hug. "Are you sure you don't want to stay? If she's okay…if she comes back…"

He shook his head. It had been over a month. She wasn't coming back. She'd told him she didn't know how she came in the first place. So now they were trapped, separated by decades. "I need to go to New York," he said. "It's for the best."

Blythe nodded. "Did you get your scripts?"

"*Goodnight: Los Angeles?* No. Why would I take them?"

"She loved that show," Blythe said. "You should keep them with you."

He wanted to argue. To tell his sister that she was crazy, but oddly the idea didn't sound crazy at all. "Fine. I'll be back."

He dropped his briefcase and hurried up the steps to the house. His case was in the drawing room, and he burst through the doors, so intent on finding the leather portfolio that he almost missed the prone figure on the carpet.

"Dear God in heaven," he whispered, praying that he wasn't hallucinating. "Sylvia?"

He bent down beside the woman and turned her gently, his breath catching in his throat as he saw her face. He tried to speak but couldn't quite manage it.

Her eyes fluttered open, and she smiled. "Tucker," she said weakly, reaching out for his hand. "I came back as fast as I could."

He laughed, the sound bubbling up inside him as he fingered the cloth of her robe. "Tell me you haven't been wearing this for a month."

"Only minutes," she said. "I'm so sorry. I didn't mean to leave."

"It doesn't matter. You're back now." He touched her face. "You're staying?"

"Oh yeah," she said. "And you're staying in California."

He leaned forward and brushed his lips with hers. "Wherever you are, I am," he said. "Whenever, too."

"I love you, Tucker Greene," she said. "And our love's going to be one for the history books."

He looked at her curiously, trying to read her face. "Really? They write about us in history books?"

But Sylvia only shrugged and smiled. And when she pulled him in close for a kiss, Tucker decided that history could wait. At the moment, all he cared about was now.

PISTOLS AT DAWN
Nancy Warren

CHAPTER ONE

"WHAT ARE WE DOING in Paris?" Natalie Bowman wailed, shoving a pillow under the laptop that was overheating her thighs. She stretched her neck and tried to find a more comfortable position on the hotel-room bed.

"Huh?" her fiancé said, glancing up from his own computer and blinking owlishly. He'd snagged the one desk in their room—a charming gilt-and-white affair with spindly legs that looked as though it were meant for writing love letters with a fountain pen, not pounding out multimillion-dollar deals. But Andrew had received an emergency call hours after they'd checked in to their romantic suite on the Rue Rivoli. A huge deal his firm was financing was heading south. He'd been e-mailing, text-messaging and phoning back to his Wall Street office ever since.

Her disaster, since it happened later and was less severe, meant she got stuck working from the bed. One of her major clients in the advertising firm of Mortiffee Morrisson was throwing a hissy fit over the new ad campaign.

The fact that the client had already approved the concept, storyboards and even the casting of models and spokespeople didn't seem to matter a bit.

Mostly, she thought, Ephram Schneider was annoyed that she'd taken a vacation. A much deserved and overdue vacation.

After two years together, she and Andrew had decided to get married. The sparkling solitaire on her left hand still felt foreign and a little clunky when her fingers were flying over the keyboard, but, hey, she and Andrew were perfect for each other. Everyone said so. They both knew it. With so much in common, it was a match made in Manhattan.

They were both successful, ambitious and charitable. Okay, so the amazing fun they'd had in the early days had worn off and they'd started putting off sex for Letterman, then falling asleep before the opening monologue was over. They'd reached that point, the inevitable fulcrum in a relationship, where change was inevitable.

Move forward or go back?

Break up or hook up?

They'd chosen the latter. They were engaged to be married, and to celebrate their personal merger they'd decided on a holiday in Paris.

But, apart from eating in the greatest restaurants on earth, they'd done almost nothing required by the city of love.

Love? They'd only made love once in four days. That was the first morning. After a nice bout of early-morning sex, they'd walked from their hotel to the Eiffel Tower, ridden up that amazing monument where the world was spread below them, all the sights they'd try and cram in seeing thoughtfully pointed out from on high. After arguing in a carefree way about whether to see the Pantheon first—his choice, because he wanted to see Foucault's Pendulum—or the Louvre—her choice, because she'd dreamed about seeing all those great works of art ever since she'd discovered she loved to draw—they'd taken their argument to a sidewalk café and enjoyed flaky, buttery croissants and café au lait.

Then Andrew's cell phone had rung. After that, forget the Pantheon, the Louvre. Paris. Forget sex.

They might as well have stayed home. No, they'd have been better to stay home. At least there she had a proper ergonomic desk, an assistant, and she could physically meet with Ephram to soothe, flatter and calm.

"Is this what our life is going to be?" she asked aloud the question that had plagued her since Andrew's emergency call. "You on one computer and me on another?" She stared at Andrew, who'd taken off his glasses and was rubbing his eyes.

He looked tired and a little stunned. "This really isn't a great time to discuss our relationship. We're here. Let's make the best of it."

"Why did we choose this hotel? Do you remember?"

He narrowed his eyes a little, which he did by habit when he wasn't wearing his glasses, as though he could bring the world into focus with the power of his eyelids. "It's close to everything. Great location."

"High-speed Internet access," she reminded him.

"Well, naturally," he said, as though she'd mentioned that the bathroom included running water.

"Andrew, people don't come to Paris for the Internet." She stood and stalked to the double doors that opened onto a tiny balcony above the street. "There's life down there. A cop is riding by on a bicycle with a baguette under his arm. Over there is the Jardins des Tuileries and the Louvre and the Seine. The cafés are crowded and the people out there on the street are living. They're out there on the streets of Paris and we're in here."

"Look, I'm sorry it's been so nuts, but—"

"If not this emergency there would have been another one. What's happened to us? We can't even have a holiday."

"You're on your computer, too."

"I know! I hate it." She hesitated, then walked back to the bed. With a decisive click, she turned off her laptop. The computer whined a little as it began shutting down, but she ignored the "come on, you don't really want to shut me down" tone. "Let's ditch this work and go out. Let's walk by the Seine. Maybe we'll take one of those hokey boat tours. And we'll go to Napoleon's tomb and Versailles, and—"

"Honey, I'm up to my ass."

A searing pain struck right behind her eyeballs, as though a tiny rocket launcher had fired inside her brain. "Your ass is in Paris," she yelled.

"And if you hadn't insisted on coming here, then my ass would be in my office, which would be a hell of a lot easier," he yelled back.

She hated herself for being unreasonable, when she knew he was stressed with work, but she suddenly saw their future stretching out, with this scene playing over and over. They both wanted kids, and she wondered if they could get together long enough to conceive, and if there was any point having kids if no one but the nanny would ever see them. How could they ever have a holiday if they were both so bloody important they couldn't get away for even a week?

"This is insane," she said. "Our life is insane."

"Sure it's busy now, but after this merger—"

"There will be another merger. And if Ephram's not throwing a hissy, somebody else will. Andrew, this isn't what I want. We just got engaged. When we're in this room you should be throwing me on that bed, not rushing to your computer."

He rose, but instead of coming over to her and throwing her on the bed—as she secretly hoped he would—he leaned against the desk, bracing his hands behind him.

"What do you want?" he asked quietly.

He wasn't talking about Paris anymore and they both knew it. A deep sadness crept through her system like fog.

"Not this," she whispered.

There was a long pause. He regarded her steadily while she held her breath. "I can't change."

"Everybody can change if they want to."

He stared at her for another moment and she saw the sadness reflected. "I'm sorry."

"Yeah. Me, too."

Her body felt cold and she clasped her hands behind her for something to hang on to.

Outside, one of those police sirens that sounded like a child's toy beep-beeped its way past.

"I should get back to New York. This deal's important to my firm."

"I know." She wasn't going to cry—that would be weak and clingy and manipulative. She tugged her brand-new engagement ring off her suddenly cold hand and placed it on the bedside table with a click.

"Are you coming back with me?"

She had plenty of reasons to return to work, too, but if she wanted a different future she was going to have to start working on it right now. She was taking her holiday, damn it, and she was going to enjoy Paris with or without Andrew.

"No. I'm going to stay."

"Okay." He pretended not to notice that she'd removed her ring, or maybe he was so nearsighted—in every sense—that he actually hadn't noticed. "Call me when you get back to New York."

He came over then and hugged her. It felt awkward,

as though they were old friends who hadn't seen each other in years.

"I'm going for a walk," she said, picking up her bag that was prepacked with her guidebook, digital camera, bottle of water, French phrase book, fold-up umbrella and tissues. She tossed her wallet in, stuffed her feet into sandals, collected her sunglasses and was ready.

She turned when she got to the door, but Andrew was already back at his computer.

Out on the street, Natalie had a sudden moment of panic. She'd ended her engagement to the man she'd been with for more than two years. She loved him, or thought she did. He was leaving and she was staying on alone?

In Paris?

She took a step back, hovered. A couple walked by arm in arm. They were young, both sporting denim but making it look ultra hip.

Parisians seemed born with the chic gene, she'd noticed. He had soulful brown eyes, thick, curly black hair and cultivated stubble. She had cropped blond hair and slanted green eyes. Their chatter was in French, but Natalie didn't need a translator to catch the intimate tones of lovers.

That was what she wanted, she realized. Intimacy, connection, feeling her life was unbreakably linked to another's. She was not looking for a business merger.

Okay, so here she was in Paris. Alone. Now what?

A short stroll brought her to one of a million outdoor cafés. She sat at the small round metal table, ordered a café au lait, which came in a thick white china cup and saucer with two rectangular wrapped sugars on the side. No fifty-five options on the coffee, no take-out cardboard container. Here, when you drank coffee, you sat. And enjoyed.

That, she realized, was what her life was missing. She wanted to be a sit-down café on the Champs-Elysées; instead she was Starbucks.

Well, she'd told Andrew that people could change if they wanted to and she believed it.

Today was the day she would change. Deliberately she sipped her coffee, took the time to savor the rich, smoky flavor and watch the people around her. A young intellectual looking guy at the next table glanced up from the newspaper he was reading and flirted with her with his eyes. She loved Paris.

Today she would do something only for her. After consulting her guidebook she decided on the Louvre. The art museum was so huge that the guidebook recommended taking days to tour the entire museum, or picking one section and spending several hours. She'd spend a few hours this afternoon, which would give Andrew time to vacate before she returned to the hotel.

Besides, if a woman was going to reconnect with herself, she ought to go back to her dreams. She'd started out as a graphic artist, which she'd loved, and she'd been so good at it that she inevitably got promoted right out of the creative side of advertising. Now she was a vice president. Pretty big deal, but her creativity had limited scope, and most of her energy went to client relations.

That same love of color and design and art that had led her to graphic design now led her feet to the Louvre.

Of course the lineup was amazing. Thank you Dan Brown, she thought, knowing that *The Da Vinci Code* with its spooky Louvre connection had a lot to answer for.

Luckily, her trusty guidebook had suggested the quickest way to get into the Louvre was to buy tickets online ahead of time. She had two in her bag. Sadly, she'd only need one ticket.

Once she'd entered the museum, she stood, like many a visitor before her, she imagined, completely disoriented and confused. Where to go? With so much on display, where to begin?

Four staircases led to different quadrants of the museum. She found a selection of museum guides in every language. When she picked up the English one, she noticed a rack of brochures and instinctively she glanced at them, subconsciously judging design, impact and creativity. Her eye was drawn to the word *sex* that made one brochure stand out from the others and, as she reached for it, she thought, huh, sex really does sell.

Sex Through the Ages was a traveling exhibit and it was coming to Paris. The sex exhibit included costumes, historic sex aids and, of course, paintings, lithographs, photos and film. The exhibit, which began in New York, was going to travel to selected cities around the world, including Paris. One of her clients was a condom manufacturer with international distribution. Maybe they could help sponsor this thing and get some publicity, she thought, looking more closely at the cover.

The brochure pictured a pencil drawing of a nude looking up with sexual intent. Behind her stood a man who obviously planned to take her up on her offer. Little color photos showed what had to be an antique vibrator, some kind of corset with enough whalebone to double as a torture chamber, and a mug shot of a kindly looking older man in a cap. Was he the curator? A random security guard? Whoever he was, he posed in front of a wall of erotic paintings.

She tucked the brochure in her purse, unfolded her map and tried to figure out where to go first. Denon, Richelieu, Sully—each wing had a separate staircase and each was crowded.

People swarmed around her and sudden loneliness struck her in the chest. Andrew should be here with her, damn it. She pulled out her cell phone and stared at it, and knew she wouldn't beg Andrew to stay. With a sigh, she obeyed a tactful sign and turned her phone off.

Where to begin? With some of the greatest art in the world in one building, where to start? With the pre-classical Greek sculptures? The entire room of Rubens? Oh, hell. She was a tourist. Why shouldn't she act like one? She followed the largest crowd of all up the Denon staircase and began following the signs for La Joconde—the *Mona Lisa*.

As she wandered, painting after painting astonished and compelled her. These were works she'd studied in school, gazed at in coffee-table books, dreamed of. And they were there in front of her, so much more powerful when she could lean close enough to see the brush strokes, smell the paint. She felt humbled and awed by the sheer volume of artistic works of such genius that she ought to devote time to savor each one rather than march on. The *Mona Lisa* smiled down graciously over the crowd before her so jammed that Natalie doubted anyone could see. Arms shot up with cameras to snap photos, a child emerged from the jam in tears. Natalie gazed from far away and then moved on—from Fra Lippo Lippi to Delacroix, from *Winged Victory* to Vermeer's *Lacemaker*. It was almost too much.

Walking in a daze as her feet began to throb and her brain began to overload, she found herself in a gallery that was quieter and less crowded. As she entered, a kindly looking older man in a cap nodded to her and smiled. She had the strangest sense that she knew him, then realized that he looked like the guy on the cover of that Sex Through the Ages exhibit brochure.

Stress, she thought. Must be stress.

CHAPTER TWO

WITH A TINY SMILE at the man, she walked into the gallery. These paintings seemed more modern, she thought, than what she'd seen so far. And some of the landscapes were surely American. She took her time in front of the pictures, but she was having trouble concentrating. She kept thinking about Andrew and wondering what he was doing now. She glanced at her watch. If she left right this second she could probably catch him before he left for the airport. She could...

She could what?

Beg him to stay? Plead with him to put the woman he'd sworn to love ahead of his business deal?

Or move on.

The paintings in front of her eyes blurred at the edges, until she blinked furiously, refusing to give in to tears. There'd be time for those later.

Her attention was caught by a sad and rather bloody scene. *The Duel*, it was called. Louisiana, 1859. Odd. She hadn't known the Louvre contained American art. Emile Gascon was the name of the artist. Hmm. She thought she knew American art, but she'd never heard of this guy. He was good, though; she couldn't believe how much feeling the canvas exuded. She felt rage, despair and grief emanating from the canvas in waves.

Oh, such grief that her throat caught. She never understood dueling—what a way to end a quarrel, by stabbing or shooting your opponent. She gazed more closely and realized that there was something odd about this duel. The loser of the duel was obvious, since he was sprawled facedown on the grass, blood seeping into the ground, his pistol beside his open hand. His opponent had turned away and was slipping into his coat.

But there was a woman, her body covering the corpse as though she could press life back into her dead lover, her blond hair running down his back like endless tears. Natalie had the strangest urge to reach out and comfort the distraught young woman. What an artist this Gascon was. You couldn't even see the woman's face, but her attitude and posture expressed such anguish that Natalie wanted to cry.

After a moment, she moved on to more paintings of Louisiana, and she spotted more works by Gascon.

There were social scenes from New Orleans in its crazy, lawless pre–Civil War days, rural scenes, pictures of plantation life, and then a painting on the back wall that stopped her cold. Her neck began to prickle as she stared at the canvas. There was an air of blatant sensuality and a hint of danger. And talk about nineteenth-century exploitation of females.

A woman reclined, naked, on a red chaise that even in the painting had the texture of velvet. She had her arm crooked and her head rested against her palm, blond curls spilling. She gazed out at the viewer as though distancing herself from what was going on. But she was the focus, not only of a casual Thursday-afternoon art lover wandering into the Louvre, but also of half-a-dozen black-clad men who stared at her. Something about her helplessness enraged Natalie. She stepped closer. And in that moment gasped. The woman's face—it was like looking into a mirror.

She backed away as a wave of panic swept her. If a painting could communicate, this one had sent out a sharp warning. *Run*, she heard in her mind, in an echoing voice curiously like her own. *Run*.

Natalie took a step backward, realizing her heart was pounding.

"She's beautiful, isn't she?" an older man's voice said behind her in English. The voice sounded American. Startled, she turned to find the security guard smiling at her.

Natalie nodded. She wanted to leave. She felt spooked and miserable. She was going to head back to her hotel, find a dark corner of the bar and enjoy a stiff drink.

Maybe two. "Yes," she said, nodded and made to walk away.

"She looks as though she's helpless, but she's not. She's much more powerful than she knows," the older man said. He smiled and she found his pale blue eyes both wise and full of meaning. He gave the impression he'd seen everything mankind had to offer. Maybe it was from a lifetime of being around great art.

"Really?" She was intrigued. "You think she has power? I thought exactly the opposite."

He shook his head. "She's the focus, the one in control. Her sexual power will save her."

It was such an odd interpretation of the painting that Natalie moved closer for a second look. Perhaps the whole Andrew thing had shaken her more than she realized. Instead of a stiff drink, she probably needed an hour or two with a good therapist. The guard hadn't mentioned the uncanny resemblance to herself, so maybe it was in her mind. But, when she turned she again had the feeling of staring into a mirror.

Wondering if she was completely losing it, she asked casually, "Do you think she looks like me?"

He put his head to one side, studied Natalie and then the women in the canvas. "Perhaps a little. The artist obviously had great affection for her. Look at the way he's threaded the hair with light, so it glows." He indicated the painted curls and Natalie leaned closer. Even as the voice that was and wasn't her own yelled, *No,* she felt a push at her back and tumbled forward.

She was going to bash into a priceless work of art and end up in the Bastille, or wherever they put prisoners these days, she thought in momentary panic. She put out her hands to take the blow, but there was nothing but blackness.

She screamed, one of those dream screams that have no sound.

She felt as though she were falling, but the floor kept moving away and wouldn't break her fall. She'd tried skydiving once and that's what this felt like. The rush of sound that's almost deafening, the feel of cool air hurtling past, the terror of free fall. In this case, though, she didn't have a pull tab to activate the parachute. She was dropping helpless, the scream a silent wave of panic all around her.

And then, after endless, rushing blackness she felt the jerk and pull, the steadying. Her heart pounded and she felt she was going to throw up. She was in the dark.

Had she fainted? Fallen into a coma?

"Open your eyes, *ma chérie*," a commanding male voice ordered. The words were in English, but with a French accent and the tone of the voice was chiding, almost as though she'd been reminded before but was deliberately being difficult.

She found, when she tried, that her eyelids lifted. Then widened. What the hell?

She was staring directly at a painter. He was a familiar-looking man, but she couldn't place him. Everything felt strange. She surveyed her surroundings and the nausea increased. Six men stared down at her. All of them were similarly dressed in some kind of old-fashioned costume. Dark suits, top hats. One held an ebony walking stick.

There was a common expression on their faces that made her feminist blood boil. Lust? Desire? Speculation? The one with the cane made her the angriest for his gaze seemed to contain cruelty. And, she realized with a shudder, ownership.

Wherever she was, she needed to get out of here. She made a move and felt the soft scrape of velvet against her hip. She looked down at herself and gave a small scream.

She was naked.

Instinctively she tried to cover herself, but the cruel-looking man stopped her with a hand on hers, pulling it away from her breast. "You are too delectable to hide yourself, my precious."

Natalie ran multimillion-dollar ad campaigns and managed a staff of ten. She made very expensive decisions every day, dealt with monstrous egos, creative tantrums and demanding clients.

Nobody called her "precious" in that condescending way and walked away with their gonads still functioning. Yet here, she was a naked nobody on a couch. On display and completely vulnerable. The same instincts that made her a success at work, however, jumped to save her now. She knew her best bet was to stay still and shut up until she had a better handle on what was going on.

Maybe she was having a dream or a hallucination, or a brain tumor. Soon she'd come out of it and back to herself. Unless it was a brain tumor, of course. Then she wasn't sure.

She remained still, feeling her skin crawl as they stared at her. She gritted her teeth and stared straight ahead, ignoring the voyeurs.

"Good girl, that's right," the painter said, nodding and giving her an encouraging smile.

"You're the one from the gallery," she said. That's why he was familiar. He looked exactly like the security guard she'd talked with. But what was he doing here? Wherever "here" was. Her voice sounded strange. Scratchy, as though she hadn't used it in a while. She tried clearing her throat. She was thirsty, she realized. "I recognize you."

There was a rumble of male laughter. "You're becoming too famous, Monsieur Gascon."

"Monsieur Gascon? *Emile* Gascon?" That was the name of the painter. She was *in* the painting. But, he'd painted it in—she brought the plaque beside the picture to mind—1859. "What's going on? Why did you push me? Where am I?"

Gascon didn't answer her, Instead he put his finger against his lips in a "shh" gesture.

"She'll fetch a fine price," a man of about thirty, with a Clarke Gable mustache said, ignoring her outburst as though she hadn't spoken.

"Damn and the devil I wish I could afford her," a younger man said. He had soft brown hair, big blue eyes and a baby face. He glanced around. "I don't suppose several of us could pool our resources and share?"

"No," said the cruel man, his hand tightening on the

cane handle. "I do not." She saw that he wore a curious ring with some kind of black insignia.

In fact, each of the men wore the same ring. Some kind of club? Her father wore a Masonic ring. Maybe these men belonged to a fraternity of some sort.

She didn't think this bunch raised money for new hospital equipment and kids' summer camps, though.

She wasn't entirely sure what they did, but the mention of price and they way they looked at her made her more determined than ever to get out of here.

"We could all take her now, try her out before—"

"No!" This time the cruel man pulled at his cane and a wicked-looking steel blade gleamed.

"No need to take offence, Count," said the one with the stupid idea. "Just a thought."

She had to do something. But what?

Get out of here. Somehow, this wasn't feeling like a dream or a hallucination. It was too real.

"Could I speak to you for a moment, privately?" she asked the painter.

"In a moment, my dear. Just remain still until I've finished." The voice was pleasant, but there was a note of warning in his eyes that told her to shut up and remain where she was. Great. What was she supposed to do? Lie back and think of Paris?

Oh, God. Paris, and Andrew. What if she never got back from whatever bizarre place this was? What if no one ever saw her again and Andrew thought she'd abandoned him? Or worse?

As panic threatened, she forced her thoughts away from Andrew. Hysteria wasn't going to help. She had to remain calm. There had to be a way out of this. And somehow this bizarre dress-up artist with the paintbrush was the key. She wouldn't let him out of her sight, and as soon as this sextet of funeral directors left the studio, she'd make Picasso over there put her back where he'd found her.

She hated this. Hated everything about it. Their eyes on her, her naked body out on display for strangers, her own absolute helplessness.

"What do you think she'll fetch?" asked a young man in his midtwenties.

"The price of any object of beauty depends solely on the value the purchaser is willing to pay."

"Aye, and the competition the item encourages."

"With that lovely smooth skin, the plump breasts and a belly made for pleasure, she'll make a fine mistress."

Breathe, she told herself, as her fists automatically clenched. One naked woman against six men, one of whom she knew was armed, was not a smart move. But just let one of them try to make her his mistress, and he'd be singing soprano for the rest of his life.

"She's a bit old, though," said the baby-faced one.

"Experience, my child. A woman like this could teach even you to be a man."

"Maybe I'll buy her, then, at the auction, right from under your nose."

"You'd best improve your fortunes by tomorrow night."

"You're going to auction the painting?" She addressed her question to the young man with the Clarke Gable moustache.

He chuckled. "No, my dear. We're going to auction you."

"You think you can sell me? Like a slave?" The whole notion was as ridiculous as it was revolting.

"You'll find it more amusing, I'm sure, to be a rich man's mistress than to continue as a lowly servant. We've bought you a lovely gown to wear tomorrow. The first of many if you behave yourself. Besides, your master can no longer afford to keep you. You can serve out your indentures to one of us. We won't ask you to dirty your hands with the washing or dusting."

A low chuckle made her shrink back into the couch as much as she could.

"You'll be far too busy for housework."

CHAPTER THREE

ANDREW COULDN'T concentrate. The hotel room felt strange without Natalie in it. Voices floated up from the street and he strained to hear her high-school French among them. Twice he made simple arithmetical errors—the boneheaded kind that could wreak unimaginable havoc on a financing deal.

Natalie was gone.

He wouldn't even turn his head to where her engagement ring sparkled on the night table like one of those warning signals on the car dashboard that light up when the engine's about to blow.

How had such a small disagreement led to her taking off the ring? Couldn't she see he was busy?

But then he was always busy. They both were. Did she think he wanted to choose business over the woman he loved?

A man looked after those he cared about. Doing it with money was the only way he knew. With bad eyes and more brain than coordination, he'd learned early that his intelligence and hard work were his tools, his weapons, his ticket to a good life.

Naturally, he worked out three times a week in a gym, played the obligatory golf games and charity tournaments with clients, and could scramble around a squash court without embarrassing himself too badly, but he was very happy to be a man of his time. In the days when a man's success depended on hunting mastodons to feed his family, well, he'd have been the entrée on the mastodon's family table.

Natalie was feeling anxious, that's all. Worked up about this wedding thing, worried they'd made a mistake. He understood her feelings of uncertainty. This was a big step. Neither of them wanted to screw up.

Once they were home, things would be better. He'd apologize, they'd talk. He'd get that ring back on her finger. He would.

Soothed by the thought that this was a temporary glitch and not the end of their engagement he wondered, for about the fiftieth time since she'd left, why he hadn't gone across the room and taken her in his arms? Kissed her the way he used to. Thrown her on the bed and shown her a few of the ways they were so very good together.

Why hadn't he done that? Thought before action was a great strategy in business, but with an angry woman, he suspected that sometimes action was required. Immediate action.

His concentration was so shot he went back to packing. Heard the ding of a new e-mail.

He was starting to hate the sound of that thing. It was like a servant's bell ringing—and he'd drop everything to run to the beck and call of his masters.

He didn't ignore that e-mail, of course. Things at work were too precarious.

But the message wasn't at all what he'd expected.

It was from some weird-ass Paris server he didn't recognize. The subject line was *Natalie*.

His heart skipped with embarrassing eagerness and he felt relief wash over him. She was e-mailing to tell him to stay, maybe she'd even apologize. She'd be back to the hotel soon. He clicked open the message, read it quickly once. Frowned, then sat to read it over again.

Natalie's in trouble. Go to the Louvre. Tell no one.

What the…? He read it again, first baffled, then worried.

Who in Paris knew Natalie? Was this some kind of practical joke? A sophisticated hacker with a sick sense of humor? Something told him that wasn't the case. He hit Reply. *Who are you? Send more details.* Pushed Send. Within seconds the e-mail came back undeliverable.

Now he was getting concerned.

He called Nat's cell phone and got voice mail. He left a message asking her to call him immediately.

Think, he told himself. Think.

Corporate kidnapping? But who would want to kidnap an advertising VP in Paris? It made no sense.

Natalie. He had no idea what was going on, but he had to see Natalie.

Shoving his wallet into his pants, he left the hotel and headed for the Louvre, suddenly thankful that they'd chosen this hotel not only for high-speed Internet but also for its easy proximity to the tourist sights. Including the famous art museum.

Normally he was cool under pressure—he used his brains. But with Natalie involved he found panic beating at the inside of his skull as he raced to the Louvre, skirting tourists, families of unhurried Frenchmen, guys ambling along smoking foul-smelling cigarettes. He mumbled *pardonnez-moi* as he jogged and sprinted his way to the Louvre, until haste overcame good manners, then he simply ran, pushing by people like a cop in a TV show.

Even as he ran, he began marshaling his wits and thinking of resources he could call on. The American embassy, the local police, Interpol—he'd use every contact he'd ever cultivated in business and politics.

He'd do whatever he had to do.

He'd save her.

He didn't even know from what.

Why had he let her go out like that? Why hadn't he stopped her?

Why?

He arrived at the glass pyramid outside the Louvre panting and sweating. "Oh, shit," he said when he saw the line-up. Didn't anybody in Paris have anything better to do on a Thursday?

He jogged around to the front of the line, where a very uninterested door guard spoke no English but used sign language to point him toward the back of the line. "Emergency," he panted. *"Urgence."* He had no idea if that was the right French word but it sounded pretty good.

Not to the guard.

He pointed to the line and said, *"Pas possible."*

This time the guard pointed him in a different direction.

Miracle of miracles, he found somebody who could speak better English than he could speak French and discovered the museum pass. Yes. He bought a three-day pass for a bunch of euros and bypassed the lineup to the special museum pass-holders entrance.

By the time he'd entered the hallowed halls of the Louvre, he was sweating and his hands were far from steady.

His mild sense of triumph disappeared as he glanced around the crowds of people, all his senses on alert for…he had no idea what.

A hostage crisis?

Natalie standing there laughing at him? What a great way to get him away from his desk, ha-ha.

A frigging note?

Nothing. Nothing. A tour group, families, students who seemed unbalanced without their backpacks. People milled everywhere, talking a dozen languages, giggling, lounging, carrying gift-shop bags.

No Natalie. No sign or hint where to look.

Not a soul seemed to note his arrival or appear with instructions.

He started walking, faster than anybody in the crowds surrounding him, so he wanted to yell at them to get the hell out of his way.

Had every tourist in the world and every Parisian decided to pick today to visit the Louvre?

Think, he ordered himself again.

Perhaps they could make some kind of announcement, the way department stores do for lost children, he thought. It was a long shot—first that he'd be able to make himself understood in phrase book French. Somehow he didn't think Berlitz had a handy phrase for "excuse me, my fiancée went missing and I got a weird-ass e-mail from out of the ether saying she was in the Louvre and needed my help."

Or maybe he could…or maybe he could what?

Freaking out would help no one. He approached an official-looking desk, trying to dredge up a few phrases. The one he most hoped would work was, *Parlez-vous anglais?*

An old guy in an official uniform of the Louvre crossed his path. Perfect.

"Excusez-moi," he said, already feeling like an idiot.

"How can I help you, sir?" the guard asked in American-accented English.

"You speak English, great. I'm looking for my fiancée. I know it's a stretch, but I got a message to meet her here and I really need to find her."

The guard nodded gravely as though finding needles in haystacks was his specialty. "What does she look like?"

"Blond, about five-six, slim, beautiful. She was wearing a blue tank top and a white denim skirt." He pictured her as she'd looked right before she walked out of their suite. Why the hell had he let her go? How could he ever let her go?

The guard nodded gravely. "I believe I did see her. Right this way, sir."

"How could you possibly remember one woman out of thousands?"

The guard smiled, kindly blue eyes twinkling. "She's also American. And very beautiful."

"Yes. Is she okay?"

"Perfectly, sir. This way."

"Thank you," Andrew said, allowing himself to relax a bit. Something about the old guy inspired trust.

The guard led him to an elevator tucked away behind a marble post and they ascended rapidly. Still, he wanted to hurry. His sense of disquiet wouldn't leave him until he found Natalie.

Once out of the elevator, the guard led him down a corridor packed with people, then to a quieter hallway and finally into a gallery. There weren't a lot of people in there and he saw at a glance that Natalie wasn't among them. His heart sank.

"She's not here."

"Come this way. I believe I can take you to her."

Andrew followed, wondering if the old guy was out of his mind. At the end of the gallery was a bank of paintings. He didn't bother looking at any of them.

Instead he grew irritated. There was no door, no archway. Where the hell was Nat?

"I thought you said you were taking me to my fiancée," he said.

"You mustn't panic, sir. You must use your intelligence."

Well, he certainly had enough intelligence to know when he was being conned. "What the hell's going on?" he asked. "It was you who sent me the e-mail, wasn't it?"

"I think you'll find this painting interesting, sir," the guard said.

"I'm not here to look at art," he snapped, turning away. "I have to find—"

"Does your fiancée look like this woman?"

Irritated, Andrew cast a swift glance at the painting the guard indicated, then stilled. He stepped closer to the indicated picture. "What is going on?"

"She's very beautiful indeed. Unforgettable."

"How can that possibly be…" He glanced sharply at the guard. "What kind of—is this a joke?" He looked around for hidden cameras and some smirking Frenchman with an appalling sense of humor. There was no one in the gallery but him, the guard, and a few other tourists. He heard a couple speaking in German in the corner, and a mother attempting to explain Impressionism to a bored-looking young girl.

No cameras, no one at all paying attention to him except the guard.

But it was the painting that pulled his attention once more. It was Natalie—but Natalie as he'd never seen her. He was no historian, but the painting had to be from some time in the 1800s. He knew her so well, and the painter was enough of a master that Andrew could feel her fear and anger through the paint. She stood on a raised platform in a white dress. Her hair was up, which wasn't a style she usually bothered with, except maybe for the odd gala. She was the focal point of the painting, staring out at the viewer—at Andrew, while a room full of dark-suited men and women in historical costumes stared at her.

He glanced at the wall plaque which said, Emile Gascon. *Lady in White*. 1859.

Andrew's heart thudded unpleasantly—1859?

"How did a painting of my fiancée, who is living in 2006, end up in the Louvre, dated 1859?"

"Please, sir, try to keep your voice down," the guard admonished.

Andrew wasn't a violent man, but he pulled the guard up by his lapels. "I don't know what is going on here, but I'm not about to be conned. Produce Natalie now or there's going to be trouble."

The guard appeared unruffled by the rough treatment. Andrew had never been the physically aggressive type and he began to feel foolish, knowing the German couple and the mother and daughter were staring at him.

He let go and the guard said, "I think if you take a closer look at the painter's date and signature, down in the bottom right corner, all will be revealed."

All will be revealed. Sounded like some corny magician's line, but Andrew was willing to look for clues to Natalie's whereabouts wherever he could find them. And he wasn't letting the old geezer out of his sight until he found her. In the flesh and not some cheesy painting.

He leaned closer to peer at the squiggle of letters and numbers in the bottom right corner. Felt a shove at his back and then all but blacked out.

It felt as though the air had been sucked out of him

and he was squeezed into a dark, cold tunnel. He struggled but didn't seem able to move any part of his body.

So this, he thought, is what death feels like.

CHAPTER FOUR

HE WASN'T DEAD. Andrew wasn't entirely sure what he was, but he wasn't dead.

He was able to draw air back into his lungs and the awful sense of hurtling through blackness stopped.

He opened his eyes. Blinked. Christ. Natalie. There she was. Standing up on the platform in the white dress, exactly as she'd been pictured in the painting. But she was real. He could see her, in the flesh, not fifty feet away. He noticed that there was silver thread woven through the fabric of her dress, but that hadn't come out in the painting.

Her face appeared calm, but he knew her, oh, he knew her. The jawline was rigid, her skin pale, her lips tightly compressed. She was furious and—he had a shrewd notion—barely holding it together.

Which pretty much summed up how he felt. He glanced down at himself and saw a lot of black fabric. In some ways, it wasn't unlike the suits he wore to work, though tighter, and with tails.

A buzz of mostly male conversation ebbed and flowed around him and he noticed a ballroom full of men dressed as he was, and a number of women who—even though they were dressed in what he had to assume was the height of fashion—didn't look entirely respectable. In different clothes, he'd have recognized them as the call girls and grifters who worked Manhattan.

A headache pounded in his temples, and he felt dizzy and unsure of his footing, as if he'd just got off a boat that had sailed through a storm.

Nothing made sense, except that he'd found her.

He'd found her.

Now all he had to do was figure out how to get the pair of them back to where they belonged.

"She's the best one we've had in years," said a friendly voice beside him with a Southern accent. But it was Southern-accented English, he was happy to note. Not French.

"She is?"

The young man looked at him curiously. "I haven't seen you before."

"No."

"First time at the Coeur de Lion auction?"

The what? "Yes."

"Trust me, you picked the best year ever. Not that either of us has a chance at her. She'll go to the count over there. He's been licking his lips over her since she was brought down. Not that he needs another mistress, but the count likes variety."

"I'm not entirely sure how this works," Andrew said, feeling rage spurt through him at the expression on the so-called count's face. He was looking at Natalie with X-rated thoughts printed all over his thin, swarthy face.

Andrew's hand tightened involuntarily, some caveman reaction he barely understood, and he realized he was gripping something cool and metallic. He gazed down to find it was a sword hilt.

The young man who'd been talking to him saw the gesture and grinned. "I wouldn't. He'd carve you to ribbons. Of course, all of us like to think we're masters with sword and pistol. Members of the Coeur de Lion have brought the ideals of French nobility with us, even to this lawless society. But the count is the undisputed master of the sword."

Deliberately, Andrew forced his hand to relax. "I have to say, I don't care for the look of the man," he said softly, striving to use the same formal sort of speech as his new acquaintance.

"A word in your ear, my friend. Count d'Homerge makes a better friend than an enemy. Especially in the society."

"Thanks for the tip." He looked up at Natalie and saw that she had the fringe of some lacy-looking scarf thing in her hands and she was pulling at it with jerky motions. He'd never seen her so agitated. He wanted to run up there, scoop her into his arms and race out of here, but he was, first and always, a man of intellect over action. A second's thought showed the flaw in that plan. His was not the only sword in the room. And, if his new friend was to be believed, he and Natalie had landed in the middle of some wacko secret society that prided itself on fighting to the death for their honor. He'd be shredded like a confidential document before he got to an exit.

No. For some bizarre reason, he and Natalie had found themselves living a scene from a painting, and he had to figure out where they were, when they were, and how to get them both back again. Preferably without getting killed.

If this was a nightmare, he thought, now would be an excellent time to wake up. He pinched himself on the off chance that it might rouse him, twisting the skin between his forefinger and thumb until he was sure he'd bruised it. All he got for his trouble was a sore thumb. This did not seem to be a dream.

Natalie. How could he have been so stupid as to fight
with her? He felt her courage even as he understood her
fear. She was beautiful, a white-gowned goddess, and
he'd almost let her get away.

That was the real nightmare.

"I haven't seen you before. Usually we all approve
the new initiates," the other man said chattily.

"I'm from New York," Andrew said, hoping that
would explain why no one here could possibly know
him. The fact that it was New York almost two centuries
from now, if the date on that picture didn't lie, he kept
to himself.

Luckily, New York did mean something. "Oh, Bannerman must have sent you."

"That's right," Andrew said, glad that there weren't
any cell phones or instant-messaging devices so his
story could be checked in real time.

There was an air of expectancy in the room, and he
could feel a strange eagerness pulsing. He'd felt something similar in strip clubs and at bachelor parties.

"Gentlemen," a commanding voice said, and an
older man with white hair and a beard reminiscent of
Wild Bill Hickock stepped forward on the stage.
Another Southerner. He looked like he should be
shilling tobacco in some ad. "Gentlemen," he repeated.
"We now come to the highlight of our annual Coeur de
Lion ball. Who will win this fair flower for his own?"
He smiled with courtly grace at Natalie, who did not
smile back.

"Gentlemen," she said, stepping forward. "Please.
I'm here against my will."

Two men stepped forward and she clamped her
lips shut. Obviously, she'd been threatened with
something.

The older man chuckled. "An unwilling mare can still be tamed to bridle, and much of the pleasure is in the taming."

He saw Natalie's face flame with two bright spots of color. This was the überfeminist they were talking about taming. He knew she was quelling her instincts to fight or flee, and he was proud of her for her restraint. In this room full of armed men, she was helpless.

He wasn't in any better shape, but at least he had a sword, not that he had the faintest idea how to use the thing.

It seemed when he'd been transported or time-traveled or whatever had happened to him, he'd come without his contact lenses or glasses. Damn. Everything had that irritating blur around the edges.

"This fine young woman comes to us from Boston, an indentured servant with three years yet to serve. I will start the bidding at fifty dollars."

There was some immediate groaning from men, including the man at his side. "That's too rich for me. Not that I had much hope of her anyway."

"You'd take a woman as your mistress who was unwilling? That's rape."

He got a goggle-eyed stare in return. "She's been a house servant, man. Her life as the mistress of one of us will be far superior. No doubt, she will receive some of the money and her protector will keep her in style. She'll have clothes, jewels, parties—she'll have everything she ever dreamed of. If she has children, they'll be looked after. We treat our women like queens." He glanced uneasily at the count. "Most of us."

Andrew bit back the urge to tell the guy what he thought of his morals, and watched the bidding climb to sixty dollars. He knew that money was worth a lot more than what the same sum would buy in the future, but the idea that Natalie could be auctioned off for the price of a couple of DVDs or an economical meal out was almost comical. Almost. If it weren't actually happening.

Well, Andrew might know diddly about swords, but finance was his world. He patted his pocket and felt the reassuring bulge of his wallet.

He waited until the majority of the bidders had fallen out of the competition. The count and two other men were in the bidding and the price had risen to one hundred and thirty-five dollars. Andrew moved slowly forward. By one hundred and forty dollars, there was only the count and one man left. His knowledge of people and money told him that the other guy was about to drop.

"One hundred and fifty dollars," he said calmly. He had around four hundred cash in his wallet plus a wad of euros, not that he figured anyone here was going to get too excited about a currency that hadn't yet been invented. But the four hundred bucks should be plenty. He tried a quick mental calculation using the historical average wage, and guesstimated that in the mid–eighteen hundreds, a hundred and fifty bucks would have been worth close to thirty-five grand. His four hundred ought to be enough to buy Natalie.

God, she'd be hating this.

He spoke loud enough that Natalie could hear him. She'd been staring at the ground, her posture one of defeat, but he knew Nat. She'd have figured out where all the exits were and would be calculating her moment to escape. She wasn't going to be bedded by some creep with greasy hair and an accent, not without the greasy guy in question ending up short a few body parts.

He watched her shoulders jerk and her head lift.

She glanced up and their eyes met. And that look said it all. He felt her anguish and her helpless rage, but he also felt her enormous relief. He telegraphed a warning, but he needn't have bothered. She was too smart to give him away. She held his gaze for one amazing moment when he felt his heart squeeze with love for her.

There was a general stir of interest. The bidding had been all but done, and now a new bidder had entered the lists. And who was he? He felt the buzz go around the room.

"And who is this man?" the count said aloud, staring at Andrew with dislike.

"Andrew Greenwood," he said calmly.

"He's a Yankee," the man said through clenched teeth. "And besides that, he isn't a member."

"He's wearing the ring," a voice said near to him. He was? He raised his right hand and there it was, a strange black-and-gold design. He saw now that they all wore one.

"I'm from New York," he said, and remembering his earlier conversation, added, "Bannerman will vouch for me."

"That's fair." There was general assent. Clearly, everybody looked forward to a little more drama before the prize was carried off.

"One hundred and fifty dollars is more than any woman's ever sold for," someone said near him.

"One hundred and sixty dollars," the count said, narrowing his eyes and glaring at Andrew. If this battle were over anything but the woman he loved, he'd back off at the menace in the man's expression.

It wouldn't do to act like the money he was throwing around was the product of close to two centuries of inflation, so he paused, and waited a couple of beats before saying, "One hundred and seventy-five dollars."

An ugly expression came over the count's face, but Andrew knew he'd won.

"You must be from a very wealthy family, Mr. Greenwood. I congratulate you on your prize."

He hadn't realized he was sweating until the moment the count bowed and stalked away.

He looked up at Natalie to find relief in her eyes and knew the same emotion must show in his.

"Congratulations, Mr. Greenwood," said the courtly Southerner. "You're going to enjoy a rare treat."

"Thank you, sir," Andrew said, holding to his role with difficulty when he wanted to grab Nat's hand and start running. "If you'll excuse us, I'd like to take my new mistress to a hotel." He flashed what he hoped was a self-satisfied grin. "I have much to celebrate."

The old man chuckled. "Of course you do. But don't forget our traditions." He wagged his finger. "You spend the first night right here. Tomorrow you can take her home with you."

"Of course," he managed, cursing inwardly. Couldn't anything in this nightmare be easy?

"You are one lucky dog, sir!" said his new found friend and, with a sudden whoop, all hell broke loose. It was like a wedding night where the guests were the tackiest known to man. With great whooping and hollering and ribaldry, he and Natalie were hoisted high and carried up three flights of stairs in a walk-up that was masculine looking, genteel rather than fancy.

No problem. All they had to do was sneak out in the night and…well, they'd figure out that part when they were away from this house of dark lords or whatever the hell they called themselves.

"No," Natalie whispered urgently, when they approached a hefty wooden door on the third floor. "Don't let them put us in there."

"I've got an idea," he said loudly, before he had any ideas at all.

"I bet you've got a few," his new friend said, and received a raucous volley of laughter.

"I'd like to stand my fellow bidders and new brothers a drink," he shouted above the din.

More laughter. "Hedging off?"

"Need some help with the girl?"

He protested, but the merriment continued. "Tomorrow we'll drink with you," said the guy whose shoulder currently supported one half of his ass, looking up with a half-drunken grin. "Tonight we drink *to* you."

And before he could come up with anything better, he and Natalie were carried into a high-ceilinged room dominated by a four-poster bed that would be puny by today's standards; a needlepoint screen, the kind where a lady changed clothes, coyly tossing stockings and things over the top; a marble-topped table with a washbasin and jug and a nightstand with a brass candlestick. The windows were small, with wrought-iron lacing that appeared as difficult to break through as prison bars.

A few pieces of loud and extremely rude, not to mention politically incorrect, advice were hurled his way before the door banged behind him. Even as he ran to it, he heard the key grate in the lock.

He turned around and Natalie was looking at him as though they were the only two survivors of a disaster. "I'm so happy to see you," she said, sounding more vulnerable than he'd ever heard her.

Suddenly, it didn't matter that they were locked in here together. Nothing mattered but the fact that he'd found her.

"I'm so sorry," he found himself saying as he strode to her side.

"Me, too."

She was so infinitely precious to him—how had he been so blind? He pulled her to him and kissed her, letting her feel all the love and passion he had in stock. And that stock had been rising mightily in the past few hours. Her lips trembled beneath his and she clung to him.

"I've been so scared," she whispered, when they came up for air.

"Me, too."

"What's happening?"

"I don't know, but we've got to get out of here."

"No chance. Don't you think I've tried? The windows are barred, the door's locked."

He went to the window anyway, and of course she was right. The window opened to let in air, but the grillwork was well bolted. Plastic explosives would do the trick, but sadly he hadn't thought to bring any with him.

"I thought you must have flown home by now." She looked at him. "Or did you?"

"No. I got an e-mail that you were in trouble. I'm only a few hours behind you."

She shook her head, her forehead wrinkling. "I've already spent a night and a day here. Time isn't consistent, then." But he didn't want to talk about the mysteries of time.

"You've been here overnight?"

She nodded.

"Alone?"

Once more, she nodded. "I've never, ever been so scared. Or so helpless. Or so angry."

He'd have time to talk about their differing experiences later. Right now he needed to concentrate on escape.

"Do they open the door to bring food?"

"Yes. An armed man and a female servant."

"Maybe now that I've bought you, they'll assume I'm with them and won't bother with the armed guard. Between us we should be able to deal with a serving girl with a tray."

"She's pretty hefty," Natalie said, looking at him doubtfully.

"Are you saying I can't take her?" Andrew asked, stung.

"You've always been a lover not a fighter." She smiled at him, but the corners turned wobbly. Then she seemed to pull herself back together. "You're right, of course. We'll overpower her, escape from here and then…" She gazed toward the grated window but didn't have to finish the sentence. He knew what she was thinking. And then they'd be out in the middle of New Orleans in 1859.

Maybe they'd get back home; maybe they were doomed to stay here as long as they could survive. Maybe all they had was now.

In that second he realized that if now was all they had, at least they'd be together, and that was still a hell of a lot better than a long and tedious life back in his own time without Nat.

"Natalie, there's something I have to tell you."

She turned startled eyes his way. "What is it?"

"I love you."

"There were long stretches in the night when I was thinking about never seeing you again. Not that we'd ended our engagement, but that I would never see you again. We might not even be in the same century. And I wanted to tell you the same thing. I love you, too."

"Come here."

Her smile trembled a little, but she managed one.

"You think because we're in some chauvinistic history lesson that you can order me around?"

"No. I think that because I paid the equivalent of about forty-seven thousand bucks for you that you should come over here."

"You got a bargain."

He couldn't argue with that. "I know. Come here and let me show you how much I know."

"Maybe you should come here."

"Why?"

"I'm closer to the bed."

CHAPTER FIVE

IN HALF A DOZEN steps he was close enough to touch her. Andrew pulled Natalie to him and closed his eyes, holding on. He smelled a fragrance he didn't recognize—something spicy and exotic—from the dress? Whatever soap was she using here? And he caught the elusive scent of her, of her skin and essence and everything he loved about her. She felt so right in his arms, her body fine boned and long limbed, her skin soft and yet resilient with muscle.

"If we ever get back," he said against her hair, "I am never letting you go."

He tipped her chin up and kissed her, letting all of his usually tightly controlled feelings out.

"I don't know what will happen in the morning."

"We may only have tonight." Her eyes were misty. "We've wasted so much time."

"No more."

His hands trembled as he undressed her. There was something vaguely wedding dress–like about the full-length gown of heavy white silk with the silver threads running through the fabric. Her upswept hairstyle was a formal one brides often chose, though somehow he doubted Natalie would.

He'd thought she looked tiny and frail, but he'd assumed it was because she was the lone female on a stage with men. Now, he understood his mistake.

As he undid the hooks running down the back of her dress he saw the corset beneath.

"Is that thing as uncomfortable as it looks?"

"More so. Get it off me, will you?"

He fumbled and swore, but he managed to get her out of the tightly laced corset. Her pale skin showed a few red patches and lines where the stays had pinched.

He turned her slowly, enjoying the sight of her freed breasts and the smooth expanse of belly above huge white bloomer things. "What are these?"

"I think they're called pantalets," she said.

"Sexy."

"You're nuts."

"Probably."

Then he kissed her again, letting his hands roam.

"Ouch," she complained. "Something scratched me." She stepped back and then grinned. "Is that a sword in your pocket?"

By unspoken agreement they'd decided to let their worries about the morning go and enjoy this night together. He was astonished to see the excitement already tinging her cheeks with pink and the humor that sparkled in her eyes. How long had it been since they'd enjoyed each other like this?

He glanced down at his attire. Since he hadn't dressed in it, he had no idea how to get out of it. The sword hung from a belt, and he took that off first, laying the weapon far away as though it were loaded. The heavy wool coat, satin waistcoat, starched shirt came off layer by layer. His trousers were of fine wool and his leather boots shone. "I think I'm a bit of a dandy," he told Natalie, looking at the pile of fancy clothes.

NATALIE HAD NO attention to spare for anything but Andrew. When he was naked, she looked at him—really looked. For the first time in a long while, she let herself live completely in the moment.

When had she stopped being able to simply be? Without a million things on her mind, the next meeting, the next job, the next quarter-hour block on her time sheet?

In the past few months, she'd been so tired and work focused that it was sometimes easier to fake an orgasm than put the time and effort into achieving one.

No wonder they'd had such a terrible time in Paris.

Now, she looked at the man standing naked before her, a quizzical gleam in his eye. He wasn't superbuff, but he kept himself in shape. She liked the look of him, the wiry limbs, the quietly sensual mouth. His eyes were a little unfocused without his glasses. "Can you see?"

"I seem to have time-traveled without my contacts," he admitted. "You have a soft halo all around you. It's nice."

He reached toward her and surprised her by picking up her foot. His hands were warm as they wrapped around her ankle and heel. He sat beside her on the tester bed and kissed the arch of her foot before kneading the muscles, rubbing her toes until the tension began to flow out of her.

"It's nice to be able to take our time," he said, rubbing in hypnotic circles, his thumbs over the soles of her feet.

"Mmm," she purred.

"No phones will ring, no beepers, pagers, e-mail."

"No TV news, sports highlights you have to catch or late-night talk shows."

"Only us."

She shivered. "Until morning."

"Morning's a long time away," he said soothingly. "And we're together now. We'll be okay."

The candlelight added a warm glow to their surroundings. In the grate, the fire popped and then made a quiet sizzling sound.

"It's going to be all right," he said, and for some odd reason, she believed him.

Tomorrow there would be danger and confusion and fear. Tonight there was only room for comfort, intimacy and pleasure.

Having massaged both feet to his satisfaction, Andrew moved up to her calf muscles. When he reached her knees, he parted them gently, stoking the skin of her inner thighs. "You're so soft here, so sensitive," he murmured as she shivered beneath his touch.

She'd never felt so sensitive, or so responsive to his touch. With perfect timing, she slipped her legs apart at the very moment he moved closer. When his lips followed the path his hands had taken earlier, she trembled all over. It was so quiet. No traffic noises from outside. Once she heard a carriage rumble by, and then nothing. There must be movement inside the house since there were plenty of servants, but up here it was silent, cocooned from the world and, for this night, from reality.

The fire was a soothing crackle in the background, the only other sounds coming from her and Andrew. The sound of his lips moving against her skin, their breathing, the shifting of the canopy bed beneath their weight, the sound of linen sheets against naked skin.

How many times had they made love? Hundreds. How had it never felt like this before?

Her breath trembled as he took his sweet time moving his mouth to where she needed it most.

Her breath became the loudest sound in the room.

He took her slowly with his mouth. Odd that this moment should feel like such a luxury when for all she knew they had very few of them. They were out of their own time, and somehow this made her feel weightless. Not burdened by the thoughts of clocks and schedules and the pressure to get on to the next thing, be it sleep, an appointment or her climax. What was the hurry? So she let herself relax as she never had before, enjoy as she never had before.

She knew with uncanny certainty that Andrew was feeling the same. He never went this slowly, or reveled so completely in the experience of lovemaking.

When at last he put his mouth on her, she cried out, her hips jerking crazily as sensation spiraled through her. She was so hungry for the feel of his tongue, wet and curling around her, lapping and dipping that her hunger grew. She was beyond want and edging into intense need.

He backed off, slowing her down, but she was too far gone. In one of her less subtle moves, she grabbed his head and held him against her, moving her pelvis in time to his tongue.

It was too good, too amazing, and she felt herself rising, emotion and pleasure merging until, like a glass when the bartender forgets to stop pouring, she overflowed, spilled over, with a wild cry.

He held her through that first explosion and the aftershocks that rocked her, then he kissed his way up her belly, spending a long time playing at her breasts and then moving higher until they were kissing, not like two people saying good night but like two lovers who could never get enough of each other. The first climax had taken the edge off her urgency but she still floated, still hummed with desire.

He rose up, hovered on the edge of entering her, and then lifted his head so they were staring into each other's eyes in the wavering glow of candlelight as he slowly, but slowly, entered her.

Tears pricked at her eyelids as she saw the fierce love in his eyes. She clung to him, wanting to hold him inside her body, revel in this intimate connection.

"I love you," he said, but he didn't need to say the words. She felt his love in every stroke, and in every brush of his skin against hers, heard it in the beats of his heart against her breast.

"I love you," she replied huskily, feeling a single tear roll down her temple.

He wiped at it with his thumb, then kissed the damp spot.

He moved a little harder, delving deeper inside her with each thrust. The friction built and so did her level of desire. She raised and lowered her hips in the same rhythm until their skin was slick with sweat and their breathing harsh.

"Let go," he said softly. "I'll wait for you."

And so she did. Closing her eyes and tilting her head back, she gave herself over to the ancient needs gathering, listened to the pulsing of her blood grow wilder and more urgent until there was no stopping the wave of exquisite sensation that rolled over her and through her.

The minute she cried out, grabbing mindlessly at his sweat-damp shoulders, sliding down his back to grasp his hips, he slipped his own leash and bucked hard and furiously until they were crying out together, into each other's mouths.

Her heart thundered, her blood pounded, and she'd never felt more thrillingly alive.

Afterward, they lay entwined, arms and legs curled around each other. Perhaps they were unconsciously making the point that they were one. Whatever happened now, they would share the same fate.

"Why was it never like that before?" she asked quietly. They'd extinguished the candle and only the faint glow from the fire shed any light into the room.

Normally, Natalie wore pajamas to bed, but her hosts hadn't provided any, so she was unusually aware of her own nakedness, the feel of her skin brushing Andrew's and the slightly coarser feel of the linen sheets against her.

She traced her fingers over his chest, absorbing his warmth and the amazing fact of him being here with her. The nightmare didn't seem so bad somehow now that she was sharing it with him.

She thought he wouldn't answer. Maybe she'd offended him by implying that their sex life wasn't always this good. But then she heard the low rumble of his voice.

"I think maybe we took each other for granted." He touched her breast and skimmed his palm down her belly. "Took this for granted."

"Love seemed too easy?"

"Yeah, maybe. Now we know how quickly you can lose what you most treasure."

"We almost threw it away."

He shifted, turned to face her. She could barely make out the shape of him in the darkness. "I don't want to sound like a jackass, but I'd like to make you a promise."

"Okay."

He took her hand in his and held them clasped loosely over her heart. "I promise never to give up on us again."

Her heart skipped a beat. Did he feel it through their joined hands? How long was "never" going to be for them anyway? A day? A week? An eternity of skipping around in time trying to rediscover their own place in the history's chronology? She realized it didn't matter.

"I make the same promise to you."

"If I let work take over, if I ever stop appreciating you, I want you to say two words to me."

"Two words?"

"Remember Paris. It will be our code."

"Remember Paris," she repeated slowly, then nodded. "That's good for me, too. If I'm ever trying to walk away before we've finished a fight, or if I get too caught up in some advertising campaign, then you can say those same words to me. I want to love you and live with you for my whole life and I want that a lot more than I want to suck up to a client or bag the next account."

"Okay."

She lay with her head on his chest, feeling surprisingly content considering the mess they were in, but then she was so much better off since Andrew had arrived. She realized now how truly terrified she'd been when she'd arrived all alone, naked, on a different continent in the wrong time.

She was still a continent and a couple of centuries off, but at least she was with the right man. That counted for something.

"We should get some sleep," he said, his fingers smoothing her hair.

"Yes."

But they didn't sleep. Time was suddenly too precious. Instead, she leaned over and kissed him slowly on the lips, and they made love again.

CHAPTER SIX

APART FROM A FEW snatched hours of sleep, they made love all night.

But, like all nights, no matter how amazing, this one ended with sunrise.

Daylight crept in through the shutters, pink tinged and vague. Then it whitened, brightened, and the reality of their dilemma faced them once more.

They left the bed. Natalie poured water from the ceramic ewer into the washbasin and had a quick sponge bath before dressing herself back in the heavy white satin, since it was the only clothing she had. With Andrew's help she was able to dress without the necessary but unwelcome help of a lady's maid.

Andrew followed her lead and sponged himself down before scrambling back into the clothes he'd arrived in last night.

"Where's the bathroom?" he asked.

She walked to the bed, bent down and retrieved a ceramic chanber pot. "Welcome to the eighteen hundreds."

"How long before they invent indoor plumbing and hot showers?" he wondered aloud.

"Longer than I'm planning to stay," she informed him, sitting at the dresser in front of the mirror and re-pinning her hair.

"How do you know to do that?" he asked.

"I watched the maid when she did my hair. I want to fit in well enough with the general population that I can disappear if I need to without calling attention to myself."

"That's great. Um. How about me?"

She glanced over her shoulder, her brows raised.

"Am I going to blend in, in this evening dress?"

She surveyed him slowly. Then she bit her lip. "I have no idea."

"Well, let's get out of here first, then we'll worry about fitting in."

"Right. So, the plan is to overpower the woman who brings the breakfast and make a run for it."

"Yes. Exactly."

"Then we…"

"We find that guy," she said. "The one I saw at the Louvre."

"You mean that guard?"

"You saw him, too?"

"Yeah. He said he knew where you were. He showed me a picture. It was an old painting, but it was you."

She nodded. "I know. I was naked, God, I can't believe all those people at the Louvre saw me naked."

"What are you talking about? You weren't naked." He stepped closer. "I'd like to see that painting though."

She glared. "Later." Holding him at arm's length, she said, "Tell me about your picture."

"It was you, at the auction. One minute I'm looking at you in this picture and the next—"

"The old guy shoved you?"

"You, too?"

She nodded. "But when I got here, I'm naked on this couch and the same guy, the guard from the Louvre, was the artist. I'm telling you he's the key to this."

"So you were…spirited here to the house?"

"No. I think when I first…landed—" she shrugged helplessly "—whatever you call the arrival, I think it was the artist's studio. It was weird. I was there, and about six men were watching him paint me." She shuddered. "I have never felt so vulnerable in my life. Or so mad. And I couldn't do anything, but stay still and wait for the men to leave."

"Did they…hurt you in any way?" He looked fierce enough to take on the six of them. And angry enough to murder them all.

"No. The guard at the Louvre said something strange, right before he pushed me back in time. Now I think it was a kind of warning. He said that the woman in the picture had the power. When I tried to look more closely, he shoved me into the frame and you know the rest."

"How could you have power when you were alone and naked in front of men who sell women to each other for money?"

"I don't know. I didn't feel powerful. I felt—exposed, obviously."

"Speaking as a man, a naked woman has a lot of power, but it's all sexual."

She nodded. "That's what I thought he said, too. But maybe that's not it." She turned to him. "Don't you think there must be some reason we're here?"

"I haven't had a lot of time to think. You mean, we were sent back for some purpose?"

"Well, I've been here longer than you. I've had more time to think. What if the power I have isn't sexual. What if he meant something else?"

"Those paintings were both dated 1859. What do you think you're going to do? Prevent the Civil War?"

Her clear blue eyes met his. "I don't think one person can change history that easily." She shook her head. "I don't know. But obviously this wasn't random. For some reason you and I were both sent back here, together. Why? Did he say anything to you?"

"Not really." He sat on the bed, and frowned at the braided rug on the wooden floorboards. "I was so frantic to find you that I didn't pay all that much attention to what he was saying."

She rose and joined him, sitting beside him on the bed, so it wavered on its ropes for a second. "Try and remember. Maybe there's a clue."

He shook his head. "He led me straight to the back and started yammering about some picture. He'd said he was taking me to you, so you can imagine that I wasn't exactly interested in looking at art. He had to pretty much force me to look at the one of you in the auction."

"Do you remember the name of the artist?"

He narrowed his eyes, obviously trying to recall the plaque. "Some French name. The last name started with a G, a name like garçon."

"Emile Gascon?"

His gaze moved to lock with hers. "Sounds right. Is he your guy?"

"Yes. There were quite a number of paintings on that wall by this Emile Gascon. There was one that moved me. It was a duel scene. A dead man on the ground and a woman weeping over him." She shivered slightly at the memory. "Looking at that artist's work made me feel that woman's grief as though it were my own. Whoever, or whatever he is, the man is a great artist."

"Or some kind of magician."

"Then there were more pictures, mostly landscapes, a few portraits, nothing that jumped out at me until I saw the picture of myself. Naked."

"Yeah. That would give you a shock." He glanced at

her from under his eyebrows. "I'll still have a couple hundred bucks left over from buying you. Maybe I'll buy that painting."

"Could you please think about something else besides seeing me naked?"

"Hey, you misjudged me. I'm thinking of it as an investment. If he's good enough to hang in the Louvre in 2006, this guy is collectible."

"Quit joking. Say one serious thing. Please."

He flopped backward so he was staring up. "My great-great-something grandfather was killed in a duel."

She felt something had stabbed her in the chest. "He was?"

"Mmm-hmm."

"When did it happen?" Her tongue felt suddenly clumsy in her mouth, so she had a hard time getting words out. "When?"

"I don't know exactly. It's an old family legend. Very romantic. He was from a well-to-do family, and fell in love with a servant in the house. The family got rid of her, but he found her again, somehow. I've never known any more details than that he fought a duel over this woman."

"In New York?" But she knew, even as she said the words.

Andrew raised his head and looked at her. "Louisiana."

Her mind flew to the picture hanging in the Louvre, the woman whose grief had called to her. "What happened to the woman? After the duel?"

"No one knows for sure."

"It's such a sad, romantic story. Someone must have passed along some information."

"There are two versions. We're not sure which is true. One story says she married the guy who won the duel."

"What's the other version?"

"It was a long time ago, Nat. Stories are always garbled when they get passed down, you know that."

"I'd still like to hear the other way the story ends."

"She killed herself." He reached out and took her hand, pulling her down beside him on the bed.

"When I was being painted, and then again at the auction, they said I was an indentured servant."

Outside a carriage rumbled by and the coachman called to his horses to slow. "You know what I think?"

"What?" She felt cold suddenly, and wrapped her arms around him for warmth and comfort. And simply to feel him beside her, alive and whole and breathing.

"I think this Gascon character is like a time-traveling relationship counselor. We broke up, he put us in a position where we were forced to realize that we were meant to be together."

"So he pushed us back in time? Isn't that a little drastic? He couldn't have said, 'Hey, you two. You love each other. Quit being pigheaded and work it out.'"

"Would we have listened?"

She stared at him. "Probably not."

He traced a finger over her eyebrow, then down her temple and the curve of her cheek. "I was going to go back to New York. I was packing. I was angry, and hurt and feeling like you just didn't get it."

She nodded. "I know."

"I figured you'd come to your senses when you got back to the city and we'd get back together. Or we wouldn't." He cupped her cheek in his palm. "I was going to walk away from the greatest thing in my life." At this distance, she figured he could see her pretty clearly, certainly read the truth in her eyes. "You wouldn't have come back to me, would you?"

"No. I saw my whole life in that awful moment when

we looked at each other and you told me you were going back. I knew I was always going to be less important than your work." Her throat tightened and the rest came out huskily. "And I couldn't stand it. No. I wouldn't have gone back to you."

"I don't love my work more than you." He blew out a breath and his eyes crinkled in concentration. "I...it's all I'm good at. Business. I've never been the sweep-a-woman-off-her-feet type. I make money. It can buy you everything you'll need, everything I don't have. I guess it's how I learned to show love."

She was about to tell him that that was the stupidest thing she'd ever heard, but then he continued.

"I've done stupid things before, lots of them, but nothing stupider than almost walking away from you. I won't ever do it again. But don't you see that, if it hadn't been for the time-traveling guard, we would have lost each other."

"I still think that this is a pretty big stunt to pull to get two people together."

"Well, maybe he can see into the future, too. Maybe—I don't know." He got off the bed and walked to the window, his boots echoing. "Maybe we're destined to have a child who'll cure cancer, save the environment, get that world peace thing figured out."

The idea of their child, no matter how talented or mundane, filled her with a quiet joy. "Maybe."

"Well, let's go find the artist's studio, figure out what is going on, then tell him thanks but no thanks and get him to push us back to the future."

She hesitated, then nodded. Fear was niggling at her, an irrational and mainly groundless fear, but she gave in to the urge to get out of there and back to her own time. "I agree. We find Gascon and ask him to send us home."

"Could you find the studio again?"

"I think so. I stared out of the carriage window when I was brought here and tried to memorize the route." She glanced up at him in amazement. "You know, some of the landmarks are the same. Jackson Square is already built—the carriage passed it on the way here. And I saw an honest to God riverboat paddle wheeler."

"Great. You can be the tour guide. Don't worry. You'll find the studio." He moved closer and kissed her hard.

"Yes. I'll find it."

There was a knock on the door.

They exchanged glances. This was the moment they'd been waiting for. Once they overpowered the servant with the breakfast tray, they'd be out of there, hunting down the artist and finding a way back to their own time.

He kissed her again, quickly, a surprising light of adventure in his eyes and whispered, "Showtime!"

CHAPTER SEVEN

"JUST A MOMENT," she called out, watching Andrew retrieve his sword and buckle it on. He picked up one of the heavy candlesticks, and Natalie was briefly sorry for the headache the servant would suffer when she came to. Then he moved to stand out of sight behind the door and Natalie walked forward, ready to distract the woman. She drew in a deep breath and tried to put a calm expression on her face.

"All right. You can come in now."

She heard the key turn and, when it opened, wanted to scream in frustration. It wasn't the servant with breakfast at the door. Count d'Homerge stood outside, and with him a few of the men who'd watched her being painted.

The memory of the way they'd watched her, naked and helpless, had her chin rising. Somehow, she and Andrew would get out of their clutches. "Count. Gentlemen. I thought this was breakfast." She spoke clearly, doing her best to warn Andrew.

"No, my dear, it's not breakfast. We're here to say good-bye to you," the count said.

Several of the men from last night were with him. She glanced around hopefully, thinking that if the artist was here, he'd save them the trip to his studio, but the artist wasn't among the men.

"May we come in?"

It was obviously a rhetorical question since he walked into the room as he spoke. Andrew was by the empty fire grate, his back to the room. The candlestick rested innocently on the narrow table behind the door.

"Ah, Monsieur Greenwood. I hope you passed a pleasant night?"

"Very pleasant, thank you."

"You let your fire go out, I see."

"I'm sure he was kept warm enough, eh?" joked the young man with the baby face. He motioned his head toward the bed and, despite the fact that Natalie, an incurable neat freak even in times of personal distress, had tidied the bed, the memory of their night of passion brought a blush to warm her cheeks.

Involuntarily, she glanced at Andrew and their eyes met.

"Well," he said, "if you're not bringing breakfast, I hope you plan to let us out of here so we can procure our own."

"Most willingly. Though I am sorry that you should be desirous to leave mademoiselle's bed so early. Perhaps your expensive purchase was not such a bargain after all."

"I'm very well satisfied, thank you. But I've some business to attend to. I'd like to leave now. With my…prize."

"Of course," the count said. "You'll want to make an early start."

"Yes."

Could it be this easy? No need to overpower the servant? They exchanged a glance and Andrew put a proprietary arm around Natalie's shoulder.

"Just one last thing, sir."

Andrew raised one brow.

"The money."

Andrew smirked ever so slightly. "Of course. One hundred and seventy-five dollars, I believe." He put a hand to his pocket and withdrew his wallet. Natalie felt his body suddenly tense and glanced down. The leather folder in his hands wasn't his—she knew, because she'd bought him a Prada wallet for his birthday. This was not it.

He shot a quick glance at Natalie, and then gave a shrug that didn't fool her, and probably didn't fool anyone else, either. If his wallet hadn't time-traveled with him, then they were in serious trouble.

He opened the leather and frowned.

"I'm afraid I've left my money at my hotel. I will need a couple of hours to bring the money."

For one long moment there was utter silence in the room.

Then an oath, a flurry of motion and suddenly the count reached out and struck Andrew across the face.

The crack of flesh on flesh was loud and so unexpected that Natalie gasped.

Andrew's head snapped back and she saw rage flare in his eyes. "What the—" he said, surging forward, his fists rising. The other men formed a casual ring around the two opponents, too much like grade-school kids at a school fight for Natalie's peace of mind.

"You have insulted me and made a mockery of this society," the count said furiously, his thin face mottled with rage. "It will be my pleasure to kill you in a duel."

"Oh, my God. No," Natalie moaned. The fear that had haunted her, since Andrew had mentioned his little piece of family lore involving a dueling ancestor, choked her.

Andrew had always used his wits as his weapons. And she was happy to see that this macho crap hadn't taken him over completely. He cocked an eyebrow. "A duel? Isn't that a little harsh? All I did was forget my money."

"Do not trifle with me. You have been struck, sir. No man lets such a challenge pass unless he is a coward."

"Please, Andrew. Don't," she moaned. "He's baiting you, deliberately."

Andrew rubbed his reddened cheek and glared at the man who'd struck him. "I'm not a violent man, but sometimes bullies have to be put in their place," he said quietly, and she had the oddest feeling he was explaining his actions to her.

"Name your seconds, sir," the count sneered.

"I would be happy to act for you, sir," said the young man he'd met the night before.

"Thank you."

"And, since you are a stranger in town, may I present my friend Laurence as another suitable second?"

It was a nightmare. A nightmare that simply wouldn't end. One of those where you evade the monster, killer, hideous terror only to turn the corner and find something worse.

"Andrew," Natalie said urgently, "You can't fight a duel. This is crazy."

But no one was listening to her. The guy who'd offered himself as a second was saying, "As the challenged party, sir, you may choose swords or pistols."

"Well, there's a catch-22," Andrew said with grim humor.

"A what?"

Right. That term wouldn't be in use for a long time yet. "Andrew, you can't," she said, throwing herself against his chest.

"He must fight to keep his honor, *mademoiselle*."

"Pistols," he said over her head. "I choose pistols."

A curt nod and then the men turned to leave. "Wait," Andrew said. "I've things to do. Preparations to make. I must leave this house."

The count glanced at him coldly. "*Non, monsieur.* Your seconds will prepare everything to perfection. Stay. Enjoy the charms of your lady."

"But—"

The count flicked a glance at Natalie and she felt her skin crawl at the expression within them. "It will be the last night of your life. You should take all the pleasure you can."

With that, the men were gone, and the door locked once more behind them.

"This is ridiculous," Natalie shouted, suddenly furious with Andrew. "You can't fight a duel. You don't even know how to shoot."

"Yes I do. I used to be pretty damn good at target practice."

"Not since I've known you. When did you practice?"

He calculated silently. "About ten years ago."

She stared at him, then stormed to the window and shoved at the iron grille with her bare hands, grunting with the effort. "There has to be a way out of here," she said with suppressed fury.

"And then what?" he said quietly.

She dropped her hands and her whole body slumped. "I don't know."

He went to her and took her hands in his. The metal grille had indented cruel lines in her palms, like a squiggly tic-tac-toe scoreboard. He kissed the palms, one at a time.

"Why are we even here?" she asked. "None of this makes any sense."

"Something occurred to me when that brute was in here throwing around his challenges."

"What?"

"You're not going to like it."

She snorted. "I haven't liked anything since we broke up in a Paris hotel room."

"It's more about my family history."

"What happened?" If he was telling her his ancient family history, she had to assume there was a connection between what had happened to his family and the fact that Andrew and she were here now.

"There have been a lot of Andrews in my family. He was one of them. Andrew Greenwood. That was his name."

"So what?" A bubble of hysteria danced at her throat. "You're here to repeat history? You time traveled back one hundred and fifty years so you could get shot in a duel? And what about me? What part do I play in this morality play?"

"I don't know. I don't understand any of it. All I know is he's famous because of his last words."

"His famous last words." She groaned. "No. I don't want to hear them."

"He said, as he was dying, 'I give my life, not for my country, but for the woman I love.'"

"Well that's about the corniest, stupidest, most ludicrous…" She yanked her hands out of his and scrubbed at her eyes. "I don't want to lose you. I can't lose you."

"We almost lost each other," he said solemnly. "Last night was…"

She wrapped her arms around him. "Last night was the best thing that ever happened to me."

"Or me. Don't you see? Maybe that's what this is about."

"What?"

"Maybe we had to lose each other to find each other."

"If that's all there was to it, then why aren't we falling back to our own time?" She ran to the window and yelled, "Okay, Gascon. Lesson learned. Send us home."

Silence greeted her outburst.

"I have a feeling getting home is not going to be that simple."

CHAPTER EIGHT

ANDREW WOKE TO THE sound of scratching. He blinked slowly, aware at first of the darkness and unfamiliarity of the room. Then, coming fully to himself, he remembered he wasn't in his own bed, or Nat's apartment. He was in Louisiana, and when daylight broke, he'd prepare to fight a duel.

Was he to have his much-needed pre-duel rest interrupted by mice? He and Natalie had talked and made love all that day and most of the night before falling asleep exhausted. If you could share a lifetime of intimacy in a couple of days, that's what they'd done.

Even so, he wanted to touch her again, pull her closer in the dark and find as well as dispense comfort. He reached for Natalie, but her side of the bed was empty. He raised himself to his elbows and called softly, "Natalie?"

"I'm over here."

"What are you doing?"

"I'm setting fire to the door."

"What?"

"It's the only way out of here."

"But we could both be killed."

"If we have to die, I want us to go together."

He was suddenly furious and stomped over to where she was crouched by the door. "What about my honor?"

"I don't care about your honor. How can you even think of leaving me alone?"

"I won't." He got to his knees beside her on the cool floorboards. "I've never killed a man in my life, but I promise you I'm going to shoot that count and I'll aim to kill."

Her eyes filled with tears. "You're not the violent type."

To Natalie's amazement, she saw his fists clench hard, an action mirrored by his teeth. "That slimy creep only has to look at you and I want to kill him. I mean, I really want to kill him with my own hands. The hell with due process of law and all the rules I've lived by until now. We're in a different time, a different world. The rules are different."

She looked down at the bits of cloth she'd gathered to make a fire. Then she looked up at him. She supposed, like any knight about to do battle for his lady, what he needed was her trust and her belief in him.

She gave him her hands and they rose together.

"I can't lose you again," she whispered.

He took her hands, kissed each palm and placed it against his naked chest. She felt the beat of his heart, strong and regular. Felt the warmth of his skin and all the life there inside him, all their future together. "You won't," he promised.

They gazed at each other.

He bent and lifted her, like a man taking his bride across the threshold and he placed her gently on the bed. She felt her hair brush her shoulders as it fanned out around her. Watched him with eyes that grew unfocused. He gave her all his attention. She had never felt more treasured. Or more determined to save the man she loved.

"You know, I was just thinking about what you said before, that money's always been your tool. It's also been your weapon. But you were sent here with no money. Only a sword."

"It's going to be okay," he whispered. "Don't worry."

"I'm not. I believe in you. I'm sorry I lost my nerve for a second there. I won't do it again. You'll win tomorrow. I have faith." And that, she thought, was the power she had. The power of her love and faith in Andrew to make him the man he'd never known he could be.

He sat beside her and molded her form with his hands, running his palms, warm and sure over her body, bringing it to eager life. Her nipples tingled, puckering to attention.

Her well-loved body still sprang to life at his touch, and she let him do this his way. She lay passive beneath him, somehow divining that this was what he wanted—to discover her, rediscover her, imprint her on his memory.

She wouldn't think about tomorrow. Only now, only this moment out of all the moments of her life. She and Andrew were out of their time, and yet they'd never been so in harmony with each other.

When he urged her to lift her torso, she complied, and his focus on her naked skin was so intense she felt a flutter of shyness. Ridiculous, they'd made love hundreds of time. But this was so different. Almost like the first time.

When he lay beside her, she turned to him, no longer able to remain still. Her hands traced his body, the curves of skin and muscle and bone. She felt the strong beat of his heart, the softer echo of a pulse, and heard the soft rhythm of his breathing.

She hooked her bent knees over his hips and then turned her head to kiss him while he entered her. His fingers trailed over her, touching her the way she liked. In some ways this felt like the first time, but when they started to move, it was with the familiarity of practice. They knew each other, had found their rhythm and so she felt the new intimacy with the familiar patterns of seasoned lovers who are comfortable with each other.

They stared into each other's eyes as their breathing grew harsh and their movements frenzied. She felt herself begin to slip over the edge of pleasure and into ecstasy and she gripped his hips, pulling him hard against her. She felt the moment he tumbled over the edge of the world with her, but their gazes held and, more even than the wash of pleasure, she felt the sweet pain of intimacy. She might lose this man tomorrow, but for tonight, he was the missing piece of herself, the man who was now, and forever would be, her mate.

Because she didn't want him to see her cry, she buried her face in his chest, clutching at him, kissing the damp, warm skin until she had control of herself.

"How come the sex is so good here?" he said, with an attempt at lightness.

"No subduing your own cries of pleasure in case your cell phone rings and you have to answer it," she said.

"My cell? What about your new-message alert on your e-mail. It's louder than your alarm clock."

"That's another thing we don't have here," she mused. "An alarm clock. In fact, it's quieter."

"Yeah. You can hear yourself think."

"Give all your attention to your partner."

He regarded her ruefully. "When we get home…"

She finished the sentence for him. "Things are going to change."

They listened to the quiet around them. The house slept. The city slept. And finally, though they'd both vowed not to waste a minute, they slept.

LOUD KNOCKING roused Natalie from a dream that had her heart pounding and her throat dry. He'd been shot.

In her dream, Andrew had been shot.

"Who is it?" Andrew called as he shoved himself into his pants and walked, shirtless, to the door.

"Your seconds, sir."

Andrew cocked an inquiring brow at Natalie, who pulled the sheet tight around her breasts and said, "Tell them to wait. I'll get dressed."

"We're in bed. Give us a moment to dress."

The loud laugher and ribald comments were thankfully muffled by the thick door, but Natalie was still appalled at the joviality of young men who were about to participate in a bloodthirsty battle between two men, each trying to kill the other.

"If women ran the world," she muttered, "things would be a lot more civilized."

Andrew sent her a glance and said, "If you'd keep your feminist opinions to yourself while these men from a less-civilized time conduct their business, I'd appreciate it."

She sniffed, turning her back to him so he could do up the row of tiny buttons on her gown.

After two days, he was getting pretty good at it. He stopped when the buttons were three quarters done and kissed her between her shoulder blades. It was her weakest spot, and he knew it. If she were a cat, she'd have purred. As it was, her toes curled and an irrepressible shiver made its way down her spine.

"I love you," he said against her naked skin.

She turned, heedless of the fact that the buttons weren't all done yet, and threw herself into his arms, kissing him, clutching him to her. He met her passion with his own, but too soon, put her gently but firmly aside and strode to the door. "All right," he said. "You can come in, now."

The key grated once again, and then two young men entered.

"I thought you'd at least bring breakfast," Andrew complained, with a kind of insouciance that made her blink. He was about to face either death or murder and he was worried about his bacon and eggs?

It seemed he'd said exactly the right thing, though, for the heavier set of the two men slapped him on the back with a laugh. "That's the spirit. Don't worry. I've ordered breakfast for after at a nice little place I know."

THE CARRIAGE rattled its way out of town. It was early, she realized, the sky still dark and an unpleasant chill in the air. Of course, her meager wardrobe didn't include a cloak, so she huddled against Andrew for warmth.

And, truth to tell, for comfort.

"I've brought my own pistols," the heavyset young man said cheerfully. "I thought that would be best. No chance of any…mistakes that way."

"Excellent," said Andrew. "I thank you."

The carriage smelled of leather and body odor, and the way it bumped and rattled over the streets made her queasy. Still, she gritted her teeth and kept silent.

Somehow, they'd come through this. Together. They hadn't learned such valuable lessons about themselves and each other only to die. It wasn't possible. She hoped.

After a while, she noticed the carriage wasn't jostling her as much. They were out on open road. The city was left behind, and she saw fields and the large, dark green sentinels of sturdy oaks, many draped with Spanish moss. To her fanciful eyes, they looked like upright young women in mourning, wrapped in their dark shawls and weeping.

Too soon, far too soon, the carriage drew to a halt. The seconds opened the door and jumped down. Andrew exited, then turned and held out his hand to help her down.

Their gazes met and held. She saw resolution and courage, and his hand on hers was steady. She had to be as strong, for his sake. So she smiled and said, "I love you."

His eyes flashed the same message back. It occurred to her that they'd said that phrase to each other more in the past two days than in the previous two years.

Another carriage was drawn up under a tree, almost as though it were hiding. She saw four more figures in the dew-drenched grass. One held a case and she realized with an unpleasant shiver that he must be the doctor.

Some centuries-old quack who didn't know about bacteria and germs and would as likely treat a wound with bloodletting. Well, she couldn't do much, but one thing she could do was keep Andrew out of the doctor's hands.

There was another figure, she realized, one she hadn't noticed at first because he was seated on a stool in the background.

The painter.

He had an easel set up and was calmly dabbing paint onto it as though he were painting a still life of fruit instead of the background to the scene of a duel.

The painter glanced up and for a moment his attention rested on her, then he nodded, once, and went back to his painting. It was as though he were pleased she was there. Congratulating her on being part of this insane tableau.

Andrew had obviously never fought a duel before. But you wouldn't have known it from his demeanor. Did that sort of knowledge hide inside a man's DNA just in case he was ever thrown back into time?

Andrew walked calmly forward, looking every inch the Louisiana gentleman of the mid–eighteen hundreds, though she knew him to be her contemporary. If she didn't know better, she'd have thought she was watching a costume drama on a public broadcast station.

He stood proud and confident and, for all her nervousness and utter horror of what was going on, she experienced a surge of pride.

He and the count nodded to each other and then the two groups moved to opposite sides of the clearing. A pair of pistols in a wooden case was opened, presented. Each man studied the pieces.

Lord, would Andrew even know how to shoot an old-fashioned gun?

Her skin grew cold and she felt that she might, for the first time in her life, faint. For this wasn't a televised costume drama, or a bad dream. For reasons still unknown to her, she and Andrew were themselves, but somewhere else. As simply as they'd been transported from New York to Paris, they'd then, through some method other than Air France, been transported here. They didn't belong, but their bodies were stuck here, which meant that whatever happened was real. Andrew's blood would spill as freely, he could be killed as surely. She simply could not let that happen.

The key to this whole mess was the artist, sitting so quietly on the other side of the green, his easel set up as though he were about to paint a croquet tournament or a ladies' tea.

He had a palette of paints and appeared engrossed in his work. She stomped over to him, though stomp was not the right verb. The grass was slick with morning dew, her shoes ridiculous button-up boots, their leather soles providing poor traction, so she slipped and slid her way in baby steps. Even if she'd had a decent pair of sneakers, she wouldn't have gone much faster, she realized, as she began to pant. The infernal corset made deep breathing an impossibility. She felt as though she were running in a dream. The more urgently she hurried, the slower she seemed to proceed.

Unlike the duel, which seemed to move forward at astonishing speed. By the time she reached the artist, panting and sweating, the seconds were measuring out the paces with stiff legs and serious, solemn faces. Death hovered in the air like a vulture, waiting, watching.

"You have to help me," she panted when she reached the painter. "We have to stop them."

The old artist gazed up at her with his calm eyes. She remembered when she'd first seen him in the Louvre and his eyes had seemed kind. Now she thought he was some kind of evil wizard. He shook his head gently.

"This is their destiny, my dear."

"But it can't be. We aren't even from this time. You pushed us both. It wasn't destiny shoving me and Andrew through time, it was you."

"Have patience. All will be revealed."

"Patience?" She almost screamed the word. "I'm not going to sit by and watch my fiancé get killed by some madman who lived two hundred years ago."

"Time is a strange concept," he said, calmly stroking his brush over the canvas. "Like destiny. Sometimes, mistakes are made and must be rectified."

She glanced, with growing impatience, to where the two men were already pacing off, back to back. Andrew's back was straight, his head held proudly.

"Andrew wouldn't know how to shoot that ancient pistol, and anyway, he doesn't have his glasses. He can barely see without them."

"You need faith, Natalie. Faith in Andrew, in yourself, in your future together."

"Faith?" she shrieked again. Like the word *patience*, this one seemed an entirely foreign concept now that action was imperative. "What I need is a time machine out of here. Please. It's not too late. Whatever you did, do it back again. You have to send us home."

She was glancing at Andrew and his opponent, sick with fear, then back to the artist to plead.

"It's out of my hands," he said in his slow, calm way.

"A man's about to be killed and you'll do nothing? A man you brought here against his knowledge and will?"

The artist glanced up from his work once more. "You're wrong. Andrew was desperate to find you. He said to me that he'd do anything, anything to find you."

She'd think about the warmth those words sent gushing through her later, when she had leisure. Now she had a duel to stop if she was to save the man she now realized, beyond any doubt, that she loved.

Natalie wasn't a woman of violence, but then she'd never faced life and death on a dueling field before. Without even considering what she was doing, she grabbed the artist's palette knife and held it to the old man's throat.

He didn't even pause in his painting.

"Stop the duel. Take us out of here," she ordered, her voice strong even though she was terrified.

"You would kill for him?"

She pressed the knife harder. "You bet I would. This knife isn't very sharp, but I am a desperate woman and I'm strong. This," she said, pressing the blade against a throbbing pulse, "is your jugular. If I sever it, you'll die within minutes."

Amazingly he kept painting. She pressed the knife harder.

"Please, I don't want to hurt you, but I'll do what I have to."

"You're too late," he wheezed.

Almost before the words were finished, she heard the blast.

"No."

She turned and heard the second gunshot.

"No." Two puffs of smoke wafted like pipe smoke in the still air, and one man crumpled slowly to the ground, an expression of furious surprise on his face.

Amazingly, it wasn't Andrew on the ground, holding his arm, but the count.

Andrew was unscathed. He was holding the pistol in a calm, steady hand as though he practiced shooting men every day.

"He did it," she cried, amazed and trembling all over with reaction. "He did it."

She took her hand from the man's neck and moved to replace the knife on the ledge of the easel. As she did so, she saw, for the first time, the painting.

And she saw that it was the precurser to the painting hanging in the Louvre. As the meaning sank in, her elation burst like an overfilled balloon. She shook her head and said, "No," the word no more than a tendril of sound.

The painting showed the scene as it was now, the wounded man on the ground, Andrew walking toward her, pride and confidence in his gait. But the fallen man was raising a second pistol, aiming it at Andrew's back.

In the painting she'd seen hanging in the Louvre, a

man had been facedown, blood pooled beneath his lifeless body. That man had worn the same coat Andrew wore, he'd had Andrew's hair and build. And the woman she'd seen prostrate over his body, her hair a sorrowful tumble as she wept out her grief, that woman had been wearing this dress. That woman was her.

The man was lying facedown because he'd been shot in the back. Murdered in cold blood.

Andrew.

"No," she screamed, and started running. "Andrew, get down."

Her feet barely touched the grass as she scrambled to reach the man she loved, her lungs burning. In some part of her brain she realized that in the short time they'd been here the sun had already dried most of the dew, but still, she couldn't move fast enough.

Andrew didn't seem to understand. No one had seen the gun but her, and only because it was painted in the picture. She reached Andrew. He pulled her into his arms. She tried to push him to the ground, but he was drawing her closer, to kiss her.

Instinct took over. She had no breath left to warn him, and no time. With desperate haste, she spun them, so it was her back to the count.

The shot was inevitable. She heard it as she'd known she would. The sharp crack.

Andrew's lips were on hers and she welcomed them, even as she accepted the inevitability that they would die together. Because she'd make certain they would die together. She could not be that grief-stricken woman in the painting, widowed before she was a wife, losing the love she'd so recently found.

She felt the metal ball strike her back below her shoulder blade and then she was falling into blackness.

"I love you," she said, wondering dimly if her spine had stopped the bullet, so at least Andrew would live.

Then there was nothing.

CHAPTER NINE

NATALIE HEARD MOANING. She kept her eyes closed tight. If she wasn't dead, with an assassin's ball in her back, she soon would be. Please let that surgeon not touch her.

"Natalie." It was Andrew's voice, frantic and helpless. She smiled. He was okay.

"You're not dead. Thank God, you're alive."

Strangely, apart from a dull ache in her back, like a bruise, there was no pain. She lifted her eyes and there was Andrew, bending over her, his eyes damp, his hands touching her face.

But something was different. She narrowed her eyes to concentrate, then realized. "You're wearing your glasses," she said.

"Are you okay?" he asked. "Can you move your hands or your feet?"

"I don't know." She tried and found that she could. "Huh. That's funny. I thought I was dead."

"You were willing to die for me." Andrew wasn't usually given to drama, but then she realized he wasn't being dramatic. She had turned them at the last moment. But not for noble reasons.

"I couldn't bear to be without you." She shuddered. "Don't let that surgeon near me or I will end up dead."

"Honey," he said softly, "we're home. We made it back."

She blinked and turned her head. She wasn't on grass, but on the much-trodden parquet flooring of the Louvre. Amazingly, there was no one in the gallery but them and the guard who'd sent them back into time.

"You!" She glared at the calm old guy who seemed perfectly unruffled by the fact that she and Andrew had almost died. "I think you'd better explain what's going on."

"The story's there, on the wall," the guard said, pointing.

"I'm not falling for that trick again, thanks all the same," she said, rubbing her side.

"It's all right," he assured them. "Your work is done." He glanced from Andrew to Natalie. "You changed history, you know."

Curiosity overcame her. With Andrew's help, she struggled to her feet and stepped close—but not too close—to the painting of the duel.

"No, we didn't," she said, feeling tears prick her eyelids. "The painting's the same." The grief felt even sharper, fresher as she looked at the woman, so like herself, slumped over the man so like Andrew.

"The ball from that pistol hit the young lady first. And then Andrew Greenwood. Her sacrifice saved them both, since both were injured but neither died."

"So she didn't kill herself from grief."

"No. They went on to marry and raise the child she doesn't yet know she carries."

"You mean we—" They stared at each other in awe.

The old man's eyes twinkled. "Oh, Andrew, I believe you forgot this." He held out Natalie's engagement ring.

"I left it on the bedside table in the hotel," Andrew said, then shook his head and reached for the ring. "Thanks."

"Don't be too long, now. Closing time is in ten minutes."

Suddenly, they were alone. Andrew picked up Natalie's left hand and she felt the trembling coming from both of them. "Natalie, we've faced death together, and it seems we've made life together. I've been a fool, but I hope I've learned my lesson. I promise to love you forever, to put you and our children first in my life, and always, always, to remember Paris." He gazed at her and she found his precious image wavering as her eyes grew misty. "Will you marry me?"

"Yes."

He slid the engagement ring back onto her finger and, taking both her hands in his, leaned forward to kiss her.

Their kiss contained all the pain and joy of the past, all the uncertainty and hope of the future and the knowledge that they'd be sharing all of it together.

She threw herself into his arms. "Oh, yes."

TIME AFTER TIME
Jo Leigh

CHAPTER ONE

"ONE MOMENT, I'll connect you."

Betty put through the call, then slipped her headset off, anxious to get out of the cubicle. She only had forty-five minutes for lunch, and she wasn't about to spend any more time inside than she had to.

She grabbed her purse and her sack and headed for the elevators. Of course, everyone else on her shift had the same break, so she'd have to wait. She smiled at Bill Corrigan and he smiled back before turning to his friends. Then there was Sharon and her bunch laughing at something Betty didn't quite catch. In fact, wherever she looked, people were chatting, engaged. Except her.

The elevator arrived, and they all got in. None of the customary silence reigned. Conversations filled the car all the way down, mostly about what a nightmare it was to work for the phone company and how if it wasn't for the benefits every one of them would quit.

Betty didn't care much for being an information operator, but she wasn't about to complain. Those benefits were incredibly important to her. Like so many in Manhattan, she was living on the edge. Just barely making her monthly nut, what with her graduate work at NYU and the cost of an apartment in the city.

The elevator came to many stops before hitting the lobby, but finally she was free to head out to her bench. Well, it wasn't her bench, but it was where she liked to eat on days when the weather was nice—like today. August was usually too muggy for her taste, but this week had been exceptionally wonderful. She enjoyed the two-block walk to the tiny little park that was a meager oasis in the middle of the bustling city.

She sat and opened her bag, pulling out her tuna sandwich as she tried to focus on the trees across the way instead of all she had to do tonight.

She had a major paper due next month and it was giving her fits. The topic was one she adored—The Social Impact of Sexual Mores During WWII—but it was difficult to find the original material she was looking for, made even harder by the fact that she never got enough sleep. With her full-time job and her full-time studies, there was no room for much else. She couldn't remember when she'd last gone to a movie, or taken a day off just to explore the city. It was probably a good thing that she didn't have many friends. Where would she fit a social life into her schedule, let alone something as radical as dating?

She took another bite, fighting her ongoing battle with ennui. Sometimes she just got so tired, not from lack of sleep, but from the weight of being so out of step with the world around her. She'd always been the odd one, the girl who wore the old-fashioned clothes, who didn't know anything about current movie stars or popular songs.

Her parents had tried, but they'd lived in their own

world long before she'd been born. Her mother was forty-two when she'd gotten pregnant, and her father had been fifty. They'd raised her to love what they loved—music from the 1940s and 1950s, black-and-white movies, sewing, gardening. None of which gave her a clue how to survive in her own generation.

Not that she hadn't tried. But every attempt to blend in had ended in some form of humiliation. Her boyfriend—if she could call him that—when she was an undergrad had been more interested in science-fiction conferences than in her. Hell, he'd been more turned on by old *Star Trek* episodes than sex.

Finally, she'd accepted her fate, finding solace in her studies, in her books, in her love of vintage clothes. She'd taken on eccentricity as a trademark, and while it didn't win her a lot of friends, it did give her a modicum of dignity.

She ran a hand down her plaid skirt, one she'd made from a Sears pattern circa 1946. When she did have a moment that she wasn't working or sleeping, she was in secondhand stores, finding treasures from the past, which seemed to be the only place she truly belonged.

When her hand went back into the paper bag to pull out a gorgeous peach, she knocked her purse to the grass. A few things fell out, nothing too embarrassing, thank goodness, but her brochure for the new exhibit at the Met made her smile in anticipation. She was going tomorrow evening, right after work, and even though she'd only have an hour or so to browse, the subject matter was everything she could ask for: Sex Through the Ages.

She'd already made sure that part of the exhibit dealt

with WWII, and for that she was incredibly grateful. She couldn't wait to see what the curators had found, and she fully intended to get the name of everyone who'd worked on the exhibit so she could pump them about their source material. Something told her she was going to hit the mother lode there, both in actual artifacts and anecdotal sources.

She stared at the brochure, captivated already. A pencil drawing of a nude woman with a man standing behind her, both of them timeless in their sensuality and intent. Surrounding the drawing were inset pictures, one of an antique sex toy, the other an older man in a what looked to her to be a railroad cap. She didn't understand that one, but perhaps it would make more sense when she saw the exhibit. Or perhaps it was as simple as the fact that he stood in front of an arrangement of erotic paintings, and that he hid the naughty bits.

Inside the brochure were pictures from the exhibit, and one was Betty Grable in her most famous pinup pose. Other paintings came from other times, but she just stared at Betty, the woman she'd been named after.

As she slipped the brochure back into her purse, she glimpsed a picture she'd clipped from *People* magazine just last week. With a sigh, she brought it out, her tummy tightening even before she saw the familiar face.

Matt Stevens. She'd grown up with him, in that tiny little hometown of hers. Gone through kindergarten through the end of high school. He'd lived two blocks from her house, and if she sneaked past Mr. Snedeger's garden, she could be at Matt's in three minutes, if she ran.

Not that she'd ever been invited. Matt was one of the popular guys at her school. A jock, but not a dimwit, he had looks that drew every girl in town. Tall, dark hair, perfect green eyes and the kind of physique that made her beg for a steamy hot day so he'd take off his shirt.

She'd loved Matt since first grade. He'd barely acknowledged her existence. Not that he was mean or anything, but she was Weird Betty, and no one really paid any attention to her. Occasionally, he'd ask for some notes from a class, and one time he came by her house to see if he could mow their lawn. When it came time for yearbooks, he'd signed hers, but only just his name. There was really nothing more to say.

And now, he was a hero. A bona fide hero, worthy of newspaper headlines and TV interviews. He'd saved over a hundred lives in a fire in Washington, D.C. The tenement had been old, the smoke detectors hadn't worked, and he'd woken up the tenants, many of whom were elderly and handicapped. He'd nearly gotten himself killed getting everyone out before the fire department arrived, and he'd been hospitalized for a week with burns and smoke inhalation. He hadn't known anyone in the building, and had only been on that street because he'd taken a wrong turn.

Fate had put him there, but character had made him a hero.

She'd read every article she could find, up until the one that talked about his fiancée. Even so, she'd kept the picture, although looking at it hurt. He was the only boy she'd ever loved.

She tucked the pic back in her purse and ate the

peach. It wasn't as sweet as she'd hoped. Most things weren't. But things would change. They always did. Sometimes for the better.

IT TOOK A LOT longer to get to the Metropolitan Museum of Art than she'd counted on, what with traffic and the crowded subways. It hadn't helped that she'd been asked to stay late at work. She'd been tempted to say no, but even fifteen minutes of overtime helped. By the time she got inside the museum, she was hot, winded and irritable. Instead of going right to the exhibit, she hit the ladies' room to gather a little calm.

She washed her hands, put on some fresh lipstick and brushed her hair. When she was done, she gave herself a once-over and wasn't displeased. She'd worn a 1940s dress, one she hadn't made herself, but found at Grandma's Attic in the Village. She'd worn her hair in a classic pageboy, and she'd even picked out shoes that wouldn't have been out of place during the war.

Nodding once, she set off to find the exhibit, anxious because she knew she wouldn't have enough time.

It took her a bit to get to the right place, but when she entered the space, she felt immediately transported, and she wasn't even close to the WWII wing. Oh, for more time to linger over the pictures and ornaments and statues and clothing that were so lovingly displayed. From the Arms and Armor to Ancient Asian Arts, there were treasures everywhere she looked. Maybe she could come back. She had to. Even if it meant taking time off of work. This was too wonderful for words.

She forced her eyes front as she made her way to the

WWII display. There weren't many people there, given that the museum would close in under an hour. As she walked into the hall that started "her" era, her heartbeat accelerated with sheer happiness.

One step inside and she knew she was about to have her socks blown right off. She'd devoured everything she could find about men and women and war. She'd read memoirs, watched newsreels, studied magazines and newspapers until she had filled notebook after notebook. Everything about the era sang to her, and she felt as if she'd walked into the symphony.

There were the little comic books that featured popular characters of the day in very sexual situations. They were called Tijuana Bibles or Eight Pagers, and they'd sold for about a dime.

Things had gotten tamer as the war went on, and the men's magazines started featuring virginal gals in patriotic costumes, reminding the men what they were fighting for.

But as in any era, there was a thriving underground of strippers and sex shows, and once the boys went overseas they were exposed to kink they'd never dreamed of.

Betty inched her way past the American men's magazines toward the more interesting foreign influence, where she saw a whole range of dildos, many in the likenesses of Hitler, Mussolini and other enemies of the time.

She jumped as someone coughed behind her. Her cheeks heated as if she'd been caught looking at dirty pictures, which, of course, she had.

"Didn't mean to startle you."

"That's okay," she said, eyeing the older man. He was in a blue uniform and he had that cap on, the one she'd seen on the brochure. With his gray hair and pocket watch, he reminded her of the character from that Christmas movie with Tom Hanks. She expected him to yell, "All aboard," any minute. Instead, he gave her a small smile as he took in her outfit.

"I see you're a fan of the forties."

She nodded toward the wall behind him, covered in pinup-girl posters. "This is right up my alley. In fact, I'm hoping to find the curator. I'm doing my doctoral thesis on sex during the war."

He nodded back. "I'm sure I can dig up some information for you. In fact, why don't you come with me." He started walking toward a hallway to his right. Looking back, he said, "I believe I have a contact list. Should be a big help."

"Thank you," she said, glancing at the memorabilia on the walls, torn between her desire to really study them and getting the list. In the end, the list would be more help, but she knew she'd have to come back. There was simply too much wonderful stuff here not to.

He'd turned the corner, so Betty had to hurry to catch up with him. There were more pictures here, some she recognized from magazines she had collected. He stopped in front of one that made her smile. It was a picture taken at the Stage Door Canteen in New York. The joint was jumping, and there was a band on the stage complete with a girl singer. How she'd dreamed of doing just that. She'd always been in love with the big-band sound, and she'd memorized almost every song of the time. If she'd had any guts at all, she would have done something about her love of singing, but instead she settled for performing in the privacy of her shower.

The guide had stopped and he looked at her quizzically. "You have a question?"

"Oh, uh, I was just wondering…" Her thought splintered as she looked more closely at the picture. It was the singer that grabbed her attention. Someone she recognized, but for the life of her, she couldn't remember the woman's name. If only the picture had been clearer, she'd surely figure out the band, the woman's name. But there was something odd about the woman, too, something Betty couldn't put her finger on.

"That's quite a picture, isn't it?"

Betty glanced behind her to find the guard standing close to her shoulder. He was staring at the girl singer, too. "Do you know who she is?" she said.

"Can't say I remember her name. The picture is more focused on the boys in the foreground than her, although I do think she was a looker."

Betty smiled. "It's odd. Her name's on the tip of my tongue."

"Lean in a little," he said, stepping even closer to her. "Now that's interesting."

"What?" she asked, squinting so she could see the details.

"She looks a lot like you," he said.

"Oh, no. I don't think so."

Leaning far in, brushing her shoulder with his, he brought his finger to the photo.

Betty took one more small step, staring for all she was worth, when she felt his hand on the middle of her back, shoving her forward. She gasped as she put out her hands, but there was nothing to touch. Nothing but dark and falling.

The dark became total blackness and her hands grasped at air as she felt herself tumble through the cold. Her heart thudded in her chest as panic swallowed her whole. The only coherent thought in her head was that she was dying, but it didn't feel at all like she'd expected.

There was a jolt, as if she'd bumped into something soft yet resilient. The rushing air stilled, but the dark still held. Her stomach turned as she thought that if this was death, it sucked. And then…

Music.

Big band-music. Artie Shaw? Glenn Miller?

Lights, so bright she had to shield her eyes, and then more sound. Talking, lots of it, indecipherable but surrounding her. Waves of laughter mingling with the drum beat, the saxophone riff.

Her hand came down and there were people in front of her, to either side. Men in war uniforms and girls in striped aprons. Sailors and soldiers, many from Britain and Australia, and she knew this place, recognized the banners and the posters on the wall, and oh, God, she had really died. Died and gone to heaven, otherwise known as the Stage Door Canteen.

CHAPTER TWO

SHE DIDN'T FEEL DEAD. In fact, she felt a little nauseous. The room was warm, bright, and the energy level was frenetic what with the live band on the tiny bandstand, the kids out on the dance floor, and the tables crowded with men and women from Allied countries.

Betty stood in the midst of a tightly packed crowd, all of them in the period clothes she loved so much. She looked at faces, trying to see any of her relatives who'd passed on, but no one looked familiar. She hadn't seen any kind of white light when she'd slipped the mortal coil, which upset her for some reason, and hey, she'd been in the Met, for heaven's sake, so what the heck? Why had that guard killed her? And why hadn't it hurt?

She looked down, wondering if she would see any evidence of the killing blow, but she seemed just fine. Her hand went to the back of her hair. Nope, nothing there, either.

This was very confusing, and while she loved that heaven was everything she could have hoped for, a little adjustment time would have been nice.

Maybe if she sat down for a bit, got her bearings, she'd feel better. Or maybe there would be a guide, someone like in that movie *Heaven Can Wait*.

"Betty, you're on."

She turned, shocked to hear her name, to find a tall man with a shiny bald spot and thick horn-rimmed glasses looking from her to the bandstand and back.

"Excuse me?"

"Come on. They're just about done with this number."

Betty blinked at him, wondering if this was some kind of test. "You're talking to me, right?"

He gave her a startled look, then he smiled. "Honey, this is the Canteen. They'd love you if you sang *Mary Had a Little Lamb*."

"Sang?"

"What's with you tonight?"

She had no idea what to say. He wanted her to sing? In front of all these people? Was he insane?

"Betty?" he said again, putting his large hand on her shoulder.

The contact helped. It felt real, unlike everything else. "Um, this is heaven, right?"

He laughed. "I don't know that I'd go that far. It's a hell of a booking, though. Last week they had Tommy Dorsey up here, and last night it was Doris Day. This could be the break we've been waiting for. Now be a good girl and don't give your nice manager a heart attack."

The band ended their song with a flourish, and the whole place applauded. Betty put a hand to her stomach, nauseous again, but for a whole different reason. Maybe this wasn't heaven, but hell. She couldn't sing in front of people—she'd die.

Oh.

Too late.

She took a deep breath and let it out slowly. Okay, so here she was in some bizarre recreation of the Canteen, and she was supposed to provide the entertainment. She'd always dreamed of being a singer, and in this era, too, so clearly this was a form of afterlife where she was supposed to live out her wildest dreams and fantasies. Which was scary, yes, but also pretty interesting.

If it was heaven, she couldn't fail, right? That would be totally counterproductive and not make any sense. Which meant that all she had to do was step up to the plate.

"And now, ladies and gentlemen, the subtle song stylings of the sensational…Betty Kroger."

Her heart pounding like a Gene Krupa solo, Betty headed for the bandstand, winding through the smiling crowd. There were only three steps to climb and then she was there. The band—a drummer, three horns, piano and a bass player—waited expectantly. It probably wasn't a good time to pass out. But she couldn't seem to move her feet.

Maybe it wasn't heaven. Maybe it was a dream. An amazingly realistic dream, like none she'd had before, but it had to be something like that, right? She couldn't be at the Stage Door Canteen. Those couldn't be real servicemen, and most certainly, she couldn't be the singer.

She'd never sung in public. Never. Wait, she had. Once when she was about ten. It was a school program, and she'd rehearsed until her parents had begged her to stop. When she'd finally stepped on stage, she'd promptly thrown up. And that had been that on her singing career.

But she had wished.... So this *had* to be her fondest wishes come true. Right?

The sax player walked over to her and put his hand gently on her arm. "'For Sentimental Reasons'?" he whispered.

It took her a moment to get that he meant the song. Not why she should sing. It was a favorite of hers, and she knew the words by heart. She could do it. She could. This was the time to live out her dream, not to curl up in the fetal position and whimper. She squared her shoulders. "Let's do it."

He gave her a squeeze and walked back to the band while she went to the microphone. Looking over the crowd, she thought it was a remarkable simulation. The people looked real, the Canteen, which she'd seen in lots of pictures, looked perfect to the last detail. Heaven. Yep, heaven made much more sense than a dream.

She had a decision to make. Either go with the flow, or kiss it all goodbye. Since she couldn't bear to leave, not once she'd actually seen her dreams in the flesh, she squared her shoulders and sent her doubts out the window. Whatever the truth was, she didn't want to know. From this moment on, she was here, and come what may, it was one-hundred-percent real.

Behind her, she heard, "One, two..." and then the music started. The song, gorgeous and familiar since childhood, made her smile, and even though her heart still hammered, when it was her cue, she sang.

To her amazement, it felt wonderful. Like coming home. Couples, servicemen and girl volunteers, came together to dance, and for a moment she thought about the last place she'd been where there was dancing. It had been a blind date at a hip-hop club, and she'd been totally out of her element, with the music and the guy. This, she knew. She'd learned to dance in her living room when she was very young, standing on her father's shoes as he moved her around the room.

Closing her eyes, she let the music take her. It seemed insane now that she'd never done this in public. But then, not many karaoke bars carried her kind of music.

She didn't open her eyes again until she'd sung the last note. Until the applause.

In a very Sally Field moment, all she could think was, "They like me. They really like me." Fortunately, she kept it to herself, but oh, my, they clapped so hard and she heard whistles and cheers. Her heart nearly burst with pleasure. However she'd gotten here, she was so grateful tears filled her eyes and she had to blink them back before she messed up her makeup.

"Great job, Betty," the sax player said, touching her once more in that gentle way. "What's next?"

"'Guess I'll Hang My Tears Out To Dry'?"

He gave her a wink, then went back to his boys. A moment later, her hands were on the mike stand, the lights had dimmed, and once again she poured her heart into the music. This song always made her think of Matt Stevens. Knowing she'd never see him again made her incredibly sad, but she knew deep down that she wouldn't have seen him anyway. Of course, if this really was her personal heaven…

But that wouldn't be fair. He'd have to die, too, wouldn't he? Were there rules here? Lines that couldn't be crossed?

She stopped thinking, concentrating on the touching lyrics, knowing most of these young men were thinking about their sweethearts, the girls they'd left behind.

As she sang the last line, she looked into the eyes of some of the boys standing just this side of the dance floor. They truly were boys. So young. And yet, in the real war, they'd all joined up, seen things no one should ever see. Scarred in so many ways, they fought proudly, knowing the cause was just.

She wished she could talk to each one of them, hear their stories about the farm or the office, about Mary Sue back home and how she was working at the local Red Cross rolling bandages, or taking his place at the factory until the fighting was over.

The sacrifices were hard, but met with enthusiasm. War Bonds, salvage drives, blackouts, brownouts, civil defense drills. Amazing what people could adjust to, when they had to.

The songs went on, faster numbers to get the place jumping, then she'd slow it down, give them a chance to touch, to hold a pretty girl, even if she was just a substitute for the one they longed for.

They took a ten-minute break, and when she walked off the stage, the crowd parted for her as if she was somebody. As if she wasn't Weird Betty at all, but a star.

A young G.I. wearing the U.S. Army collar tabs of the coast artillery came over with a cold Coke.

She accepted gratefully, loving the small bottle, knowing this was a treat supreme, donated to the Canteen for the pleasure of the fighting men. It tasted wonderful, and different. It occurred to her that even if she'd wanted one, they didn't have Diet Cokes yet. And since this was her heaven, she didn't have to think about calories, not even for a second.

She laughed out loud.

The young man, who was probably in his late twenties, looked at her curiously.

"Don't mind me, soldier. I'm just happy."

"The way you sing, ma'am? I think you're about the best singer I've ever heard in person."

"Have you seen quite a few?"

"Not that many. But Dorothy Lamour came out to see us. She was with Mr. Hope. That was a great night."

"I'll bet."

"And then, when I was on leave, I saw Dinah Shore. She was real pretty. Not as pretty as you, though."

Betty blushed and hid her smile with more soda. Her, pretty? How could that be? She was overweight Betty. Awkward Betty. "What's your name?"

"I'm Billy Henderson, ma'am. From Salt Lake City, Utah."

She stuck out her hand. "Nice to meet you, Billy. I'm Betty."

He blushed just as much as she had a moment ago. But his grip was firm and his smile genuine.

"I'm Terry O'Brien, ma'am."

She turned to find another soldier, tall, red haired and grinning like a kid on Christmas. She took his hand, only to find another G.I. to his right, wanting a touch, a smile, some kindness.

It took the sax player to get her back onstage. He'd waded through the gang of boys, all of them eager to meet her, and pulled her to the stairs. "We've got time for about four more songs, Betty, then we do 'Good Night, Sweetheart.'"

"Sounds great. What's your name?"

"I'm Jeff Griggs and I normally play with Artie Shaw."

"I'm delighted to meet you, Jeff. You guys are the best."

Jeff pointed to the piano player. "That's Mike Travoy, and he's here from Xavier Cugat's band."

In fact, all the guys played for big-time names. But they volunteered every couple of weeks at the Canteen. No pay, no glory. Just pride in the fact that they were doing something good.

Betty went back to her mike. She had them play something upbeat, something fun. "Accentuate the Positive." Everyone loved it, and the dance floor overflowed. She saw a sailor leaning on crutches tapping his one good foot to the beat.

This was the most incredible thing that had ever happened to her. By so much, it wasn't funny.

She'd thought getting into NYU had been a great day, but it was nothing like this. She felt reborn. Maybe she was. Maybe that's just what happened after a person dies at the Met.

It didn't matter one whit that she didn't understand

why or how. All she knew was that for whatever time she was allowed to stay here, she wasn't going to hold back. Not at all. She'd sing with all her heart. Eat every damn thing that appealed to her. She'd stay out late, sleep in to all hours, and if she was very, very lucky, maybe she'd find a nice lonely G.I. who looked a little like Cary Grant and wanted one last fling before he went overseas.

Time slipped by with a saxophone accompaniment, and Betty tried to memorize every single second. She'd never get over how they all wanted to meet her, to shake her hand. The stars she saw in their eyes. It was every fairy tale she'd ever heard, all wrapped up in one glorious night.

A guy whose name, she discovered, was Rob found her just before she had to go up on stage again. He pulled her into the tiny kitchen where volunteers were making sandwiches for the boys. "You're doing a great job, Betty. They're crazy about you."

"Thanks," she said, her head still in a whirl.

Rob pulled a room key from his breast pocket. "Here's your key. I had Jonesy take your stuff to the hotel, so you're all set. It's the St. George, if you've forgotten."

"Right. The St. George."

"But the big news is, they want us to come back. Two more nights. How's that for knocking 'em dead?"

"It's incredible," she said, leaning against the wall. "Two more nights?"

"Hell, rumor has it they pushed back Jo Stafford, just for you."

"No—they didn't."

"Oh, yeah. So give 'em all you got, kitten."

"I will, thank you."

"The sky's the limit. We're goin' all the way."

She smiled, wondering where in time all the way would be. Here? In a hospital in 2006? It was so bewildering all she could do was put one foot in front of the other toward the bandstand.

She found her purse on one of the speakers, and slipped her key in there, glad to know she'd have a place to sleep tonight. Of course, she had no idea where the hotel was, but that was the least of her problems.

Problems? She laughed out loud.

Jeff sidled up beside her. "What's up?"

"Nothing important. Let's get this joint jumpin'."

"You got it."

He swung around to the boys as Betty took the mike. She took requests from the boys, thrilled that she knew each and every song. But like all things, even this fairy tale had to end. It was her last number. She turned to Jeff. "'Sentimental Journey.'"

He nodded and raised his shiny sax.

As she sang, she watched the mood of the room shift. They all knew it was coming to an end. Who knows, for some of these boys it might be their last night in America. For most, the last real good time they'd have for a long, long time. But then again, if it was her personal heaven, none of them would be hurt or alone or scared, not ever again.

She sang with her eyes wide open, not caring anymore if her tears streaked her makeup. As she got to the final refrain, her gaze moved over the crowd.

A boy standing at the side of the bandstand, dressed in navy whites, blue tie, hat in hand, stole the last of her breath. She stared, hardly believing. It wasn't true, it couldn't be. *He* was alive. Engaged to another woman. No way he was standing there, looking up at her with heartbreakingly beautiful green eyes.

But he was. Matt Stevens. The one boy in all the world she'd ever loved. All her doubts vanished with the first notes of "Good Night, Sweetheart." It truly was heaven.

CHAPTER THREE

DAMN, SHE WAS PRETTY. From her dark hair to her full red lips. Not so skinny, like that actress he'd seen here the other night. She was a real lady, with curves in all the right places. That she sang like an angel was a bonus, one he wouldn't forget. He wondered if she was on the radio, or if he could find her on a record. Course, that would mean buying a player, but he should be able to do that.

He checked his watch, knowing he should be heading out but not ready to go back to his hotel. Not ready to face the rest of the night.

Maybe he'd go to that bar, the Night Cap. It wasn't bad. They had music, the drinks were cheap. And there weren't too many fights.

If he was lucky, they'd let him drink until he was ready to pass out. Then he wouldn't dream. Of course, he'd have another killer hangover in the morning, but what the hell. It was better than the alternative.

A junior hostess, another pretty young gal, smiled up at him. "Hey, sailor. It's that time."

He nodded at her, wondering if she could be a day over seventeen. "Thanks for everything."

"No need. We're here for you."

He turned away, embarrassed at the sudden wetness in his eyes. Darn it all to hell, what was the matter with him? He never cried, not once, since he was a kid, and now, the oddest things would set him off. All he could do was blink it back, try to hide his weakness. He hated this like fire, but he couldn't make it stop. It didn't matter what he told himself, the names he called himself, the tears came until he wanted to knock himself out.

He focused on the stage, on the singer. Her smile made him forget his own foolishness. Wistful, sweet, she seemed to be saying goodbye to her lover, and her gaze—why, she was looking straight at him.

He wished the crowd would hurry, but one thing the navy had taught him was patience. Standing in line for chow, for the shower, for the torpedoes. He wanted to get closer to her, maybe say thanks instead of just wandering away. He'd remember tonight, more than most. And this memory wouldn't hold anything horrible. Just the sounds of home. Of the man he used to be.

"Move it, sailor."

Startled, he realized he'd let the crowd in front of him dissipate, and he hustled forward with regret. He wished he was brave enough to go up to the bandstand, to meet Miss Kroger in person and tell her how much he'd liked her songs. Instead, he followed a group of Australian soldiers, their accents strange, their voices loud without the music.

"Excuse me."

He stopped at the feminine voice, turned with an

awkward lurch to the tap on his shoulder. He blinked in surprise when he saw who it was.

"Hi," she said. "I'm Betty."

For a long moment he couldn't do anything but stare. She was just so darn pretty. Dark hair that had looked brown on the stage was actually a deep red that made her blue eyes shine. Her skin was as pale as a moonbeam and it looked too soft to touch. It was her smile, though, that made his guts tighten. Ruby-red lips curved in a smile that stirred things he'd thought he'd never feel again.

"I'm John," he said, surprised his voice worked at all.

"Nice to meet you, John." She looked down at her feet, then touched her hair, as if she was nervous about meeting him, but that was crazy. "Uh, is this your first time at the Canteen?"

"No, ma'am. I've been here almost every night for a week.

"Wow, okay. So you know the area?"

"I do."

"I'm staying at the St. George Hotel, but, well, I'm not ready to turn in yet. Maybe you could suggest a place I might go to get a drink?"

John looked around, wondering if this was some kind of a joke, but no one here would try and pull anything on him. Practical jokes were done among friends, among shipmates, and he had none here.

"You know where the St. George is?"

"Yes, ma'am."

"Betty, please."

He took in a deep breath, then let it out with a smile. "Yes, I do, Betty. And they have a real nice little bar right next to the restaurant. You should have no trouble getting a drink."

"Maybe you could come with me and make sure."

He stared at her, not believing she'd said the words. She was beautiful, a singing star, and they were surrounded by men of every shape and size, a lot of them officers, and it didn't make sense. He didn't have this kind of luck, not by a long shot.

"If you've got other plans…"

"No, ma'am. Betty. Ma'am. I don't have any other plans."

"Wonderful. Let me tell my, uh, manager that I'll be going." She looked behind her toward the bandstand. "I'll meet you by the front door."

"All right," he said.

Betty smiled at him then walked away. He watched her go, the way her hair shimmied on her shoulders, the sway of her hips, the curve of her calves. He knew if he turned, if he walked to the door, he'd wake up, hopefully in his bed, but probably some alley with a hangover.

He sighed. Every dream comes to an end sometime. As he headed toward the door, he thought about another dream from another time. Another pretty girl.

It wouldn't do to think about Sarah. Instead, he'd head for the bar, not the fancy one at the St. George, but the old dive. It was going to take a lot of drinks to quiet the voices tonight.

"Good night, sailor."

He smiled at the hostess. Gosh, she looked young. Rosy cheeks, crooked smile, freckles on her nose, she looked like she'd still be in school, barely old enough to go to the store by herself. But she also looked tired. Of course, most everyone did. No one had slept well since Pearl Harbor, he'd imagine. Too much work on the home front, too much death in the battlefield. Sleep was one of the first things to go.

He stepped outside, and put his cap back on his head. All around him the men mingled, not ready to leave the Canteen for the night. In the dark, he couldn't make out much about the faces, but the energy bled from man to man, enlivened by arguments about nearby bars, about finding some hoochie girls over in Harlem, about finding a warm bed, with or without a gal.

All John could think of was the way Betty had smiled at him, and that made him warmer than any sheets. Damn, but that had been a good moment. One he'd remember over and over, and maybe if he could remember it often enough it would take over from the other memories, and maybe give him some peace.

"John?"

He turned, immediately recognizing the voice, stunned to find it here on the sidewalk. There she stood, her smile bright in the dim light from the round globe outside the Canteen.

"I thought you'd left without me."

"I… no, ma'am. Betty. I'm still here."

She nodded once, then her gaze moved from him to her surroundings and he had to wonder at the look of surprise that took over her soft features. It was as if she'd expected to be somewhere else. Her eyes grew wider and the longer she studied the browned-out

corner of Forty-Fourth and Broadway, the more per-
plexed she seemed. He looked, himself, trying to
discover what was puzzling her, but it was the same
tonight as it had been since he'd arrived. Behind them,
the stairs leading down to the basement USO club,
across the way, dark theater marquees, Times Square
shadowed in dimmed-out streetlights, the headlights
of taxi cabs and buses painted black. Even the famous
things, like the Camel cigarette sign, the RKO theater,
the news crawl around the Times building, were dark
and hiding. He remembered thinking, that first night in
New York, that regardless of what you couldn't see, you
still felt the city. The rumble of the subway, the honking
horns, the bustle of the crowds as they headed here and
there. It was still New York, and it was miles and worlds
away from where he'd grown to manhood.

"Of course," she said, although he didn't think she
was speaking to him so much as to herself. Then she
touched his sleeve. "What's the date?"

"Today? It's August twelfth."

Betty looked as though she wanted to say something
else, but she just shook her head. "Is the hotel far?"

"Not too far."

"Shall we walk?"

"You bet," he said. He held out his arm, and she
took hold of him. He didn't have to see how the men
around him reacted to this unprecedented moment. He
could feel their envy wash over him in waves.

He escorted Betty in silence, not quite sure what to
say, still not understanding his luck. Why him? He was
just a sailor, no one special at all. Waiting, just like all

the others, for new orders, for another ship. He had a few bucks saved up, but he wasn't keen on spending them on anything frivolous. A room and food had been necessary, and he'd gone to see *A Tree Grows In Brooklyn*, and that had been nice. Mostly, he just went to the Canteen. Two, three hours before it opened, he'd find himself in line, being jostled by all the other men, hungry for music, for light, for the pretty hostesses who liked to dance.

This felt as unreal as being shot at, but this, he had to admit, was a whole lot better.

"Tell me about yourself, John," she said. "Where are you from?"

"Milford, Kansas," he said.

She paused, and he looked down, checking to make sure she hadn't tripped on some hidden rut in the pavement. "Milford," she repeated.

"Yep. My folks have a farm there, and before I left I had fifty acres of my own, just on the other side of their place."

"That's wonderful," she said. "You have such a bright future ahead of you."

He didn't say anything as they crossed the street. The streetlights still worked, although they were dimmed by a wash of black paint that didn't hide the color, just made it difficult for the planes to see. Next to them, a soldier kissed his girl, the kind of kiss he'd never seen in public before the war.

Betty didn't seem upset by it. In fact, she smiled, and he had to wonder if she had someone over there. If she was missing him right now.

"Do you have a girl back in Milford?" she asked.

He opened his mouth to answer her, but the words didn't come. He'd had a girl before he left, and she'd had him. Only, he wasn't that fellow anymore. Not by a mile. "Not really," he said, hoping like hell Betty wouldn't press for more. "What about you? You have someone?"

"Nope, not me. I'm footloose and fancy-free. Except, of course, for tonight. I'm with you tonight."

He smiled, liking the sound of that. "It's just a few more blocks," he said.

"Good, I'm ready for a drink. Don't get me wrong, I'm not a lush. It's just been quite a day."

"It must be great to sing like you do. I have a voice like a frog on a bad night. But you, you sing like an angel."

She laughed, and that was a sound he'd not soon forget. Light and high and full of joy. She sparkled when she laughed, and it made him think of sunnier days, of standing in a field of corn so high it knocked the hat off his head.

But as she walked, she never stopped looking around, staring at the buildings and the people and the cars. She'd pause at storefronts, peek in doorways. All he could do was stare at her. Marvel at her beautiful smile.

"John?" she said, stopping him in front of a newsstand. She picked up a copy of newspaper, and looked at the headline for a long moment, then she looked up at him. "I didn't ask. What's your full name?"

"John Matthew Stevens, ma'am. I mean, Betty."

Her mouth went into a ruby red O. She blinked

twice, and maybe it was a trick of the light, or maybe it was nothing at all, but he could have sworn her eyes filled with tears.

CHAPTER FOUR

AUGUST 12, 1945. Two days before the end of the war. Betty stared once more at the date on the *New York Times*, then back at John. John Matthew Stevens. From Milford, Kansas. Which, by her calculations, would make him Matt Stevens's grandfather.

An interesting way of having her fondest wishes come true. She was in the era she loved; she got to sing her favorite songs in front of an adoring crowd. For the first time, she actually felt comfortable in her own Weird Betty skin, and she was with the man she loved—twice removed. It was more than a poor grad student could process.

"Are you all right?"

"I'm great," she said, loving the way John looked at her. He had Matt's eyes. Or was that the other way around? But there were differences, too. John's lips were fuller, his cheekbones stronger. His hair was shorter, of course, given that he was in the navy, and it was, well, sixty-one years ago.

John was taller, too. Maybe not. She hadn't stood next to Matt since high-school graduation. She winced, remembering that less-than-stellar moment. Matt had been so busy with his friends and family that she'd actually sneaked up slightly behind him and had her friend Stacy take a picture. If you looked at it just right, it almost seemed as if they were together.

But she really was with John. Who cared if it wasn't real? It felt real. The night air was cool, the sounds of a darkened New York filled her with excitement, and when he looked at her, even in the shadowed light of the browned-out newsstand, she felt it all the way to her toes.

She put the paper under her arm, anxious to read every word, and opened her purse. It was her purse on the outside, but not on the inside. There was her room key, a wallet she didn't recognize but assumed to be her own, her lipstick, and aha, a coin purse. She paid for the paper, a whole three cents, then slipped her arm around John's. "Let's go find that hotel."

He smiled at her, and something told her he hadn't done it that much. Not lately. Maybe that's where she came in. Maybe in his afterworld, he'd always dreamed of being with a singer from the Stage Door Canteen. Wow. She was someone's dream girl. Go figure.

As they walked, she couldn't help but smile at every single person they passed. All of them smiled back. Well, not the ones who were kissing, but everyone else. They all seemed so happy to be alive. She'd think about that dichotomy later.

"So, you just came to New York today?" John asked.

"That's right."

"Where from?"

She blinked as she tried to come up with a believable story. Because her plans of enjoying this reality to the limit would be severely curtailed by a trip to Belle-view. "Connecticut," she said. She'd been to Connecti-cut.

"Were you singing there?"

"Singing. Yes. I sang. At a small club."

"I'm sure glad they brought you out here. How long will you be at the Canteen?"

"I'm booked for two more nights."

"I hope I'm still here to see that."

"You might be leaving?"

They turned a corner, and there was the St. George. It looked like a decent enough hotel, with a uniformed doorman and everything. The lobby was nothing re-markable, not even the deco architecture that she loved, but it was clean and well-appointed, with comfortable overstuffed chairs and a bellboy with one of those circular hats above his uniform. The restaurant entrance was to the right of the lobby with the bar to its left.

John held the door open for her, and she walked into a film noir set. Dark, smoky, with an elegant raven-haired beauty at the piano. She expected to see Bogey and Bacall sitting in the back booth next to the one they chose.

She scooted in, noticing all the men in uniform. Every one of them looked handsome and courageous. The women, some in uniform, but most in demure dresses or white blouses and skirts, gazed at their men with longing, laughed at their jokes, sipped their drinks, leaving bright red lipstick stains on the rims.

A waitress in a dark dress with big shoulders came to take their orders. Betty had a Rob Roy, John, a Scotch rocks. When they were alone, he turned to her, his eyes shining from the small candle on the table. "I'm waiting on orders," he said, and it took her a minute to remember their interrupted conversation.

"You have to go back?"

He nodded. "I'm fine. I wasn't hurt. There's no reason for me not to go."

"How long have you been in the navy?"

"Four years."

"Oh, God."

The waitress came, and John focused on his drink. She could see he was upset, and that wasn't okay. Not tonight.

She held up her glass. "To the Canteen," she said, "where dreams come true."

He smiled, toasted her, and took a drink. "Can I ask you something?"

"Of course."

"Why me?"

She blinked again, not at all used to coming up with facile lies. So she didn't. "You look like someone I once knew. Someone I liked a lot."

He nodded. "Whoever he is, I owe him."

She wished there was more light, so she could see his face more clearly. The sadness she'd detected at the Canteen was still there, which was completely understandable. The idea that he'd have to go back to the fighting had to weigh heavily on his broad shoulders. All the more reason for her to do what she could to make tonight special. "You don't think you'll have time to go home for a visit?"

His smile faded. "Nope, don't think so."

"Well, then that means you need to see New York, yes?"

"I guess it does."

"What have you seen so far?"

"The Canteen."

"Oh. That leaves a bit to still be discovered."

"I think I've already found the best thing in New York."

The words that had been about to come out of her mouth stalled as she caught her breath. It wasn't just that it was a lovely compliment, it was that she knew beyond any doubt that he meant it. His sincerity was as fresh and pure as the first sunrise and she had no idea what to do with it. She wasn't the type of woman who got compliments, sincere or otherwise. Not Weird Betty. But that's not who John saw. In his eyes, she was a treat, a star, a catch. Overwhelming didn't come close.

She sipped her drink, glad now that the room was too dark for him to see her blush. She hoped like hell this wasn't her one and only night in heaven, but if it was— it was aces.

The only thing that would make it more perfect was if he…if they…oh, yeah, she was a regular femme fatale. She'd been with guys. Not many, and not very memorably, and she'd never seduced one. Gathering all her courage, she put her hand on his thigh.

His eyebrows rose, but only for a moment. It was enough to let her know that her familiarity was a surprise. She only wished she knew if it was a welcome one.

He swallowed so hard she could see his Adam's apple bob. "Have you been to New York before?"

Ah. A continuation of the conversation. His voice hadn't cracked and he hadn't moved his leg, so she just kept her hand where it was, not moving, not squeezing, just resting. "Yes. Yes I have."

"Ah."

"It was great. Fun place. Lots of things to do."

"Right."

Okay, so not a conversation so much as awkward flailing about. Why hadn't she done more? Experimented? What had she been waiting for? Life, as she now knew for certain, was very short. That was something they had in common, no? They both understood how fragile and breakable humans were, so why the tap dancing? "John?"

"Yes?"

"You've probably noticed my hand."

He nodded, looking very serious. And a little scared.

"I'm not good at this," she said, meeting his gaze head-on. "But I'd like you to join me tonight. In my room, I mean. Not just for drinks, because we're having drinks." She winced at that last part, but she didn't look away.

"I'd like that," he said. "More than you could ever know."

Instead of the sigh of relief she expected, her chest constricted and tears burned her eyes. Now, she turned, focused on the piano player, on the rest of the room. On the feel of his thigh flexing beneath her palm.

"Betty?"

"Yeah?" she said, not facing him yet, not while she was still blinking.

"Are you sure? We can just sit and talk. I wouldn't mind that at all."

Sniffing, she turned to see his concern. "How about we start with talking and see where we end up."

He nodded. "You ready for another?"

"Sure."

He signaled the waitress but instead of putting his hand back on the table, he covered hers and gave her a gentle squeeze.

"I want to know who you are," she said, her shoulders relaxing even as her heart reacted to his touch. "Please."

He didn't answer for a long moment. When he did, his voice was so soft she had to strain to hear. "I don't know who I am. Not anymore. I just know, I'm not who I was."

"Why don't we start with who you used to be?"

He smiled, a feeble affair, but she could see he was trying. "Sure. It's not very glamorous. Nothing at all like your life."

She laughed. "We won't even go there. Not yet. Come on, talk. Tell me your secrets."

His expression changed again, so subtly that if she hadn't been watching for it, she'd have missed it. It hit her what she saw there, in the furrowed brow, the wavering smile: longing. What she couldn't tell was if he wanted to share his secrets, or forget he had any.

Maybe she should change the subject, let him off the hook. But no. She was with John for a reason, and pussyfooting around wasn't going to get the job done.

She leaned toward him, moving her hand farther up his thigh, her lips closer to his ear. "Talk to me, sailor. Tell me the things you'd never tell the girls back home."

He inhaled sharply, then before she could shift back, he kissed her. Kissed her like it was the only kiss. Ever.

CHAPTER FIVE

HER LIPS PARTED beneath his and he slipped inside, tasting the hint of her drink. He knew he was holding her arms too tightly, that he was pressing too hard, but he couldn't help it. He felt desperate, as if kissing her would erase the images flashing in his mind, the images that never truly left but waited in the dark alleys for him to drop his guard.

She moaned in his mouth, stirring him, making him hard, and it had been so long since he'd felt this need that it was like the first time.

She was so different from Sarah; as bold as her lipstick, as alluring as her voice. Betty was the kind of gal he read about, not the kind he knew. And yet, when she looked at him, her eyes were kind, not calculating. There was a sweetness in her, and not just her taste. Maybe it was simply that he shouldn't touch her, shouldn't even want her.

Her hand moved up his leg, brushing the side of his erection with her thumb, and he bit back a groan. He felt frantic, uncontrolled, and he didn't want to be in this bar.

He pulled back. The way she looked at him made him harder still.

"Let's go," she whispered.

He wished he had a jacket to hide his condition, but the hell with it. He pulled his wallet out, left two bucks on the table, then stood, holding his hand out to her.

Betty took it and stood, running her free hand over her skirt. God, she was a picture. He thought about her, standing on that stage, her hips swaying as she sang. He'd wondered then what it would be like to have those hips underneath him, and now he was going to find out.

They walked to the elevator with her in front of him, mostly so he wouldn't embarrass her. A private who'd had a few too many joined them, his eyes wandering shamelessly over Betty. He'd have shown him what-for if the ride had gone on past the fourth floor.

She got out her key as they headed to her room. He took it and opened the door. She walked inside, her gaze leaving his reluctantly.

The room was high-class. A hell of a lot nicer than his. It must cost thirty bucks a night, which was way out his price range. He didn't want to spend any money in New York, not on himself. He wouldn't mind buying Betty some flowers, though. She'd like flowers.

He closed the door behind him, and watched her as she went about the room. She opened the closet, touched some of the dresses there, then, as if she'd lost something, she opened the bureau drawers, one after the other, rifling through her things. He saw bits and pieces, a little strip of lace, a nylon stocking. She seemed surprised, as if they weren't her things.

When she closed the last drawer, she stood for a long time, staring at the blank white wall behind the dresser. He wasn't sure if she was happy or sad or if she was just confused, but there was something about the way she stood there that made him want to comfort her.

He moved to her side, touched the small of her back. She faced him, tears in her eyes, her lips parted, her breaths coming in short gasps. He held open his arms, and she fell into him, and he held her, rocking gently.

"I'm sorry," she said.

"For what?"

"I'm fine, really. It's just something I realized. Something I missed."

"Shh," he said, patting her pretty hair. "It's all right. We all miss things."

She pulled back just enough so that she could look into his eyes. Her hand came up slowly and she touched his cheek. "I can't imagine what you've been through," she said. "What your eyes have seen. But for tonight, let's just be here, okay? Right here, nowhere else. You and me. No one else. Nothing else."

He nodded, wanting that as much as he'd ever wanted anything.

"Make love to me, John."

He kissed her for the second time, his hands sliding down her back, her breasts tight against his chest. He turned her around and walked her toward the bed.

When her tongue slipped between his lips, he shook with wanting her. He had to be careful not to push her down on the bed, but be gentle, make sure he didn't scare her.

She sat, brought her hands to the buttons on her skirt. He watched as she undid each one, unable to even

blink as she revealed the delicate edge of a white petticoat. Her fingers paused as she got to the button over
her breasts. "John?"

He jerked his head up. "Yes?"

"Are you going to participate, or just observe?"

"Pardon?"

"Am I the only one who's going to be naked?"

"No." He cleared his throat. "No, not at… I'm sorry,
I was staring. I just…"

"It's okay. I don't mind. I thought it might be more
fun if we were both, well, you know."

His hands went to his jumper and he whipped it over
his head, knocking his Dixie cup off. He didn't care. He
just stripped off his undershirt.

She laughed, making him grin, but she went on unbuttoning. When she stood, he forgot about his pants.
She let her dress drop to the floor, and the sight of her
in her underthings was something to behold. Her lush
curves, the way her hair touched her shoulders, the
perfume of her skin… It made him dizzy, it was so grand.

Then she lifted the petticoat up over her thighs, her
hips, revealing sweet pink panties, and then her flesh,
pale and perfect. Her bra, it was pink, too, which was
something he'd only seen in pictures. He couldn't take
it another minute, he had to touch her.

Reaching out with trembling fingers, he stroked
above her bra, that first swell of her breast. She was
softer than he imagined, impossibly soft. With all the
hard things he'd seen in the past few years, it was almost
too much.

She let him keep his hand there while she reached

behind her in the move that women do with no thought, but that makes men weak in the knees. Hands in the back, chest high, breasts thrust forward. Jesus.

Her bra loosened and as he stared she slid her bra straps over her shoulders, one at a time. He moved in closer, still touching her just there.

She let the bra drop, showing him her incredible, beautiful breasts. Firm dark nipples, pale round flesh. He whimpered, or maybe that wasn't out loud.

She reached up, took his hand and moved it down. He felt her nipple press against his palm. He listened to his own heartbeat crash in his chest, felt the tremble to his toes. She gave him a sympathetic grin. He must look like the kid from Kansas he used to be.

Betty, though, she knew what she was doing. Not that she was acting like a hussy or anything, but she was sure when she ran her fingernails down the middle of his chest. When she slipped those fingers inside the waist of his pants. Oh, yeah, when she started unbuttoning his flap.

He was near busting out of his skivvies, so she had to struggle a bit. More than a bit, evidently, as she sat back down on the bed.

He looked down, but he couldn't see her legs. He could watch as she finished her task and sent his pants to meet his shoes. He kicked them both away, toed off his socks.

"Oh, my," Betty said. "Is that all for me?"

He grinned. "Everything I have is all for you, ma'am."

She stood up again, gave him a too-brief kiss, then she bent to her left and undid the garter that held up her nylons.

He felt like a kid watching a magic trick. Too soon, she had all four garters undone, and then she was rolling her stockings down, revealing her beautiful gams. She was a knockout of the first order, and it occurred to him that maybe he'd been killed along with all his buddies, and this was heaven. It made a lot more sense than him just being the luckiest Joe this side of the Atlantic.

When she was all naked, except for her ruby-red lipstick, she sat again, only to lay her head down on the pillow, lift her arms up, curve her legs, and damned if she wasn't the most wonderful thing he'd ever seen.

"Come here, honey," she said. "Come to bed."

He almost ripped his skivvies, he was in such a rush to get them off, and then he climbed over her, spread himself out, watching her every second.

"This is what I wanted," she said, her voice low and soft. "Only with more touching."

He leaned over her, his hand skimming her side, and kissed her. With his eyes closed, all he could do was feel, and man, what he was feeling. Soft skin, tender lips, the tip of her tongue darting between his teeth. A dream made real, and his for the whole night.

She touched him, too. Her hands ran down his back, leaving a wake of fire in their path. She explored him boldly, not hesitating to touch his hind end. When she grasped his erection firmly, he nearly lost it. No one, certainly not Sarah, not even the women overseas, had ever made him feel this sexy. He thrust into her mouth and her hand, wanting to be inside her. Now.

She took his hand in hers and guided it down over her stomach, straight between her legs. He took over from there, finding her moist heat, slipping inside. He'd learned a thing or two from his shipmates, especially Tommy Hogan, who'd been stationed off the coast of France for three months, so he knew what he was looking for.

Betty's gasp told him he'd found it. Gently, he teased her right there, listening carefully for signs he was doing it right.

"Oh, John," she said, her voice all whisper thin. "Oh, baby."

He guessed he was.

She spread her legs more, prompting him to shift his position but not stop kissing her. The way she used her tongue, how she nipped his lower lip, it wasn't like any kiss he'd ever had. She was magic, she was…

Her hand grabbed his wrist as she turned her head. "I want to come with you inside me," she said. She looked up at him, and he was helpless. If she'd asked him to step in front of a moving train, he'd have done it, no question. This would be a lot more fun.

He put most of his weight on his one hand while he got himself aimed and ready with the other. He was still shaking. Hardly breathing.

She lifted her hips, and he had to close his eyes or this was going to be over way the hell too fast.

He rubbed the head of his cock just inside her, and then he pushed. Not all the way, not yet. He wanted to make this last, to feel it forever. Nothing was like this. Nothing, not in heaven or earth. It was coming home, it was finding peace, it was the closest he'd ever come to perfect.

He moaned as he filled her, as she squirmed beneath him. Her hands tightened on his sides, pulling, her hips lifted, pushing, and he opened his eyes to find her chin lifted, her eyes tightly shut, and her mouth open on a silent scream.

When he was in as far as he could go, he stopped. He was breathing like a prize fighter, his arms shaking with the weight of his upper body, all his concentration on not just going completely crazy.

It was Betty who made him move. She squeezed him, down there, squeezed him like it was her hand making a fist. He grunted, pulled back almost all the way, then sent it home. Hard.

She gasped and her nails dug into his flesh. That was it, he had no more control. For every thrust, she bucked against him, and now she was making this noise, this unbelievable sound that drove him harder. Nothing existed outside of the bed, not the room, not the city, not the whole damn world.

CHAPTER SIX

BETTY CRIED OUT again, barely recognizing her own voice. John's face was a mask of pleasure and pain, almost fierce with concentration, with intent. Every muscle in his body was taut, and she was almost there.

As he made love to her she saw the warrior in his eyes. She saw the anguish there, too, but mostly, she saw that he wasn't Matt. That she didn't want him to be.

His movements became erratic, his back trembling under her hands. She arched her pelvis, wanting to come, meeting his every thrust. It was almost there, seconds away, and her muscles tightened impossibly. Again and again he filled her, rubbed her, and she came in glorious spasms, clutching him, scratching, crying out.

He came, then, straining, moaning. For a long moment, they were, each of them, panting before slipping back into the world. Betty's ear's rang and her limbs protested, but she didn't want to move. John couldn't hold himself up on his tired arms, and he arranged himself next to her. Close. His arm went around her waist, his leg atop hers, his head on her pillow.

She sighed with contentment, wondering again how it was possible, if any of it was real. Wouldn't that be something? If she hadn't been killed at all, but swept back in time? It was equally unlikely, but she liked the idea that this wasn't all a dream.

"Are you okay?" he asked.

"I'm wonderful," she said. "Why?"

"I don't know. You looked like…"

"What?"

"A little sad, I guess."

She touched his face. "There's nowhere I'd rather be."

He smiled. Captured her hand and kissed her palm. "I keep thinking I've died and gone to heaven."

She inhaled sharply. That was too much of a coincidence for her to take it lightly. "Did something happen? On your ship, I mean?"

His smile faded. "A lot happened. But not to me."

"I'm sorry. We weren't going to talk about that."

Pulling her closer, he turned his gaze to the ceiling. "It's not easy to put it aside. But tonight, you made it seem further away."

"Let's talk about something else. Something wonderful."

"Like what?"

"I don't know. How about some happy memories?"

"I don't have a lot of those." He looked at her again. "Not that I didn't have swell folks, but every time I think about them, about the way it used to be, it feels like someone else's life. I'm not that kid anymore. I never will be again."

"But you'll be going home soon, won't you?" She wanted to tell him the war was over. That by this time two nights from now, all Manhattan, all the country, would be celebrating. But she was afraid. She didn't want to dispel this magic, whatever it was.

"I don't know. Probably not for a while. When I do get discharged, I'm not sure I'll go back."

"But your parents. Won't they be anxious to see you?"

"They'd want to see their son." He shifted, putting a little more distance between them. "I was so anxious to fight. To get out there and do my part. I had no idea what I was talking about. I was young and dumb."

"No one can know war from the outside. But in time—"

"Time can't change what happened." He swallowed thickly, his Adam's apple sliding in his throat. "They said I was the lucky one. That it was a miracle anyone survived. I don't feel so lucky. I watched my buddies get wiped out. Torn to pieces. I couldn't do a damn thing to help them. I was buried under bodies. I thought I was going to die from the crush. I couldn't see anything, but I heard the explosions, felt the ship get destroyed underneath me. I don't know why I didn't die, but it wasn't a favor. I haven't slept a night since then, not without a lot of help."

Betty turned so she could face him, hold him. "Oh, John," she whispered.

His eyes were glossy with unshed tears, and she felt like hell for stirring him up. "Tonight you'll sleep. I'll hold you and I won't let go. Not for anything. Tonight, you'll be safe, right here."

He nodded so slightly she almost missed it. Then he stretched for a kiss. Sweet, gentle, and so tender she wanted to cry.

"Come on, let's get under the covers."

Between them, it didn't take long. Once more, they curled around each other. The room was dark, the night not quite silent. She wondered, as she petted him in long, slow strokes, if she'd wake up in his arms. If she'd wake up at all. If not, she'd be grateful for this amazing night. Grateful to the end of days.

JOHN OPENED HIS eyes to a bright splash of sunlight. He winced, expecting the pain of a hangover, but nothing happened, except that he felt thirsty. And sore. And the touch of her thigh against his.

He turned slowly, not wanting to wake her. Her hair was a mess, a bit of her makeup had smudged below her eyes, and her lips were a pale pink. Beautiful didn't come close.

His gaze moved down to where the sheet rested, just covering her breasts. Mesmerized by the sweet swell, the jut of her nipple, he longed to be inside her again, to stay there forever. She'd kept him safe all night. He'd slept, actually slept, for the first time since the ship. But not until they'd talked.

He'd told her things he'd never told another soul. Not about that night, but about his doubts and fears. He'd been taught to work hard, to be the kind of man others counted on. To stand up for his home, his country. The war had not just been brutal. It had taken his long-held beliefs and shaken them to the core. He had no idea who he was anymore. What he was here for. How he was supposed to go on.

He'd have to go wherever they told him. There was only one other choice, but he couldn't do that. He'd heard too many stories about the men who'd gone nuts over there. They were locked away, disgraced as cowards. He wouldn't do that to his family.

His orders might be at his hotel right now. Waiting. He knew enough about the navy to know there wouldn't be a grace period. He'd be back on a ship in no time, back in action the moment they pulled up anchor. The thought made him sick to his stomach.

At least he'd had last night. Betty was the most amazing woman he'd ever met. To tell the truth, he hadn't had any experience to compare with making love to her. He was used to women being demure, to shy giggles in the dark. He'd been with some loose women overseas, but each time he'd come away feeling empty, which was much worse than the frustration that came from living day and night with hundreds of men. He'd stopped going to the brothels, taken the derision from his buddies with as much good humor as he could muster, and explored foreign cities instead of foreign bodies.

He felt anything but empty this morning. It wasn't just the act, although God knows that was incredible, but that he'd been plucked from a crowd of better-looking, higher-ranking, certainly wealthier men. Picked by a woman who could have had anyone, anytime. He had no idea why she'd spoken to him at all, let alone this.

It was all he could do not to touch her. Just watching

her breathe made him heat right up. Oddly, he also wanted to talk to her about things he hadn't wanted to talk about at all. But talking would have to come later. Because Betty woke up, turned to him with a smile and an invitation he couldn't refuse.

MANHATTAN IN THE daylight surprised Betty a lot more than even the brownout of last night, although it took a while to figure out exactly what was so unsettling. She expected the clothing, the cars, the skyline. But when she and John got to his hotel, it finally dawned on her— everything was in color. When she thought of the 1940s, she thought in black and white.

She followed him to his fourth-floor room, where he was going to change clothes. After, they were going to do some sight-seeing. Knowing that right now, thousands of miles away, the war was officially ending, that tomorrow, the news would hit that the Japanese had surrendered, that the world would move from horror and heartbreak into an unprecedented peace, made her wonder again how she'd gotten here. If any of it was real.

All she knew was that it felt real. The honking horns, the street vendors, even her underwear, were all too vivid to be figments of her imagination. Yeah, the torpedo bra was not something she'd voluntarily choose.

John's room was nothing but utilitarian. A single bed, a dresser that had seen better days, a carpet that didn't bear thinking about. She sat on the lone chair while John changed into his dress blues. His move-

ments were jerky and agitated, which had everything
to do with the white envelope on his dresser. He hadn't
said what it was, but she'd seen the government seal.
Orders.

As she watched him, she tried to come up with a way
to tell him the war was ending. That tomorrow, President Truman would announce the unconditional surrender by Japan. John wouldn't have to fight again. In fact,
he'd probably be discharged. He'd be able to go home.

"I'll be out in a minute," John said, as he walked into
the small bathroom and shut the door.

She couldn't stand seeing him so upset, but how
would she explain her prescience? Would he even
believe her?

On their walk to the hotel, they'd made plans to
enjoy the day, and all she wished was that they could
do exactly that. Enjoy the day, start the celebration that
would sweep the city into madness tomorrow. If she had
her way, the one thing she'd like to witness was Times
Square, perhaps figure out where Eisenstaedt took his
famous *Life* magazine picture of the sailor kissing the
nurse. She'd been there when they'd unveiled the com-
memorative statue, and it would be amazing to see it
happen live.

But that tidbit paled in the face of John's distress.
He'd talked to her in a terrible whisper, long into the
night. She'd wept, silently, not wanting him to stop,
because the fear inside him needed a place to vent. It
was very, very late when they'd finally slept, and her
dreams had been filled not with her old life, but with
John. Brave in the face of untold horrors.

He'd been in the Pacific, on the destroyer *Callaghan*, since 1943. He'd seen action in Yap, Ulithi, Woleai, and after that he'd gone to Saipan, Tinian and Guam. But the worst of it had been in Okinawa, where his ship had been destroyed. Sunk by a kamikaze pilot. So many of his shipmates had been killed.

The lump in her throat urged her to do something so she wouldn't cry again. She walked over to the window, only to find the view was of a brick wall. When she turned, her attention fell to his bedside table. To the picture in the small frame. It was a girl, a pretty girl with a bright smile. There was a lipstick kiss on the lower right corner, and Betty's heart sank to her toes.

Of course John had been spoken for. She'd known him such a short time, but she'd fallen under his spell. It wasn't just his connection to her past that had her entranced, either. It was the man. Noble, kind, a most incredible lover. There was nothing of the youthful crush in her feelings for John. Whatever had brought her to this time and place, it was to meet him. Of that she was certain. But she was an interloper in a time not her own. With a man who belonged to someone else.

"That's Sarah," he said behind her.

She started, turned to see him standing by the bathroom door, his short hair damp, slicked back.

"Your wife?" Betty asked.

He shook his head. "Supposed to be. We were engaged just before I left."

"You miss her."

John sighed as he lowered his head. "I miss what we had. What we could have been."

"I'm sure things will work out once you get back. It'll take some time to readjust, but—"

"Listen, I know I said we should do some sight-seeing, but do you think it can wait till this afternoon? There are some things I need to take care of."

She held herself perfectly still. She even managed a smile. He probably wanted to open the envelope in private, then call his girl. "Sure, whatever. I have a couple of things to do myself." She stopped herself just before giving him her cell phone number. Obviously that was impossible.

He walked over to her slowly. God, he looked good in his blues. Of course, he looked better without them. His hand brushed hers.

She forced a smile. "It's okay."

"I know. I just don't want to let you go."

It was her turn to touch him. Just a brush against that same hand. "Why don't we pick a time to meet. For an early dinner, maybe?"

"Great. That'll be…where?"

"At the Canteen? Five o'clock?"

He nodded. "I'm sorry."

She kissed his clean-shaven cheek, inhaling the slight scent of Old Spice. "Don't be," she said. "It's going to be fine. I promise."

He turned her and captured her mouth with his. The searing kiss made leaving a lot more difficult. But, as they said, war was hell.

BETTY KNEW EXACTLY where she was going, but first, she had to make sure she had cab fare. Exploring her purse, she found a nice chunk of change, especially for 1945. She caught a taxi and thought about John the entire way to the New York Central Library. She wanted to research the *Callaghan* and John's tour of duty. Not to pry, but to understand.

She climbed the steps, running her hand over the top of the rightmost lion that flanked the doors. Thank goodness some things had been built to last. Of course there were some differences inside. No computers, for one. No one on cell phones. No iPods or Palm Pilots. But the scent of books was all around her, and it was as comforting as her old bra.

It wasn't difficult to track down the information about John's ship. It was difficult to read about how the ship went down.

She sat in a small alcove on a wooden chair, surrounded by the newspapers the kind lady behind the desk had pulled for her. As she read, she was very grateful that whoever had taken her back in time had given her tissues.

John was a hero. He'd saved lives, lots of them. At great personal risk.

So Matt took after his grandfather in more ways than just his looks. She hadn't realized bravery was genetic, but John, after being nearly crushed to death by the bodies of his gunnery unit, had shot down two planes, then single-handedly put out the fire in the battery. That had been two months ago.

Thank God it was over. He'd never have to go back out there, never again have to watch his friends die, blown apart by an unseen but well-known enemy. He, along with the rest of the world, could begin to recover. As much as she didn't want to think of him disappearing from her life, to believe anything else could happen was crazy. Aside from the fact that she didn't even belong here, he had a home, a life, a girl who loved him. He needed to go back to the life he was destined to live. He needed to marry Sarah and have a child who would have a child named Matthew, who would, like his grandfather, nearly die saving almost a hundred people.

Although she might never know how she'd gotten here, she now knew why.

CHAPTER SEVEN

JOHN SAT ON THE edge of his bed, where he'd been for the last two hours. He stared at the papers on the unmade bedspread, still stunned at what he'd read at least a dozen times.

The navy didn't want him back. He'd been given an honorable discharge, and he was a free man. Even more shocking, he was going to be awarded the Medal of Honor, something he'd thought was reserved for real heroes. All he'd done was fight to keep his buddies alive. To keep himself alive. He'd done a damn poor job of the former.

He needed to make some phone calls. Let his parents and Sarah know they didn't need to worry anymore. He just couldn't seem to pick up the receiver.

What the hell was he going to tell them? That even though he was free to go home, home wasn't where he belonged? That they'd lost their son on that ship, in the middle of the night, with the fires of hell burning all around him? That he couldn't sleep anymore, couldn't seem to get through a day without the spooks coming on him. Just yesterday, he'd been having a cup of coffee when he started shaking so bad he made a mess all over the counter. He'd left in a hurry, but he hadn't stopped shaking for hours.

He didn't understand. He'd gotten out. He'd made it. And while his closest buddies had been killed, he'd helped get a bunch of men onto the rescue ship, men who were in a lot worse shape than him. So why couldn't he just get on with it? He should be happy now, looking forward to going back to his old life. But the only comfort he could find was in thoughts of Betty.

Knowing he was going to see her tonight let him keep breathing, kept his hands steady. For the first time he'd felt a bit like his old self. Maybe it was because she was so darn pretty. Or that she was so understanding. He'd never been with anyone who'd made him feel more comfortable. He looked at the window, wishing he could see her.

He turned back to the phone. He still couldn't pick it up. He just couldn't.

BETTY HAD GOTTEN to the Stage Door Canteen about a quarter to five and waited with all the soldiers and sailors lining up a full two hours before they'd be allowed in. She'd hurried after stopping at her hotel. John didn't need to see the traces of her tears. He needed her to be strong and happy, and to help him see where he belonged.

Tomorrow would change the world. Maybe once he realized the war was over, he'd feel better about going back home. Until then, she needed to keep his spirits as high as possible.

"Betty."

She turned, her whole body reacting to the sound of his voice. John was across the street, waving his cap at her, trying to dodge the heavy traffic on 44th Street. She waved back, so excited she almost tripped over a crack in the sidewalk.

Garnering more than one irate horn, he made it to her side of the street and pulled her into his arms. He kissed her, bending her back, holding her so tightly that if his kiss hadn't already stolen her breath, his urgency would have.

Behind her, she heard hoots and whistles. It was the boys, of course. They had been an orderly bunch, very polite to a young woman in her prettiest pale pink dress. They'd offered her cigarettes or to run and get her a pop. She knew their raucous behavior was harmless fun, mostly aimed at the sailor who'd found his gal.

Only, she wasn't his gal.

John must have felt her stiffen because he pulled her up, then stepped back. He blushed as he studiously put his cap back on his short dark hair. "Sorry about that," he said, making sure only she could hear.

"I'm not. You hungry?"

He nodded.

"Come on. I'm taking you somewhere special."

"You're here. So it's already special."

Betty almost tripped again, only this time, over his compliment. She didn't think she could ever get used to it. Compliments and Weird Betty just didn't go together.

She took his hand in hers as they walked down to Broadway, where it would be easier to get a taxi. Again, she couldn't help staring at the cars, at the clothes, at the very feel of the city that was still so surreal.

John did the whole taxi thing, and it took her a minute to remember that women's lib wouldn't be around for a whole lot of years. He opened the door and she scooted in, holding down her skirt, and she quickly told the cabbie where they were headed as John got inside.

The cab sped off just as John took her hand in his. "I didn't catch that. Where are we going?"

"You'll see."

"So full of mystery."

She grinned. "You have no idea."

He tilted his head a bit as he studied her. "You're not like any girl I've known."

"Again, you have no idea."

"You never did tell me where you're from."

She almost said Kansas, then quickly changed gears. "California," she said, hoping he'd never been.

"That explains some of it. I hear people are different out there."

"They are. It's all that sunshine and orange juice."

"Not to mention movie stars. And singers."

It was her turn to kiss him. But this wasn't about desperation, it was about sweetness. This man, so handsome, so brave, was more wonderful than any movie hero. His touch was amazingly tender, on her arm, on her neck. His silky tongue teased her with banked passion.

She wanted to go back to her hotel, to keep him in her bed and never let him go. How on earth was she going to convince him to return home when she wanted his home to be with her?

It was ridiculous to feel so strongly about a man she barely knew. Nothing would have convinced her it could happen to her, not like this. Certainly not like this.

"What's wrong?" he whispered, his lips still brushing hers.

"Nothing. Nothing at all."

"You look wonderful," he said, just before he kissed her again.

It took a sharp turn of the cab to pull her from him this time. "I thought about you all day," she said. "Every minute."

He nodded. "Me, too. You were my bright light. How is it possible?"

She laughed. "I have no idea."

The cab slowed and pulled to the side of the street. There it was, 21 West Fifty-Second Street. She recognized the signature jockeys at each side of the door to one of the most legendary restaurants in the world. She'd read about 21, but she could never afford to eat there. Luckily, in 1945, the prices were a lot more reasonable.

John paid the driver, and held his hand out to her as she got out of the cab. There weren't many people entering at this hour, but she'd made sure that not only would they have a table, but that John would be allowed to dine in his uniform.

"What is this place?" he asked, looking up the stairs.

"It's a terrific restaurant. And before you get all panicky, know right now that it's my treat."

"Your… Oh, no. Not on a dare."

"You can buy me something later," she said, squeezing his hand. "Come on. Let's show these yokels what real class looks like."

His laugh made her feel better instantly. It was probably a good thing that he was going back to Kansas. He'd undoubtedly freak when he found out the real depth to her independence. Although she had a feeling that if anyone around here could take on a twenty-first century woman, it was John Matthew Stevens.

HE HADN'T EVER EATEN a dinner that fine. Everything about the restaurant was exceptional. He'd actually had a steak. With all the rationing, it had been almost a year since he'd had one. He'd been wary about the wine, but damn, it had been great. He'd even had chocolate cake after, another rare wartime treat. But none of it compared to Betty. She sure was something.

He'd laughed more tonight than he had in a long time, and he'd barely thought about Kansas or the ship. They'd talked about every kind of thing. Turns out, she was a reader, too. And during those long days and nights on the ship, when the boredom all but ate a man from the inside out, books had become his haven. She'd loved *The Great Gatsby* and *The Sound and the Fury*, which were two of his favorites. He'd also taken to doing crossword puzzles, and when he wasn't doing that, he was writing long, long letters home. He'd mostly written to Sarah, but he didn't mention that to Betty.

The two women were worlds apart. Sarah was a nice girl. He'd known her since fifth grade, and they'd started dating in high school. It had seemed the most natural thing in the world to ask her to marry him before he enlisted. But as time went on, confusing realizations had come to bear.

"John? You okay?"

He blinked, saw he was gripping his wineglass too hard. He let it go, found a smile. "I've had a great night. Thank you."

"I have, too. But I know something's wrong. Do you want to talk about it?"

He opened his mouth to say no. But then he remembered who he was with. "That letter I got. It wasn't orders. It was my discharge papers."

Betty closed her eyes for a long moment. A waiter came near but veered to another table. When she looked at him again, those beautiful blue eyes were wet with unshed tears. "I'm happy for you."

"I'm relieved. God knows, I didn't want to go back."

She reached across the table and took his hand in hers. "You said something yesterday. That you weren't sure you wanted to go home."

"I'm not. I just don't see myself going back to the farm. It wasn't something I had a choice about. I was born on the farm, and I'd die on the farm. That's the way it is. But I almost died in an ocean thousands of miles from the wheat and the corn. It made me think."

"What about your girl?" she asked softly.

He cleared his throat, suddenly embarrassed. "I've known her most of my life. She's…she's a good girl."

"But?"

"I'd never been with anyone else. Never knew any of the possibilities."

"I'm thinking there's more to it than that."

He looked up at the miniature planes hanging from the ceiling. What a crazy idea. "I've changed, Betty. Everything about me is different. I know war affects everyone. I'm not naive, but something happened to me out there. I'm not just talking about the really bad times. All of it. Seeing the world, meeting so many different kinds of people. The world I came from was so small. I just never knew it. Did you ever see that movie, *The Wizard of Oz?*"

She nodded. "It's a classic."

"I don't know about that, but I did think it was kind of funny that the little girl was from Kansas. And then she got blown into this other world, full of color and mystery and adventure. I remember when I first saw it, I understood why she wanted to go back home to all the comforts she knew. Now, I think she was crazy. She should have kept on moving, explored that Oz place, every inch of it. Even if there were bad witches and flying monkeys."

"Can't you do both? Take your girl with you? Wouldn't she like to know about the Emerald City?"

He shook his head. "You don't know Sarah. She's not one for travel. She wants to stay home. Have babies. She likes to cook. Pies, mostly, that she enters in the county fair. She hasn't won yet, but she keeps trying."

Betty slipped her hand out of his grasp and leaned back in her chair. She looked troubled, and he didn't like that. "It doesn't matter. And hey, don't you have to get to the Canteen?"

She nodded. "I do, but we've got a few more

minutes. John, you're the most wonderful thing that's happened to me in ages. I hardly know you, and I have no business butting in, but I think it would be a mistake for you to not go home. I think, once you're there, that things will change for you. You've had some harrowing experiences. No person should ever have to do what you've done. But there's a place for you in Kansas."

"Used to be a place."

It would be so easy to agree. To forget what she knew about the future, and just be with John. But how could she? If John didn't marry Sarah, there was every reason to believe all those people in Washington would die, because Matthew wouldn't be there to save them. If only she could know for sure. But then, nothing in this life, no matter what era she was in, was certain. "No, John. The war changed a lot of things, but not that. It's where you belong. You need to at least try. Once you're back where you grew up, where you have your roots, you'll see."

He looked away. He hadn't even realized, until just this second, that for some crazy reason he'd thought that maybe he and Betty could… That was crazy. She was a famous singer. What would she want with a farm boy from a hick town? She'd probably go on back to California. Become real big, like Patti Paige or Rosemary Clooney. She'd forget about him in no time. But he'd never forget about her.

"Just think about it, okay?" Betty leaned over and touched his cheek. "But not tonight. Let's go sing and dance. Tomorrow, things will look different."

He nodded. "Sure. Tomorrow."

"Will you come home with me tonight?" she asked. "I mean, to my hotel?"

"I'd like that. More than you can know."

"Good. It's settled. Let's blow this Popsicle stand, big guy. And don't you be dancing too close to any of those cute little college girls, you hear?"

He saluted. "Yes, ma'am." Then he got up and pulled out her chair. When she was next to him, when her mouth was close enough to his neck that he could feel her warm breath, she whispered, "Trust me on this, sweet John. Tomorrow it will all be different."

CHAPTER EIGHT

ONCE AGAIN, Betty thrilled to the sound of the applause and the whistles. Except for convincing John to abandon her in this familiar but strange world, it was one of the best nights she'd ever had. She'd been more relaxed, her voice had never been better. The band, well, they'd been sublime. And always, John had been in her line of sight.

It was wonderful knowing that tomorrow all these kids, and God, they were so achingly young, would be off the hook. No more battles. No more death on foreign soil. But it was also tough, because she desperately wanted to tell them. To watch their faces when they found out. She wanted to shout it over the microphone, scream it at the top of her lungs. Of course, she couldn't. No one would believe her. It wasn't time.

Which, since it seemed as if she really was in 1945, was how it was going to be about everything. She couldn't warn anyone about Vietnam, about the death of JFK. About a hundred things. She couldn't change the fabric of the future, except, perhaps to make sure that all those people in that burning building would be saved by Matthew Stevens.

On the other hand, perhaps, once she was sure John would play his part, she'd go back. Or disappear. She couldn't think about it, not now.

Turning to the bandleader, she told them the song she wanted to sing. When she turned back, she sought out John, his hat in his hand, a smile on his face. To him, she sang the one song that was so perfectly true it broke her heart. "Till The End Of Time."

As she sang, she wondered if her feelings for him would have been the same if she hadn't had a crush on Matt all those years. Was it truly John she felt so much for?

Matt had been her ideal, her unrequited perfect hero. But there was a reason for that. It wasn't so much about how he looked as who he was. Kind, generous, smart. All the things she was drawn to in John. Which made a lot of sense, right? The reason Matt was Matt was because he'd grown up with John as his grandfather.

The song ended, and right on its heels, the band played "Good Night, Sweetheart." She climbed down from the stage into John's arms. They swayed to the music, holding each other tight. He kissed the side of her neck, nibbled on her earlobe.

She felt his hard length against her belly, and she thought about the night ahead. They would soon be in bed making love. Celebrating his goodbye, although she didn't want to think about it that way. Celebrating the peace. That was better.

"You have anything you need to do here?" he asked.

She leaned back to see his face. God, the want in his eyes. "No."

He stopped dancing even though the song wasn't over. "Let's go."

It wasn't quite that simple. Like the night before, so many wanted to shake her hand, to say a word or two. For the next hour she listened to boys with shiny faces and big smiles. Some of them still had bandages. She knew a lot of their wounds couldn't be seen at all.

Finally, they were at the steps that would lead them to the street. John held out his hand to her and she took it, thrilling again at his touch. Unexpected tears came to her eyes, but she blinked them away. She wanted to remember this night for how wonderful it had been, not for how sad.

It also took longer than expected to find a taxi; they should have walked to the hotel. When they did get to the St. George, they didn't bother with the bar.

The moment her room door closed behind him, she was in his arms. It was as if they hadn't seen each other for months, as if they hadn't just been holding hands. He got to work on her zipper, never once taking his lips away. Of course, she was doing the same with his buttons, but she was having far less luck.

Somehow, they got undressed, and for a long time they stood in the middle of the room and kissed. They touched, too, rubbing against each other in the hot room.

John had opened the blackout drapes earlier. They wouldn't be turning on the lights, so it didn't matter, and the warm wind over his skin felt great. But he knew he'd feel even better when Betty lowered herself to her knees, right there on the green carpet. As he watched, she opened her mouth, and took the head of his penis between her lips.

He groaned, not just because it felt like heaven, but because he couldn't believe the power of her ruby-red lipstick moving over his flesh. He fisted his hands, tightened the muscles of his legs, his back. He wanted to thrust inside her, but of course, he wouldn't. It was amazing, what she was doing. That she was letting him watch.

It occurred to him that there were two different kinds of sex and they had very little in common. One was more mutual masturbation, where there's lots of moaning and groaning and mess, but it doesn't change a man, not in his deepest parts, not in the very veins and in his blood. Then there was the kind of sex that does.

He never knew about this kind until just this minute, and even though this amazing woman was doing even more amazing things to the part of him that appreciated it the most, it wasn't even close to the effect she was having on his heart.

There was only one thing wrong. She was going back to California, and this was just wartime madness, and he was like every other Joe who figured they were going to be dead in a week, so they'd better have all the sex they could find. Only, he wasn't going to be dead. He was discharged, and oh, God, what was she doing there with her tongue?

He had to stop her this second, or it was gonna be all over. Taking a deep, shuddering breath, he put his hands on her pale shoulders. "Betty."

She paused, still surrounding him in wet heat, and brought her gaze up to meet his.

"We have to stop this. Now."

She pulled back, a little too slowly, because he almost lost it. "You don't like?"

"I do. Too much. But I can't stand not touching you."

She smiled. And he shuddered again.

THE RADIO PLAYED "Long Ago and Far Away" when he lay on top her. He was the best blanket. Not too heavy, because of those strong arms of his, and his body was hard, firm, long. He covered her lips the way his chest covered her breasts. His breath sneaked inside her before his tongue, and his follow-through stole it right back again. Kissing him was all her dreams of kisses come true. Slow and sweet, a promise of things to come.

He rolled to her right, and she rolled with him, their naked bodies sticking a bit with the heat, the poor breeze not up to its task. She didn't care. She had to touch him.

From his strong jaw down his neck, her hand slid over his shoulder but veered from his arm to his chest. The hair there was dark and curly, and it felt wonderful between her fingers. When she rubbed her palm over his nipple, she watched his muscles tremble. It made her gasp in surprise to see her touch do so much. A tiny miracle.

He rested his head on her pillow, just a couple of inches from hers, but she didn't look at him. Not yet. She still followed her hand as it traced his waist, his hip, the pale skin next to his deep tan. With just her fingertips, she drew a line from the highest part of his hip, straight down to the dark hair of his groin and the base of his impressive erection.

She couldn't stop there. She touched him in a way she'd never felt free to do with any man. Frankly, she'd never wanted to do this, to explore so intimately. "You're so…"

She heard him take in a breath and hold it.

"…beautiful."

He exhaled with a laugh. "Not the compliment I would have expected."

"It's true though. And it is a compliment." She looked up, glad to see he was smiling.

"You know, if you keep on touching me like that, we might have a problem here."

She continued, drawing little squiggles on the length of his smooth shaft. "Really? What kind of problem?"

He chuckled, making it bounce. But she didn't have long to be amused. He grabbed her wrist and, as he climbed over her again, he put her hand up by her head. "This kind of problem."

She wiggled, making all kinds of interesting contact with his body. She stopped, though, when he looked at her. His smile had gone, and in its stead was such fierce longing she was the one who trembled.

He parted her legs with his knees and very slowly, he entered her.

Lifting her hips, she pulled him closer.

He opened his mouth. "I…"

"I know," she said. "I'll never forget you. Not in a million lifetimes."

CHAPTER NINE

JOHN BOLTED UP, and looked frantically for his weapon. He had to get to quarters.

"John. It's okay."

A woman? Here? It took him a minute to realize he wasn't on the ship. It was Betty. In New York. "Who's banging on the door?"

"Are you all right?"

She seemed as frightened as he was. He put his arm around her and held her tight as his heartbeat slowed. Whoever was at the door kept banging.

"John?" she said again, her voice tender, concerned.

"I'm okay." He pulled back and let her see. "You'd better get that before there are complaints."

She nodded as she pushed back the covers.

John watched her walk to the bathroom door and retrieve a yellow robe. She tightened the belt as she went to the door and opened it a crack. He couldn't see who was there. He couldn't hear, either, and he hoped his presence in her bed wasn't compromising her. He couldn't leave; his clothes were on the other side of the room. Instead, he leaned his back against the wall, willing himself to get calm.

After a couple of minutes, Betty closed the door and turned to him. Her smile said something was up. "Oh, my," she said.

"Who was that?"

"Rob."

"Ah."

"He brought news. Unofficial, but reliable." She approached the bed, her hair all wild, her lips still swollen from his kisses. She climbed up beside him and took his hand. "It's over. Japan has surrendered."

He heard her, but the words took a while to sink in. It had been coming, after the bombs were dropped over there, and yet he hadn't dared to believe. This was the best possible news. The end of the killing, not just for him, but for all of them. If only it could have come two months ago. But it hadn't and there was nothing he could do about that.

"I thought you'd be happy."

"I am. I truly am. It's great news." He kissed her, feeling better the instant his lips touched hers.

When they pulled back, she still looked concerned. "It's not in time, is it?"

She was a smart one. He'd known that from the start. "No, not quite."

"It's still good. The world needs a break. It's going to be a wonderful, productive time, you'll see. All the troops coming home. Getting back to the business of America."

"Maybe the rationing will end, huh? Real coffee? Sugar?"

"No more blackouts."

"New cars."

"Meat for dinner."

He laughed. "That's good, because I was spoiled by that steak."

"Ah, sweetie, you'll be having steak whenever you want it. Although you need to be careful because it's not so great for your cholesterol."

"My what?"

"Nothing. Never mind. Come on," she said, tugging his hand. "Let's get cleaned up. I imagine the party's already started."

"The party'll still be there in a while. Why don't you climb back under the sheets and let's take this morning a little slower."

She breathed in deeply as she untied her belt. It fluttered to the floor, leaving her naked and beautiful as she took his advice.

They listened to the noise coming from the street. Horns honking, shouts. The unofficial word must be spreading quickly. It was going to be wild out there today. But not for him.

There was no hiding from it. Not now. Everyone at home would be getting this same news. His parents wouldn't understand if he didn't come home.

"When are you leaving?" she asked.

He turned to her, a chill running down his spine. "How do you do that?"

"It's a curse."

He took her hand in his. "I figure I'd better get out on the first train I can. It's going to be a madhouse."

"That seems right. It'll be hard to get a ticket."

"I don't know that I'm going to stay."

"I know."

"And I'll probably tell Sarah that it's over."

She squeezed his hand. "Give it a little time, okay? Be patient. It's going to be an adjustment for everyone."

"Yeah. It will."

They sat there for a while, listening as more and more noise came from down below. He should get up, get dressed. He'd have to pack, check out of his hotel. "You're going to the Canteen tonight, right?"

"Yep."

"Then what?"

"I don't know."

He kissed her on the lips, then looked at her with steady eyes. "I wish…"

"Me, too, sailor. It's not to be. But I'll always remember you. It's been the best two days of my life."

"You know what? I believe you. Because it's been like that for me, too."

"Make love to me," she said. "One last time."

SHE LAY BESIDE him, her heart still hammering from her climax. She felt the weight of his head on her shoulder, the sweat of his side pressed against her. She didn't bother wiping her tears. All she could think was that she hoped whoever or whatever had sent her back here was happy. She'd done her job. John would be going home to his Sarah. She knew that once he was there, it would be hard to leave.

He'd find comfort in the familiar things of his life. Day by day the horrors of his war would begin to fade, and he'd find himself driving the plow, eating with his family after church, walking into the dime store he'd

known all his life. And he'd marry her. They'd have a
child. And sixty some odd years later, his grandson
would be a hero, just like his grandpa.

It felt like the shallowest of victories. A cruel trick.
To bring her back to the time she fit, where she, for once
in her life, belonged completely, only to have her heart
filled with the memory of the man she couldn't have.
It wasn't fair and it wasn't right, and if she had a choice?

At least she'd been his for a moment. In her other
life, she'd been invisible. An uninvited stranger in a
world of friendships. She'd always been on the outside
looking in. But here, she was home. She was someone.
With John, she was extraordinary.

She would love him till the end of this time, till the
end of her time. It might seem foolish to even think the
word *love*. And yet there was no doubt in her mind, and
more importantly, her heart.

It wasn't so bad, him leaving. Because from this
day forward, she'd know what it felt like to love. To
be cherished.

That was something big.

Maybe that was the deal. To learn what that felt like.
To be so loved that it changed her chromosomes.

"What did you do to me?"

She laughed at his whining. "Me? I just lay there and
thought of England."

He barked out his own laugh. "Woman, you've
spoiled me forever." Lifting his head, he met her gaze.
"You have."

She couldn't let the conversation go there. Not if she
wanted to see him off with a smile instead of sobs.

"Come on, big guy. Let's shower and see how the city is celebrating."

He nodded, kissed her bare shoulder, then rolled out of bed. He held his hand out to her. "Who knows? Maybe we can get a real cup of coffee."

She wiped her face then took his hand. They walked slowly to the shower.

IT WAS TIME. She'd decided, back at her hotel, that she wouldn't go with him to the train. It was too difficult for her, and he really had no idea what time he'd be leaving. The tension would have killed her, and she was already dying.

They had found their real cup of coffee in a diner on Eighty-Second Street, although neither of them had much of an appetite. As they sipped, they spoke a little about the news, about the Canteen. Nothing of consequence, and all of it heartbreaking. But she didn't cry. Not until now.

He looked down the road, searching for a taxi. His duffle was on the sidewalk, packed with his few belongings. Revelers were all around, the word of the surrender singing through the city. Everyone seemed tipsy, even though it was just after noon. The air, warm and humid, felt electric. Betty could hardly stand the ache in her heart.

"I could stay another day," he said. "It wouldn't matter that much."

"No. You need to go. It won't get any easier."

"I hate this." He touched her face. "I don't want to leave."

She pressed her cheek into his palm, not able to speak through the lump in her throat.

"Can't you give me an address? Somewhere I can write to you?"

"I don't think that would be a good idea. You'll be busy, and I don't know where I'll be."

His hand came down, his eyes stricken. "So that's it? We say goodbye and we never see each other again?"

"No. We kiss. And we hold on to our memories."

"It's not enough."

"It has to be," she said. "Now, kiss me."

He took her in his arms. It didn't matter that they were standing on the street corner, that people streamed out of shops and across the busy boulevard. He kissed her for the last time. Deeply, painfully, with tears wetting them both. She memorized his taste, the way he held her against his chest. It was the hardest goodbye ever.

She was the one who pulled back first. It was the most difficult thing she'd ever done, but she kissed both of his closed eyes, then she turned and walked away, rounding the corner with her back straight, her head tall. Once she was out of his sight, when she knew she'd never see him again, she leaned against the cool granite storefront and let the tears come.

No one bothered her as she wept. She used all the tissues she'd tucked in her purse, and she knew she looked like hell, but she didn't care. Not a whit. She'd made a horrible mistake. The moment she'd walked away, she'd seen the error. She didn't care about those people in the future. Someone else would help them.

She only cared that for the first time in her life, she'd fallen completely, utterly in love. All she had to show for it was a handful of tears.

When she could see again, she figured she'd go back to her hotel. Crawl into bed and hide under the covers. She was supposed to go back to the Canteen tonight, but how could she? They wouldn't miss her, not with the news.

She blinked as she realized exactly where she was. Directly across the street from the Metropolitan Museum of Art, where all her problems had begun. Coincidence? Not likely.

An old Ford almost clipped her as she hurried across the street, but that's not what made her heart pound. It had all started there, at the Met, with that weird guard and that exhibit.

Some part of her mind knew that the exhibit wouldn't be there for over sixty years, but she pushed that back, certain she'd find an answer, any answer. More than that, she'd find a way to get John back.

She got inside and stopped. It felt just like it had two days and a different lifetime ago. It smelled the same. How was that possible? It didn't matter. Answers mattered.

She took the same route, walked through the same halls. And her heart nearly stopped when she saw the sign: Sex Through the Ages.

With slow, careful steps, her heels loud in the empty room, she entered the exhibit space. The same pictures were lit. Nothing was different, even though some of the displays highlighted scenes from the future. Her future.

From the corner of her eye, she caught movement. And there he was. The guard. The same man, unchanged. Not younger, not older. Same pocketwatch, same cap. She wanted to speak, but her voice didn't work.

"Welcome back, Betty."

She opened her mouth twice. Finally, she said, "How?"

"How? I don't know how it works. Just that it does." He came close to her, and she could smell his aftershave. Aqua Velva.

"Why me?"

"You love this era. You've studied it all your adult life. You feel at home here. Don't you?"

She nodded. "It makes no sense."

"I wouldn't say that."

"No? I was born in 1980. This is 1945. How does that make sense?"

He smiled at her. "How did it feel to be singing on that stage, Betty? Wasn't it better than anything you've ever felt before?"

"Yes. Now ask my about the worst feeling I've ever felt. That one's pretty fresh, because it's happening right now. You knew I would meet him. And you knew I would have to let him go."

"There were choices to be made."

"By whom? Who did this?"

"I'm sorry. I honestly can't tell you."

"Can't or won't?" she demanded.

"Does it matter? You're where you belong. In the time you belong. You know it. You feel it in every step you take, in every breath. You belong. And after all, isn't that what you've always wanted? Your dream came true, Betty. It's true right now."

"No. I didn't dream about losing the only man I'd ever love. It's too cruel, even for someone who can play with time like a toy."

"Well, if you feel like that, there's something we can do."

"What?"

He lost his smile. In fact, he looked downright sad. "We can take it back. All of it. You'll never even know you were away."

"What?"

He nodded. "All you have to do is say the word. You'll have no memory of the Stage Door Canteen. You won't remember singing, or eating at 21. And you'll have no recollection of meeting John Stevens. It'll be gone. No more pain. No more regret. But you need to decide now." He looked at his watch, then back at her. "Two minutes, and the offer is off the table."

CHAPTER TEN

GRAND CENTRAL STATION was a madhouse. Every train was full, the ticket lines stretched across the great hall. Men, women, most of them in uniform, all of them thrilled to be going home, bumped into him, smiled, and kept on going.

He'd gotten his ticket, although his train wouldn't leave for another few hours. He stood around a bunch of benches, although he doubted he'd find a seat. It didn't matter. He just leaned against a column, thinking about what he was leaving behind.

It was all so crazy. He never should have met her. Things would have been so much easier if he hadn't. Of course, he wouldn't be going home if it wasn't for Betty.

He wondered what she was doing right now. Did she hurt the way he did? Did it ache knowing she'd never see him again?

He knew for certain he wasn't in love with Sarah. It wouldn't be easy to tell her, but he couldn't marry her. Not when he knew what love really felt like.

It wasn't supposed to happen in a day, not in real life. But it had. He loved her, and he wanted her, and dammit, why was it so hard to go home?

His folks were good people, his town a good town. He'd always loved living there, never even thought about moving away. But the ghosts of his shipmates hung over his head now. George Ellers. He'd been married for just over a year, and he had a baby he'd never seen. Never would see. Scotty Tobin had been the young punk they'd all kidded because he barely needed to shave. He'd never see his mamma in New Orleans again.

He still didn't understand why he'd made it and they hadn't. Why Betty had made love to him. Why anything happened in this crazy world. But he'd given his word, and he wouldn't back out. If nothing else, his parents deserved to see him whole, to rest easy that he'd come through the fighting. He also needed to decide what to do with his land.

Someone jostled him to his right, and he saw it was a young girl, holding on to her soldier, crying her eyes out. It should have helped that he wasn't the only one leaving something great behind. It didn't.

BETTY SANG TO THE packed house, although no one was really listening. President Truman had come on the radio earlier this evening to make the official announcement. The treaty wouldn't be signed for a little while, but the war was over.

Not all the troops would be coming home right away, but come home they would. Broken, some of them, battered, all of them, and so damn happy to have won the righteous fight.

Here at the Canteen they wanted happy, and she gave them happy, even though she could barely believe she was singing at all. The choice, when it had come right down to it, was to keep John. Maybe not in the flesh, but surely in her heart. The thought of going back to the life she had before was untenable. Despite the pain.

So this was it. Her new world. No ATMs, no computers, no cable. On the other hand, there was the adventure of watching, live, everything she'd loved in the books and in the movies. Sure she was scared, but the excitement overshadowed her doubts. She'd be great in this era. Heartbroken, yeah, but great.

The song ended to great cheers. She knew the applause wasn't really for her tonight. It was congratulations to them all. For being alive. For having a future.

"What's next?"

She turned to Jeff. She'd come to like him so much. He and Rob had welcomed her with hugs and kisses, their enthusiasm so great they didn't even notice that she wasn't smiling half so brightly. But it was all right. This was her world now, and she needed to be part of it. Not an observer any longer, but a participant. This was her time. "You guys know 'I Left My Heart at the Stage Door Canteen'?"

Jeff laughed. "You bet we do." Then he told the band, and he raised his sax.

The crowd recognized the song from the first five notes, and they cheered their heads off. She doubted they even heard her sing the first few lines, but then it got pretty quiet, considering. Betty hung on to the mike and watched the dancers on the floor.

The young men and women clung to each other

like lovers. All of them. Gone were the tentative
touches, the shyness she'd seen just two nights ago. As
she sang the words that tore at her heart, she thought
about what was to come.

She'd have to talk to Rob. Evidently, she had a career
as a singer to look forward to. Travel, she supposed, to
cities she'd known only through books and movies.
She'd wanted to ask the museum guard about what was
allowed, what was forbidden, but there'd been no time.
So she figured she might as well use some of her knowledge to give herself a solid financial base. Nothing too
flashy. She didn't need to be fabulously rich. But what
the hell, right?

One of the boys tossed a rose up onto the stage. Where
he'd gotten it was anyone's guess, but she picked it up,
grateful for the token. Ah, it was a major, and he gave
her a smart salute, then blew her a kiss. It was wonderful, except that she'd promised herself she wouldn't cry.

The song ended on a high note, and it was time for
a break. She got offstage, and headed through the crowd
past the milk bar and food service counter to the small,
hot kitchen. Three volunteers, all women with brilliant
smiles, were putting together ham sandwiches on rolls.
There were great big tubs of yellow mustard and
butter—very orange butter—on plates. The women
wore white aprons.

"You hungry?"

Betty shook her head as she read the woman's name
badge. "No thanks, Theresa. I just wanted to get away
for a minute."

"You're a big hit out there. All the boys love you."

"Thank you."

"You have someone? Overseas?"

"No, no I don't. What about you?"

"My Scott is coming home. I'm not exactly sure when. Or where he is, but I feel it in my bones. He's coming home."

"I'm sure he is. It'll be a wonderful homecoming."

"That's why I'm here, you know. Me and Esther." She nodded at the woman next to her. "Because we sure hope someone over there is making sandwiches. Making sure they all get some food and maybe some music. Something to make it nice, you know?"

"I do, Theresa. You know what? I think I will have one of those sandwiches. They look very tasty."

It was Esther who wrapped her a sandwich in a napkin. "My son's name is Eddy. Edward. He's a sailor."

At the word, despite seeing at least fifty sailors right outside the door, Betty burst into tears. Not small, delicate little tears, but giant, gasping sobs that shook her body and hurt her throat.

She dropped the sandwich and covered her eyes, trying to stop the tears, the unbearable ache, and then there were arms around her. Theresa and Esther were hugging her, telling her it was going to be okay, that they understood. But of course, they didn't. They couldn't. She'd never see him again. She loved him and she'd never touch him, never make love to him. He was gone.

"Honey," Theresa said, "It's okay, honey. Please. We've all lost someone. All of us. I lost my brother. He was only twenty-eight, and he died in Normandy."

Esther, who was crying now, too, said, "I lost my nephew. He was a mathematician. Why they needed a mathematician to fight in Dunkirk, who knows. But he died there. He's never going to be a mathematician again. So we know, sweetheart. We know."

Betty sniffed, and a napkin was put in her hand. She used it, but needed another one. Finally, after a long time, she could breathe again. Everyone had lost someone. She wasn't the only broken heart in New York. All the others, they were pulling through. They were moving forward. For the men they'd lost. For the future.

"I have to go back onstage," she said. "They're waiting."

"Hold on one second, honey," Theresa said, leaving her for a moment to open her purse. She pulled out a little compact, and a tube of lipstick.

"Thank you." Betty wiped away most of the damage and she put on the lipstick carefully, even though it wasn't exactly her color. She handed the compact and the Revlon to her new friend, then she held up her head and went back to her job. To celebrate. To make this night the celebration of a lifetime for every soldier in the joint.

Jeff held a hand out for her as she walked up the stairs to the little bandstand. She smiled as brightly as she knew how, and she told Jeff what she wanted to sing. "I'll Walk Alone."

She sang the song with as much heart as she could muster. And by the end of it, she almost believed it. She closed her eyes, never letting go of the mike, but with every whistle, every cheer, she felt stronger.

"Betty?"

She turned to see Jeff, standing close.

"Do me a favor? How about 'I'll Be Seeing You.'"

She nodded. "You bet."

He bowed his head, then turned back to his band. The sweet, sad notes drifted over the crowd, and it got suddenly, touchingly, quiet.

She sang. The words to one of the most beautiful songs she'd ever heard made her ache, but in a good way. Those who weren't dancing were swaying to the rhythm. To the words.

Because it had been where John stood, she turned to the right, to the corner where he'd listened to her sing. A sailor was there, which made her voice catch, but only for a moment. He had red hair, and besides, John was on a train. But she sang to that carrot-topped sailor anyway.

As she neared the end of the song, she noticed Jeff had moved in close. She stepped aside, even though she didn't remember a sax solo in the song. When she glanced at him, she froze. It wasn't Jeff. It was another sailor. Hat in hand. Smile on his face. His eyes wet with tears.

She dropped the microphone and it made a horrible wailing racket, but she didn't care. She had to touch him. To make sure he was real, and he was here, and he wasn't on that train at all.

Her arms went around his neck, and he was holding her, tight.

"I couldn't go," he said. "Not without you. Please, please don't send me away again. I love you."

She nodded. "I love you, too."

"Thank God," he said, and then he kissed her.

Somewhere outside the bliss of his kiss, there was cheering and shouting and whistles and stomps. The squeal of feedback stopped, and Jeff's voice came out of the speakers.

"Well, boys and girls, I think we're gonna be celebrating the rest of the night without a singer. But that's okay. That's just fine. Because this is what we fought for. Right here, right now. This is victory."

EPILOGUE

February 19, 1980

BETTY SAT ON THE ugly green couch in the waiting room of Milford hospital. Next to her was a stuffed bear, very small but very cute, and totally foolish. She'd brought it, anyway. She looked up when she heard footsteps, and she smiled.

John, her husband of thirty-five years, walked into the room, carrying two cups of hot coffee and a snack cake under his arm.

He was still as handsome as the day she'd first laid eyes on him. His hair was a little whiter, but still thick. He wore glasses now, although he kept threatening to get contact lenses. He'd kept himself in fighting shape, due more to the work on the farm and their nightly constitutionals than any overt effort. And he was her whole world.

"I thought we'd split this," he said. He put down the coffee cups and handed her the plastic-wrapped cake. "It's your favorite."

"Thank you."

"Any word?"

She shook her head. "It's her first. It's going take a while."

He sat, and took her hand in his. "Our baby's having a baby. How'd we get so old?"

"I don't feel old. Well, maybe when I get up in the morning."

"You know what I was thinking?"

She leaned her head on his broad shoulder. "What?"

"I was thinking that it's about time I retired."

She had to sit up for that. She'd brought it up a few times in the past, but he'd waved the idea away. He was a farmer, and even though he had a great manager and a whole crew of workers, he still rose with the sun, got out there on his land and took an active role in his business.

He hadn't needed to work for years. Investments, of course. He'd wondered about her strange gift with the stock market, with their whole portfolio, but after a while, he'd just accepted that she was real good with numbers. They had enough money to do anything they wanted. Mostly what they wanted was to be together, which worked out well for her.

She'd given up her life as a singer, except at church, and she hadn't thought twice about it. When they'd gotten back to Milford, there were some awkward days. He'd met with Sarah, alone, but it turned out that she was waiting for him more out of loyalty than love. She'd moved to California, found herself a cameraman and they'd had three kids together.

Betty wondered about her own parents, but they never did come to Milford. She hoped they'd had a peaceful life, one that brought them happiness, but she'd decided up front that she wasn't going to look for them. She wasn't sure how she knew that was the right thing, but she knew.

The life she'd built with John was as rich and full as her wildest dreams. She'd been right about him accepting her independent ways. He didn't always understand, but he never said a word. If anyone asked, he always said it was part of her charm.

"What brought this on?" she asked.

"Now that Johnny is starting his own family, I figured it was time."

"That's fine with me. Is there something you want to do?"

He nodded. "I want to go back to sea."

"Honey, I think you're marvelous, but I don't believe the navy will take you back."

"Maybe not. But the cruise ships will."

"Cruise ships?"

He nodded. "We've got the time, we've got the money. Let's see the world, old gal. Let's do it in style. Anywhere that strikes your fancy."

"You're serious."

"That I am."

Just then, their son, John Jr. walked, in and plopped himself on the seat across from hers. He was grinning like a proud papa.

John Jr. looked so much like his father. So much like the boy she'd loved all through school. He was a good man, with good values, and she couldn't have been prouder of him. "Well, she did it," he said. "She's great, and so is our son. Eight pounds, four ounces."

"Oh, Johnny, that's wonderful." Betty went over and gave him a hug.

"Congratulations, son."

"Thanks, Dad. We'll be able to see him in a few minutes. They'll take him to the nursery. Em's pretty tired, so they're taking her back to her room for some rest. Damn," he said, resting his head in his hands. "A son."

Betty went back to her chair and stared at the two most important men in her life. She'd been given such an amazing gift. She still didn't know how or why. All she knew for sure was that she was more grateful than she could ever say.

She'd never told John about her trip back in time. Mostly, these days, she didn't even think about it. But she'd thought about going back to the Met. To see if the guard was still there. If he'd remember her.

John took her hand once more, while he looked at his boy. "So, did you two finally pick a name?"

Johnny looked up and nodded. "His name is Matthew. Matthew John Stevens."

Everything you love about romance...
and more!

Please turn the page for Signature Select™
Bonus Features.

PERFECT TIMING

BONUS
FEATURES
INSIDE

The Writing Life
by Julie Kenner

When my Harlequin editor, Brenda Chin, suggested that I be part of an exciting anthology with a time-travel theme, I jumped all over the chance. I'm by nature a writer of contemporary stories; I just don't have a head for history. But I absolutely love historical romances, having started out as a reader by glomming each and every one of Julie Garwood's wonderful stories.

My first attempt at writing a romance of my own was, in fact, a historical (a medieval, complete with an uppity heroine and a formerly noble hero now living like Robin Hood in the forest). I got ninety pages into it, then abandoned it when I realized I was overwhelmed by details. (What kind of money did they use? What was the hero's sword made of? And so on.) I considered my options: In addition to my full-time job as a lawyer and trying to finish a novel in my not-so-spare time, I could research the twelfth century. Or, I could write a contemporary romance.

Call me lazy, but I took the contemporary route (a fortuitous decision, too, since I soon learned that I have a very contemporary voice).

All of which is to say that while I love writing contemporary stories, I've still always had a secret urge to write a historical; not one set centuries ago, mind you. And not a full novel. Because while that would be fun in theory, I'd already learned that a full historical novel simply isn't in my blood.

But a novella? And a novella featuring a heroine with contemporary sensibilities—and, even more, a novella that I could set in the twentieth century? Let's just say I jumped all over that.

I picked the Roaring Twenties as the period for my story because it seemed perfect for a sexy story: an era when sexuality was being explored, when fashions were becoming more revealing and when women were enjoying a new level of freedom. And, yes, I'll admit that part of my decision to pick the period stemmed from having just watched a wonderful movie on DVD, *Bright Young Things*, an adaptation of an Evelyn Waugh novel that I highly recommend.

Researching the story was as much fun as writing it, and unfortunately with a novella there's a limited amount of space for all the fun tidbits I ran across about radio, the silent film era, flapper fashions and, of course, the lingo of the twenties, which you'll find scattered through the story.

If you'd like to check out some links to information about the 1920s (including links about radio, film and the language of the time), just visit my Web site at www.juliekenner.com and navigate to the page about *Perfect Timing*.

A Day at the Louvre
by Nancy Warren

When my editor called to ask me if I wanted to write a time-travel novella, my first thought was that I have never written a time-travel story before. I've loved many that I've read and thought, why not try a new challenge? So I agreed to give it a try, and since I was planning a trip to France at the time, I chose the Louvre as the initial setting for my story about the Sex Through the Ages traveling exhibit. A trip to Paris. Oh, the things a writer must do in the name of research!

Naturally, a great many cafés au lait were consumed in the writing of this project, as well as a bottle or two of fine French wine. Naturally, you can't drink café au lait without a croissant or a *pain au chocolat* to nibble on, and what would French wine be without a well-cooked French meal to accompany it? The sad truth is that I gained ten pounds while researching my novella. But what a way to go.

I hadn't visited the Louvre since 1984 and much had changed. Oh, not the great works of art, of course, but I don't remember three-hour lineups or the incredible crush of people crowding for a glimpse of the *Mona Lisa*. I think Dan Brown and his novel *The DaVinci Code* have a lot to answer for! In any case, I decided that standing in blistering summer heat for several hours was not going to work for me. I had coffees to sip, wines to drink, other museums calling me. It was, in fact, at the Musée d'Orsay that I discovered the museum pass. I offer this tip for anyone who might be thinking of a trip to Paris.

8 Get the pass. If you love museums like I do, you'll be glad you did. It's available at most museums, can be bought for a variety of stays—we bought the five-day pass and saw all the great museums, as well as some lesser known ones. The best part was waltzing right past the lineups and gaining immediate entrance.

I had forgotten how absolutely amazing the Louvre is. There really is too much to absorb in one day. I fell in love all over again. Walking up the stairs past Winged Victory I felt all the thrill of being so close to that marble monument carved more than two thousand years ago in 190 B.C. Wandering down the galleries is like stepping into a coffee-table book of the greatest art of history.

The Louvre wasn't always an art museum. It was built eight centuries ago as a fortified castle and later became a royal residence. It was where Henry IV died, and Napoleon married. In 1981 Francois Mitterand oversaw a renovation, including adding the controversial glass pyramid, making the Louvre the largest museum in the world. It welcomes five million visitors a year and based on my visit, I'm guessing four and a half million visit in the summer.

The museum is truly amazing. From the Egyptian antiquities that go back to thousands of years B.C. to the 140-carat Regent diamond worn in a crown by Louis XV at his coronation, it's all there, all accessible.

I used a great deal of artistic license for my novella *Pistols at Dawn*. There is no American wing in the Louvre and the artist Gascon is a figment of my imagination, as are his paintings. One thing I didn't invent, though, is the sense of history that walks with you as you tour the Louvre. Whether you are contemplating Vermeer's *Lacemaker* at work, or guessing at the *Mona Lisa*'s secrets, if there is a place on earth where time travel is possible for a few hours, it's at the Louvre.

Do-Overs
by Jo Leigh

What if you could do it all over again? Go back in time and take that incredible job? Or go on that trip you missed? What if you could fix that one mistake that haunts you to this very day?

I thought a lot about that as I was writing *Time After Time*. I wouldn't go back to World War II because I hadn't been born yet, but if I *could* go back to a certain point in my life and make a new choice? Would I?

First, I thought about this one time—it was 1977 and I was working at 20th Century Fox studios. The then president of the film division did something that was not 100 percent kosher, but nice—he told me that it would be a very, very good time to buy stock in the company. Later that year, *Star Wars* debuted. Did I take his advice? Uh, no.

But that was just about money. Would I go back in time for cash? Only on April 15.

Then I thought about high school. I know it's supposed to be the best time of your life and all, but for me, it pretty much sucked. If I went back to high school (especially if I got to retain everything I'd learned) I could change everything! First, I wouldn't even bother going to school, I'd just take the GED. Then I'd write. Become one of those Wonderkinds who publish brilliantly at eighteen. That would be cool.

As I played out the fantasy, it occurred to me that while I might be able to change something that had gone south, I also might miss something that had been wonderful. Would I still meet my best friend? My husband? Were all those mistakes I made necessary to bring me to where I am right now?

I'm not a kid anymore, and you know what? I wouldn't want to be a kid again. I've earned the lines by my eyes and those pesky gray hairs. My life has been a fascinating adventure, and yes, that means I made lots of mistakes. But they're my mistakes, and I learned from most of them. Today, I love what I do, I love where I live, I love my guy. So why would I want to tempt fate and change even one thing?

I'll take my time travel in books, thank you, and remember that this is the life I fought for. This is the life I earned.

Love,

Jo

Here's a sneak peek...

Hidden Obsession
by
Joanne Rock

The First book in an upcoming Blaze miniseries
PERFECT TIMING.

CHAPTER 1

IF THERE HAD BEEN even a hint of cosmic order in the universe, Graham Lawson wouldn't have to show up on a Hollywood set for the rest of his life.

Wrenching his practice sword out of A-list actor Brendan Jameson's hands before the guy could spend another moment checking out his teeth in the polished reflection, Los Angeles Police Department weapons expert Graham stuffed the blade in its sheath before folding the antique piece in a length of cloth for transport back to his private collection. He couldn't afford another day away from his current investigation with a new brand of flesh-pedaling gangbangers running around L.A. and keeping his department hopping. Especially since this latest crew of felons had demonstrated a prefer-ence for medieval weaponry to inflict twisted sexual pain on their victims. They showed a hell of a lot more facility with their arms than pretty-boy Brendan at Graham's sideline as a weapons consult-ant for an action-adventure flick.

"See you tomorrow, Coach?" Brendan asked, sipping his Evian between bouts of the makeup artist's brush while he prepped for his close-ups in Studio 3A.

"I don't know. I think the director said something about shooting the remaining scenes with a copied sword." Graham zipped the leather satchel he used for transporting an assortment of weapons to and from the set for the past two months. The gig started out as a favor to his ex-girlfriend, a bit-part actress in the film they were shooting and a woman who'd barely waited for Graham to finish his first sword-wielding lesson with the starring actor before she'd thrown herself at Brendan. Currently she stood by the refreshment table, leaning over to push her boobs up for more cleavage.

Nice. The kicker of it all was that Graham had made a three-thousand mile relocation from the NYPD to the LAPD in order to be with the woman he'd met while providing extra security to a Manhattan set where she'd had a role in a music video. Good thing he liked the weather out here or he might just have been pissed off at her.

"But what about the choreography of the fight sequences?" Brendan held up a hand to pause the makeup artist in midsweep of her brush full of bronzer.

Graham couldn't resent the guy—too much— since Brendan was clueless about Graham's ex-girlfriend's maneuvering.

"You're looking more at ease every day," Graham fibbed for the greater good. But then, Graham would never be able to think about dividing up action sequences into smaller vignettes to best show off his abs, either. In a world that emphasized how something looked over actual accomplishment though, maybe Brendan had an advantage.

Welcome to Hollywood.

"Killer." Brendan flashed a thumbs-up sign, tipping off both Graham and his makeup artist that the conversation was over.

Graham's phone started ringing the moment he finished packing his gear. He answered as he wound his way through the cavernous soundstage toward the studio back lot, his vintage sword secured across his back in a custom made carrying case.

"Lawson." Blinking against the bright afternoon sun that shone way too often for an East Coast transplant, Graham bummed a ride to the parking lot off a gopher speeding by in a golf cart.

Another thing he couldn't get used to about this city—you had to drive everywhere.

"It's Miguel. You done playing Gene Kelly yet?"

Graham's twenty-five-year-old partner had laughed his ass off at the idea of Brendan Jameson cutting Graham's action sequence into choreography snippets so he could remember them better.

"I'm getting in the truck now." Graham floated the golf-cart-driving kid a few bucks for his trouble and loaded the satchel into the front seat of his Sierra Denali pickup—a kick-ass ride he refused to trade even though it guzzled fuel like there was no tomorrow.

Besides, the truck had proved more loyal than most of the women in his life and that ought to count for something.

"You in the mood to maintain your highbrow commitment to the arts?"

"What's that supposed to mean?"

"There's some kind of art exhibit in town called Sex Through the Ages and our guys found a flyer for the thing in a search of a Guardian member's glove compartment this morning."

The gang calling themselves the Guardians had upped the stakes two weeks ago when they began kidnapping area women for participation in twisted, occasionally brutal, sex rituals as a form of hazing for their new members. Leads were scarce other than a few instances of weaponry with medieval flare. Maces. Scythes. Or so went the rumors. No old-school weapons had been confiscated, but witnesses claimed to see the tools in a couple of police reports. And then two women who'd escaped the Guardians came home with scythes tattooed on their thighs and tales of lurid and occasionally sadistic sex rites carried out with cultist attention to detail.

Cops all over the city had moved the case up to their first priority.

"Sex Through the Ages?" Graham pulled out of the studio lot and headed north toward the interstate. "Sounds like a docudrama on pornography. How is that an art exhibit?"

"Beats me. The brochure shows some naked paintings and a kinky costume display, but I figured you'd want to take a look at the medieval section since our guys seem to dig the Crusader tie-in."

"Right. Where is this place?" Graham didn't mind the fieldwork since—aside from his crappy sideline as a weapons consultant on the movie—he spent most of his time behind a desk these days. His field of expertise had propelled him through the police ranks with gratifying speed, but there came a point where he missed the time in the field that made the job real. Intense.

"The show is at the Getty Center. There's an exit for it off the 405." Miguel started rattling off directions but Graham could picture the place. "It closes at six, though. You'd better step on it."

"Crap. That was the most important part of this conversation, bud. You're supposed to lead with the big news and work your way down through the rest." Graham leaned on the accelerator and hit the passing lane more aggressively since his dashboard clock read 5:40.

"Then you're really not going to like this." Miguel cleared his throat and lowered his voice. "Eyewitness reports from UCLA campus say the Guardians took two other women from a summer workshop in para-psychology this morning. One of the witnesses got a good look at a weapon they were carrying and I'm going to send it over to you now. It sounded like a scythe when she first described it, but the artist's picture shows something more unusual."

"I'm on it." Graham processed the information as he flew down the highway, the smoggy breeze whipping through the open window of his truck not doing jack to clear his head.

He didn't know where a bunch of twenty-year-old street thugs were finding the kinds of weapons that few collectors could get their hands on, but obviously the Guardian organization was a hell of a lot more sophisticated than he'd first realized.

Which made them a whole lot more dangerous. And even harder to catch. Graham was pretty damn certain this group wasn't visiting museums in their spare time for inspiration on their sick rituals, but maybe these guys were pulling research from some B-movie version of battles in the Middle Ages and the helpless role of the village wenches. He'd have to remember to speak to the department's psych guys about the tight brotherhood mentality of the gang. They might be able to profile their ringleaders a little more narrowly if the Guardians were really grooving on the pseudo-historical roots of their crime ring.

Eighteen minutes later Graham jogged into the J. Paul Getty museum with the valuable historic sword strapped on his back in its protective case. He hadn't planned to make a stop on the way home and he couldn't afford to leave a ten thousand dollar weapon unguarded. Now he flashed his badge enough times to warrant the appearance of a management type who understood the need for speed and discretion. After giving the okay to keep the museum open later on a private basis just for the evening, the museum's assistant director called out a night watchman to show Graham around the Sex Through the Ages exhibit.

Progress.

The old guy was quiet, which suited Graham fine as he scanned room after room in search of anything that might clue him in to Guardian rituals or shed light on the meaning of the scythe. The drawing Miguel had e-mailed him had been an oddly shaped halberd with a curved hilt. Similar to a poleax, a halberd could be used as both a dagger and an ax, but the slight arc in the haft was a twist Graham had never come across before. He'd also never seen the style of engraving on the handle, which looked too distinct to mark the piece as an antique, although that might be an exaggeration by the artist to capture details the eyewitness had described.

Knowing the Sex Through the Ages exhibit was probably not the place to find clues about the weapon anyhow, Graham tucked away the PDA with the picture and concentrated on the task at hand. For all he knew, the traveling museum show had been just a matter of curiosity to the suspect who'd had a flyer about it. Graham needed to be open to other leads that didn't have anything to do with weaponry.

One of the echoing museum halls displayed a history of dildos. Another showcased the development of undergarments meant to tantalize. There was a sprawling section dedicated to porn, but those specialty exhibits were sandwiched between bigger rooms dedicated to various time periods.

Boot soles squeaking on the polished museum floor, Graham made tracks for the Middle Ages area that had been draped with crushed red velvet curtains tied back with golden cord.

Music had been piped in that Graham could only assume was period accurate. The sound of monks chanting a cappella provided an interesting accompaniment to racy displays ranging from provocative paintings to drawings of sexual enhancement aids and a PowerPoint projection on a blank wall depict-

20

ing various methods of medieval birth control, all of which looked fairly revolting.

Why would any of this be interesting to the Guardians? Was there a clue to their sex rites contained in the ten-minute narrated slideshow about the subversive sexuality of witch hunts? Would their group care that medieval society blatantly encouraged sex outside marriage in the subtly written code of chivalry?

"Damn." Graham muttered under his breath, resenting the lost time here if the museum lead turned out to be a dead end.

"Perhaps you would like to see the collection of paintings, sir?" the night watchman asked from a few feet behind. "Some were painted within the time period and others were crafted afterward, yet still reflect the medieval sentiment."

Nodding, Graham shifted the position of the sword sheath on his back and followed the guy past a glass display case of supposed chastity belts along with a disclaimer about the authenticity of the items that many believed a myth. As they reached the wall of paintings, Graham realized the collection resembled nothing he'd ever seen at an art gallery.

Not that he spent much time in museums, but he seemed to recall the general rule of hanging visual art was to give each piece enough white space to appreciate the works individually. Here, the canvases had been hung close together with disparate themes clashing up against one another. The rougher, two-dimensional style of period pieces butted up against soft-focus Victorian interpretations of the Middle Ages.

Graham could scarcely take it all in, other than an overall impression of numerous curvy maidens falling out of their clothes. Knights and peasants, kings and nobles filled out the periphery of the presentation, their swords brandishing at every angle like a field of strutting lovers flexing their he-man prowess in an age-old mating call.

"Do you have any questions I can help you with, sir?" the old night watchman asked in his gravelly voice, hands clasped behind his back.

"Not yet." Graham didn't know what he was looking for here, but somehow his section of paintings gave him the sense that he'd come closer. Shifting his gaze downward from the sweep of images across the wall, he spotted a weapon similar to the photo Miguel had sent.

A halberd with a slightly curved haft, although the piece bore none of the peculiar chain-link style markings witnesses claimed to have seen on the Guardians' weapon on the UCLA campus.

Moving closer to inspect the canvas, he squinted into the dark shadows of the artwork, but couldn't make out anymore detail. The blade rested at ease against a hay bale while a knight on the other side of the image removed his helm to rest at the side of a country road.

"I don't get it." Graham stood back from the painting again to see is he missed something. "How does this picture show anything about sex? Why include something as innocuous as a knight catching a few z's as part of the exhibit?"

The answers were probably here somewhere on one of the zillion little placards for patrons who wanted a self-guided tour of the Sex Through the Ages show, but Graham didn't have a lot of time for research with two more women now in the Guardians' hands.

The watchman stepped closer, blue eyes keen, as if he'd been eager for an opportunity to share what he knew. The guy probably didn't get the chance to talk to many people if his shift started at six and the museum closed early three nights a week.

"The growing church frowned on the sexual practices of societies with ancient pagan roots, so we don't have many records of private life from this time period since works of a corporal nature were often burned or destroyed in the name of protecting the public."

"Censorship has been around awhile." Gritting his teeth against his impatience, Graham stuffed his hands in his pockets and waited for more.

"Because of revisionist-style censorship, most of

BONUS FEATURE

our remaining historical evidence is subversive and hints at a society that reveled in its sexuality even as it worked hard to keep their intimate practices behind closed doors."

"Okay." Graham paced around another case containing polished wooden dildos. *Wooden?* "And my apologies for seeming dense, but I still don't understand any hidden agenda for the knight resting his tired ass at the end of a long tournament day."

"Perfectly understandable." The guard adjusted his navy blue cap over wild gray hair escaping at all angles. "And we hope that reinforces our need for placing the paintings at strategic angles, to evoke the way medieval audiences would have viewed the work. You see how the knight setting aside his arms and making himself comfortable is right beside *Madeline After Prayer* in which a young woman undresses for bed?"

Graham looked to the left at a richly detailed woman sliding pearls from her hair, her clothes slipping off her shoulders.

"Well, the story behind the painting is that the woman has said a prayer to dream of the man she will marry and her lover has hidden himself in her closet that night to make certain it is *he* who appears in her thoughts, since he plans to steal into bed with her after watching her undress." The guard gave a sly smile. "The knight in the other painting hints at the unseen man hidden in this image, waiting within Madeline's wardrobe."

"I see." Finally. Although Graham sure as hell hoped the Guardians left more overt messages in their chain of crimes. "Can you tell me anything about this weapon?"

Pointing to the halberd, he dragged his eyes off buxom young Madeline, an interesting combination of prayerful innocent and lush temptress. Not that Graham was here to gawk at women trapped in old canvas.

"Perhaps, but if I may just point out one more thing you might be interested in here…"

Graham followed the watchman's finger as he pointed toward some of the details at the edge of Madeline's image. He leaned in closer to look and then—

Wham!

The guard shoved him forward with surprising force, propelling him toward the painting. But instead of crashing into the wall of glass that protected all the artwork, Graham found himself hurtling forward through endless darkness until his mind slipped into an even blacker fog than the void through which he traveled.

LINNET WELBORNE kicked off her slipper with a thrust of one foot, sending the delicate velvet shoe hurtling into the wall on the other side of her bed where it crashed and fell to the floor with a soft thud.

Ripping off her other slipper, she shot it like an arrow from her fingertips, hitting her lyre with bull's-eye accuracy and calling forth a discordant twang of the strings. She silently damned both velvet articles along with every other item of clothing her flap-mouthed, onion-eyed, fly-bitten betrothed had given her.

She would have never worn a stitch of it if not for her beslubbering stepbrothers' insistence this eve.

"May I help you, my lady?" her maid called to her from the door, no doubt dismayed to find herself locked out of Linnet's chamber for the night. But it served Edana right. Linnet had once been attended by a beloved nurse she'd known since childhood, but these days, her maid was the snippy little sister of the monster Linnet would one day wed.

And "one day" seemed to be approaching too swiftly if reports of her betrothed's return to England could be trusted.

"No thank you, Edana. I'm sure it will please you to be excused from my company this eve since you find it so loathsome." Linnet knew she couldn't lock out the spiteful wench the whole night since all her belongings were in here, but she could not allow the woman's barbs to spew forth unchecked, either.

26

"Do you think it wise to anger me, Linnet?" Edana's words were no less sharp for the barrier of the oak door they passed through, all pretense of servitude vanished in an honest moment since Edana had never felt one bit inclined to "serve" anyone but herself.

"Perhaps you should ask yourself if you think it wise to anger *me*, Edana, since I am to have the ear of your brother when he returns from war." God help her. "I think you will find him more kindly disposed to his wife's wishes than you suspect."

She lied as smoothly as her morals would allow— which was actually a good deal—but Edana's only response was a high bark of laughter before she retreated down the corridor away from Linnet's door. At least Edana didn't try to pretend that Linnet's marriage would be a peaceful union the way her brothers did. All three of the elder Welborne males insisted Burke Kendrick would be a good husband to her because of his strength and might, or perhaps because of his wealth and prominence.

But Linnet knew Kendrick's mercilessness had brought him his coin along with the knights who swore fealty to him. Her stepbrothers had been easily persuaded to part with her when Kendrick had flashed a bit of gold beneath their noses and the promise of new lands.

For their greed, Linnet would one day have to answer to the most brutal man in all of England. And no doubt, she'd have to answer to his insufferable sister, as well.

Fumbling with the laces of her gown, Linnet yanked on the ties until she'd freed enough room to step out of her surcoat, another costly gift from her betrothed.

A beautiful body deserves to be beautifully displayed.

Kendrick's words echoed in her memory, his dark stare unnerving her that day he'd delivered trunk after trunk of new garments more worthy of her. Ha! The man had looked at her as if he'd prefer to see her naked and her stepbrothers had done naught to stop his roving hands. They'd been too busy estimating the cost of the early wedding gifts.

Now, clad in her own undergarments as she readied the chamber for bed, Linnet prayed she would not be visited by more dream visions of her future with him. Nay, she'd rather escape into the more fanciful visions she'd been having lately— images filled with wanton encounters involving a strange man she'd never seen.

Foolishness, surely. But far more pleasant than her real life. She swallowed the burning sensation in the back of her throat at the idea of marriage to a man rumored to have an insatiable appetite for virgins in his bed. Half the serving women at Kendrick Keep had been initiated by him. Even Edana admitted as much.

So, Linnet wondered as she pulled back the bed linens, how would the brute maintain interest in a marriage that would provide him with a virgin only one night?

She did not care about his interest half so much as she cared about protecting her legitimate children from the avarice of a proliferation of her husband's bastards. She would run anywhere from this marriage—gladly forsake every stupid velvet slipper and golden bauble for her freedom. But Kendrick and her stepbrothers had taken pains to ensure her isolation at her eldest brother's stronghold on the southern coast.

Escape was impossible.

Pulling the strands of smooth pearls from her hair, Linnet was about to slide beneath her sheets when a rustling noise sounded on the far side of her room. Surely she was full of foolish fancy after brooding about Kendrick, but she could not help the peculiar notion that a man's eyes followed her once again.

BONUS FEATURE

...NOT THE END...

Signature Select™

COMING NEXT MONTH

Signature Select Collection
A FARE TO REMEMBER by Vicki Lewis Thompson, Julie Elizabeth Leto, Kate Hoffmann
A matchmaking New York City taxi driver must convince three women he's found their life matches...but it's hardly a smooth ride.

Signature Select Saga
YOU MADE ME LOVE YOU by C.J. Carmichael
For six friends, childhood summers on a British Columbian island forged lifelong friendships that shaped their futures for the better... and the worst. Years later, death brings tragedy, mystery and love to two of them as they explore what really happened.

Signature Select Miniseries
SEDUCING McCOY by Tori Carrington
Law-enforcement brothers David and Connor McCoy find that upholding the law can get in the way of love as they try to convince two women not to settle for less than the *real* McCoy!

Signature Select Spotlight
CONFESSIONS OF A PARTY CRASHER by Holly Jacobs
Though her friends agree that it's a great way to meet men, Morgan Miller isn't comfortable crashing a posh wedding reception. Then again, it's better than not going at all...especially when wedding photographer Conner Danning enters the picture!

Signature Select Showcase
LOVE SONG FOR A RAVEN by Elizabeth Lowell
A ferocious storm plunged Janna Morgan into the icy water of the frigid sea—until untamed and enigmatic Carlson Raven saves her. Stranded together in a deserted paradise, Raven is powerless to resist his attraction to Janna. But, could he believe her feelings were love and not merely gratitude?

**Four sisters.
A family legacy.
And someone is out to destroy it.**

A captivating new limited continuity, launching June 2006

The most beautiful hotel in New Orleans,
and someone is out to destroy it. But mystery,
danger and some surprising family revelations
and discoveries won't stop the Marchand sisters
from protecting their birthright…
and finding love along the way.

SPECIAL PRICE!

This riveting new saga begins with

In the Dark

by national bestselling author

JUDITH ARNOLD

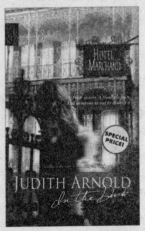

The party at Hotel Marchand is in full swing when the lights suddenly go out. What does head of security Mac Jensen do first? He's torn between two jobs—protecting the guests at the hotel and keeping the woman he loves safe.

A woman to protect. A hotel to secure. And no idea who's determined to harm them.

On Sale June 2006

If you enjoyed what you just read,
then we've got an offer you can't resist!

Take 2 bestselling
love stories FREE!

Plus get a FREE surprise gift!

Clip this page and mail it to Silhouette Reader Service™

IN U.S.A.
3010 Walden Ave.
P.O. Box 1867
Buffalo, N.Y. 14240-1867

IN CANADA
P.O. Box 609
Fort Erie, Ontario
L2A 5X3

YES! Please send me 2 free Silhouette Desire® novels and my free surprise gift. After receiving them, if I don't wish to receive anymore, I can return the shipping statement marked cancel. If I don't cancel, I will receive 6 brand-new novels every month, before they're available in stores! In the U.S.A., bill me at the bargain price of $3.80 plus 25¢ shipping and handling per book and applicable sales tax, if any*. In Canada, bill me at the bargain price of $4.47 plus 25¢ shipping and handling per book and applicable taxes**. That's the complete price and a savings of at least 10% off the cover prices—what a great deal! I understand that accepting the 2 free books and gift places me under no obligation ever to buy any books. I can always return a shipment and cancel at any time. Even if I never buy another book from Silhouette, the 2 free books and gift are mine to keep forever.

225 SDN DZ9F
326 SDN DZ9G

Name	(PLEASE PRINT)	
Address	Apt.#	
City	State/Prov.	Zip/Postal Code

Not valid to current Silhouette Desire® subscribers.

Want to try two free books from another series?
Call 1-800-873-8635 or visit www.morefreebooks.com.

* Terms and prices subject to change without notice. Sales tax applicable in N.Y.
** Canadian residents will be charged applicable provincial taxes and GST.
All orders subject to approval. Offer limited to one per household.
® are registered trademarks owned and used by the trademark owner and or its licensee.

DES04R   ©2004 Harlequin Enterprises Limited

JULIE KENNER

Julie Kenner's first book hit the stores in February 2000, and she's been on the go ever since. A *USA TODAY* and Waldenbooks bestselling author, Julie is also a former RITA® Award finalist, and winner of the *Romantic Times BOOKclub* Reviewer's Choice Award for Best Contemporary Paranormal of 2001. She retired in June 2004 from the practice of law and now lives and writes in Georgetown, Texas, with her husband and daughter. She loves writing contemporary romance because she gets to read trendy magazines and call it research. She loves to hear from readers. Visit her on the Web at www.juliekenner.com.

NANCY WARREN

Nancy Warren is the *USA TODAY* bestselling author of more than twenty sexy, humorous novels and novellas for Harlequin Books and Kensington Publishing. Nancy has won many awards for her writing, including the *Romantic Times BOOKclub* Reviewer's Choice Award for Best Blaze of 2002 and the Laurel Wreath. In 2004 she was a double RITA® Award finalist. Nancy holds an honors degree in English literature and lives in the Pacific Northwest where she spends a lot of time daydreaming about gorgeous men, and women who are a lot more adventurous than she. When not writing, she is usually out walking her Border collie in the rain or is twisted into some bizarre yoga shape. For more, including contests, articles and other fun stuff, please visit www.nancywarren.net.

JO LEIGH

The author of over thirty novels, Jo Leigh grew up in Southern California and dreamed of making movies. At eighteen, she began work at 20th Century-Fox and for the next fifteen years, she worked on location shoots all over the country. During that time, she fell in love with writing, and she sold a series idea to Cinemax, and has written several screenplays. She hadn't yet thought about writing romance novels. Not that she wasn't exposed to them—her father has been a voracious romance reader for years and years. He'd had special bookshelves built to accommodate his collection, and he still reads two or three a day! Even when he meets with the likes of the president of Boeing, there's always a romance novel tucked in his back pocket. You can imagine how proud her father is of Jo's career at Harlequin. She currently lives in Utah with her wonderful husband and loves to hear from readers at www.joleigh.com.

SCPTMAY